CHAPTER ONE

At seven o'clock in the evening of Monday 2nd September, Arthur Williams started to feel a bit unwell. A throbbing headache was accompanied by a dry mouth, and all the energy seemed to have drained from his body. Not one to complain, Arthur told his wife he was going to have a lie down. He presumed it was some kind of change of season thing – nothing that couldn't be remedied by a few hours in bed. Arthur Williams was never going to get up again.

Shortly afterwards, across the island in Vazon, Jimmy Lloyd was on his knees, inches away from the downstairs toilet. Sweat was pouring from his brow, and he was breathing heavily. The contents of his stomach had taken three flushes to get rid of and Jimmy had no idea what had brought on the sudden nausea. He closed his eyes and lay back on the cold tiles. Jimmy didn't know then that he was one of the lucky ones. He didn't feel lucky right now, but he was. The majority of the toxins he'd ingested had been expelled in time and Jimmy would be perfectly fine in a week or two.

"I'm dying."
Felicity Green didn't realise how right she was. Like Jimmy, Felicity had spent quite some time with her head over the toilet bowl. Unfortunately, she'd left it too late. The amanitin toxins had already entered her blood stream. Soon her liver and kidneys would do what they're designed to do, but it would be a case of too little too late.

"Was it something you ate?" Felicity's friend David asked.
"We all had the same thing," Felicity managed. "Fish and chips."
"Maybe there's a bug going round."
"I'm dying."
"Do you want me to call a doctor?"
Felicity shook her head. "I just want to lay here and die."

She didn't know that in less than two hours she would do precisely that. Her vital organs would fail, one by one, and she would slip into a coma from which she would never wake up.

Before the sun dawned the next day, there would be five fewer people on the island of Guernsey. Their families and friends would speak of a sudden sickness – one that had arrived without warning, and one that couldn't be explained. This wasn't the end of it – the sickness on the island was going to spread, and it was something none of the islanders could have predicted in a million years.

CHAPTER TWO

Detective Inspector Liam O'Reilly was blissfully unaware that his life was about to get extremely complicated. The Irish detective was enjoying a meal at a restaurant in St Peter Port to celebrate his birthday.
"Cheers, Dad." Assumpta raised her glass of wine.
O'Reilly's daughter was accompanied by her boyfriend, DC Andy Stone. O'Reilly's wife, Victoria, was also present.
 "How old are you now, sir?" DC Stone asked.
O'Reilly glared at the rat-faced detective. "Old enough."
"Forty-nine," Victoria said. "One year away from the big five O."
"I'm starving," O'Reilly said. "I could eat a scabby horse. I wonder what's taking so long."
 The Red Snapper wasn't particularly busy. It was a Monday night in early September, and the majority of the tourists had left the island. Soon, the place would be much less crowded, and O'Reilly was glad. As much as he liked the buzz that accompanied the mass of tourists, he was always relieved when the season was over, and he got the island he now called home back.
 The food arrived five minutes later, and it was brought out by Bertram Pink. The giant head chef apologised for the delay.
"We're short staffed," he explained. "Two of my chefs called in sick. I'm running a one-man-band back there tonight."
"Not to worry," O'Reilly said. "That seafood platter looks incredible."
"It's far too much food for one person, Liam," Victoria said.
O'Reilly winked at her. "Challenge accepted, my love."
 Victoria had opted for the fish and chips, as had Assumpta and DC Stone. O'Reilly eyed the mountain of seafood on his plate and got to work.
"How are things going at the bike shop?" Assumpta asked Victoria.

"Great," she replied. "Tommy is talking about hiring extra staff. The Kawasaki agency is thriving, and the Japanese are happy. And that's no mean feat – those guys in Tokyo are not easy to please."

"When will you be getting back on the bike again, Dad?" Assumpta said.

"Soon," O'Reilly managed with a mouth full of prawn. "Very soon. The tourists have buggered off, so the roads will be back to normal. I can't wait."

His mobile phone started to ring in his jacket pocket, and he made no move to answer it. Whoever it was could wait until after he'd finished eating. He'd polished off half of the seafood platter, and he was enjoying everything on the plate.

Life on the island had been uneventful since the fury that had reared its ugly head a few weeks earlier. A gang of cyclists had captured the attention of the islanders with their reign of terror and even though the series of deaths would never be forgotten, O'Reilly was happy to put it behind him. All he'd had to deal with recently was a spate of bizarre break-ins at a number of businesses on the island. Most of them had been shops that supplied food products and all of them shared a common denominator. Nothing had been stolen in any of the burglaries. It really was baffling, and O'Reilly wondered if they could even be called burglaries. It was more like random acts of petty vandalism.

"Good Lord, Dad," Assumpta exclaimed.

She was staring at his clean plate with an expression of utter disbelief on her face.

"You do realise that you've just wolfed down a seafood platter meant for two people," she added.

O'Reilly grinned and wiped his mouth with a napkin. "What's your point, Summi?"

"You're going to get fat."

"Nonsense," O'Reilly said. "You can't get fat from seafood. When did you ever see an obese Japanese? Who wants another drink?"

Everybody did. O'Reilly got the attention of the waiter and ordered another round.

His ringtone sounded again and this time he went as far as to look at who was trying to get hold of him. The screen told him it was an unknown number, so he ignored it. The drinks arrived and O'Reilly took a long sip of his *Scapegoat*. It had quickly become his drink of choice on the island, and he rarely drank anything else. DC Stone was sticking to coke. He was on duty in the morning, and he'd explained that he didn't feel like sifting through a mountain of paperwork with a thick head.

"Where are we with the recent break-ins?" O'Reilly asked him.

"I don't understand them," DC Stone said. "It looks like it's the same people involved. They gain access through the back, and they seem to know where the cameras are. They're also aware of the alarms, but it doesn't deter them. Most of the businesses have private security, but the response time, once the alarm is activated is a couple of minutes and the perpetrators are always long gone by the time the security company arrives. They break in, steal nothing and get out in the space of a couple of minutes."

"They break in without taking anything?" Victoria said.

"That's the weird bit," DC Stone said. "At all of the scenes of the break-ins nothing appears to have been touched."

"If they're not doing it to steal stuff," Assumpta said. "What's the point?"

"It's probably bored kids," Victoria said.

"I don't get that impression," O'Reilly said. "They're too organised to be kids looking for a quick thrill."

The conversation was cut short when a middle-aged man staggered past their table.

"Watch it," O'Reilly said when he banged into his chair.

The man didn't apologise. O'Reilly watched as he made his way to the toilets at the back of the restaurant.

"Someone's had a bit too much to drink," Assumpta said.

O'Reilly raised his glass and drained it in one go. "I'll drink to that."

He ordered another *Scapegoat* and rubbed his belly. He was feeling content. Life was grand for him right now.

The drunk man reappeared and made a beeline for his table. O'Reilly realised there was something seriously wrong when he observed the man's face. His eyes were rimmed with red, and his skin was clammy and pale. Sweat was pouring from his forehead, and he looked like he was having difficulty breathing. He gripped hold of a nearby chair to steady himself, but it didn't help. He fell to the floor and gasped for breath. Something was terribly wrong.

O'Reilly was on his feet in an instant.

"Stand back," he called out. "Give him some room."

He crouched down and looked at the man on the floor. His eyes had rolled back in their sockets and even though his mouth was open, no air was going in or out. O'Reilly checked for a pulse.

Nothing.

"Call an ambulance?" the woman who'd been on the same table as the man cried out.

O'Reilly knew that it was too late. The man on the floor was dead. He got up and glanced at the food on the table in front of the distraught woman. Half of it had been eaten already. The couple had ordered the seafood platter for two.

CHAPTER THREE

"That was a birthday I'm not likely to forget," O'Reilly told Victoria at home in Vazon.

The ambulance had arrived but the only thing they could do was remove the man from The Red Snapper. He was beyond saving. He'd been taken to the Princess Elizabeth hospital, and the cause of his demise would be determined in due course. O'Reilly hoped the answers would be revealed soon. The picture of the agony on the man's face was still imprinted on his brain, and he needed to know what had killed him.

"How are you feeling?" Victoria asked.

"How am I feeling? I'm grand. A man died next to me, but apart from that I'm all good."

"I mean, how are you *feeling*?" Victoria said. "You're not feeling sick?"

"I feel perfectly fine," O'Reilly said.

"The dead man ate the seafood platter, Liam."

"You're not suggesting it was the platter that killed him?"

"He was eating it just before he died," Victoria said.

"As was his wife – she's still alive, and I happened to scoff more than both of them combined, and I don't feel ill at all. Something else killed that man – a heart attack, perhaps."

He didn't believe this for a second. He'd witnessed victims of a heart attack firsthand and the man in The Red Snapper definitely did not succumb to a cardiac arrest. If O'Reilly didn't know any better, he would think he'd been poisoned.

"We'll know for certain when Guthrie has done the postmortem," he said. "Until then, there's no point in speculating."

"The poor wife," Victoria said. "Imagine watching your husband die like that in a restaurant."

"It's tragic," O'Reilly said. "But I imagine there'll be a perfectly reasonable explanation for it. There usually is. Do you want some coffee?"

"Love some."

"I'll pop the kettle on then. Where are the cats?'

"Where do you think?"

"Fast asleep," O'Reilly guessed. "And dreaming about whatever it is that cats dream about. I envy them."

He made Victoria's coffee and a cup of tea for himself, and they settled in the living room. The cats had commandeered the three-seater, so O'Reilly and Victoria had to make do with the two-seater sofa.

"Those moggys really take the piss," O'Reilly said.

Bram was taking up most of the room on the sofa. The fat ginger tom had stretched out, and the other two cats seemed oblivious to it. Juliet was curled up dead centre. The slender black lady was breathing heavily, and O'Reilly was sure she had a smile on her face. The third member of the gang, Shadow, had both front paws hanging over the edge. Shadow was Victoria's cat. The white brute was a bit of a fat thing and no matter how many diets they tried, nothing worked. O'Reilly had given up in the end. Shadow seemed perfectly content being a lard arse, and the Irish detective didn't see any reason to worry about it.

His thoughts turned to the scene at the Red Snapper. When the man had staggered past their table, all of them had assumed he was drunk, but according to the brief conversation with his wife he hadn't touched a drop of alcohol for over ten years. He'd been drinking sparkling water at the restaurant. That was as much as O'Reilly was able to glean from the wife. She'd gone with her husband in the ambulance, and O'Reilly didn't think she would be able to tell them much anyway.

Something was bothering him. Whatever had resulted in the man's death had come on suddenly. He didn't know all the facts, but he didn't think someone would go out for a meal if they weren't feeling well. He recalled the man's face when he returned from the toilets. The expression in his eyes was one of disbelief and absolute terror. Did he know that he didn't have long left? The idea made O'Reilly shudder.

"You're miles away."

O'Reilly wasn't listening.

"Liam," Victoria said. "Are you still with us?"

O'Reilly looked at her. "What? Yes, I was just deep in thought."

"What curious ponderings was your Irish mind wondering about this time?"

"Mortality," O'Reilly said. "You never know when it's your time, do you?"

"I have a better idea than most."

"Of course. I'll shut up."

"I'm heading up to bed," Victoria said. "Are you coming?"

"In a bit," O'Reilly said. "I think I'll stay up and irritate the cats for a while."

Victoria finished her coffee and kissed him on the cheek. "Good night."

"Good night. I'll be up soon."

He reached for his phone and brought up a number in his contacts. The clock on his phone told him it was almost ten and he decided it wasn't too late to make a call.

"Liam," Dr Lille answered after a few rings.

"Guthrie," O'Reilly said. "I didn't wake you, did I?"

"I'm a night owl. I rarely hit the sack before midnight. What's up?'

"Are you aware of the man who died suddenly at the Red Snapper?"

"I'm not," Dr Lille said. "But I imagine I soon will be."

"I was there when it happened," O'Reilly told him. "And there's something troubling me about it."

"How so?"

"I'm no stranger to death," O'Reilly said. "I thought I'd seen everything, but the poor bugger in the restaurant is stuck in my head. I know it's too early to say and I also know you're not a man who likes to speculate, but I'm asking you to humour me. If I describe what he looked like, can you give me an opinion on what might have killed him?"

"I can give you a rough guess," Dr Lille said. "For what it's worth. Why can't you wait until I've done the PM?"

"I could do that," O'Reilly agreed. "But I'd quite like to get some sleep tonight."

The line went quiet for a while and O'Reilly wondered if Dr Lille had hung up. He asked if he was still there.

"Still here," Dr Lille said. "Tell me what happened."

"He staggered past our table," O'Reilly said. "We all thought he was drunk, but I later found out that he hasn't touched a drop in years. He went to the Gents and returned a few minutes later. That's when I knew there was something terribly wrong with him. His eyes were rimmed with red and the skin on his face was pale and clammy. He was sweating like a pig and struggling to breathe. Any thoughts?"

"It seems like whatever it was came on quickly."

"That was the conclusion I came to," O'Reilly said. "You don't go to a restaurant if you're feeling a bit off colour."

"What did he have to eat?"

"The same as me. The seafood platter, and I feel fine. His wife ate the same thing."

"It's possible that he suffered some kind of allergic reaction. The fact that he was struggling to breathe corresponds with the symptoms of anaphylactic shock. The immune system releases chemicals to counter what it believes to be an attack, and this can result in airway constriction. It's not unknown for seafood to cause such a reaction."

"Surely he would know if he was allergic to seafood?" O'Reilly said.

"Possibly. Do you remember if he had any external evidence of an allergic reaction? Was there any swelling? Hives are common."

"Nothing," O'Reilly said. "He was sweating, and his eyes were red. He collapsed next to our table, and he just stopped breathing. I shouldn't have bothered you so late. You're right – I can't expect you to form an opinion based on the observations of an old Irishman who knows feck all about medical conditions."

"Put it out of your mind, Liam," Dr Lille said. "I'm sure tomorrow will bring the answers you seek."

"Thanks, Guthrie," O'Reilly said. "I'll speak to you tomorrow."

He put the phone on the table and stretched his arms. He was suddenly exhausted, but he didn't think he was going to be able to sleep tonight. The tragedy in the Red Snapper was bothering him, and he couldn't understand why it had affected him so much. He didn't know then that this was just the beginning – it was about to get much, much worse.

CHAPTER FOUR

O'Reilly was enjoying a cup of tea in his office the next morning when there was a knock on the door and DC Owen came in.

"Morning, Katie," O'Reilly said.

"I heard about the man in the Red Snapper," she said. "Andy told me."

"It wasn't the greatest way to celebrate a birthday."

"He wasn't the only one, sir."

"Sorry?"

"More than a dozen people were taken ill last night," DC Owen said. "Early indications are we have five fatalities."

"Five dead?"

"It appears so, sir. It's unheard of."

"It certainly is," O'Reilly said. "Do we know anything else?"

"Not yet. It's concerning, isn't it?"

"It is. Come on."

"Where are we going?"

"Hospital," O'Reilly said. "I want to know what the devil is going on on this island. You can drive – my gammy leg is playing up."

"Is your leg going to be OK?" DC Owen said.

They'd just turned off La Grange and were now heading south on Queen's Road.

"It's nothing serious, Katie," O'Reilly said. "The pins and plates they repaired the bone with are telling me that a change in the weather is on the cards." He'd been in a motorcycle accident a while ago and he'd broken his femur. After a lengthy spell of recuperation he'd recovered but his leg was never going to be the same, especially when the weather was about to change.

"Not many people have a built-in barometer," he said. "I suppose I should be grateful for that at least."

"How do you think those people died?" DC Owen said.

"We'll find out. I spoke to Guthrie last night and I suspect he's going to have his work cut out for him."

"It's suspicious though, isn't it? Five people in one night."

"It is," O'Reilly said. "You said there were a dozen people rushed to hospital. Do we have any news about the ones who didn't die?"

"As far as I know, they're still alive."

"Let's pray that it stays that way."

Five minutes later DC Owen parked in the car park at the Princess Elizabeth Hospital and she and O'Reilly got out. He rubbed his leg and raised his knee. The twinge in the bone wouldn't budge.

"Happy birthday, by the way," DC Owen said. "I didn't get the chance to say it yesterday."

"Thanks, Katie," O'Reilly said. "I feel old. I think it might be time to invest in a sturdy stick."

"Didn't you used to have one?"

"I'm talking about a permanent measure," O'Reilly said. "Old age isn't for sissies."

DC Owen laughed. "You're not old yet, sir."

O'Reilly showed his ID to the man behind the reception desk and explained the nature of the visit. The name badge on the man's chest told him his name was Harry Palmer.

"I've only been on duty for an hour," he said. "But from what I've gathered, it was a chaotic night."

"Could you point us in the direction of someone who might be able to shed some light on the chaos?" O'Reilly asked.

Harry's eyes fell on a woman marching past the desk. She walked with real purpose.

"Maureen," Harry said. "Have you got a minute?"

She stopped dead and turned to look at him. O'Reilly gauged her age to be mid-thirties. She was a short woman with black hair. O'Reilly thought she looked tired, and he wondered if she'd been working all night.
"Maureen is one of our senior staff nurses," Harry explained.
O'Reilly introduced himself and DI Owen.
"I know who you are," Maureen said. "I don't think there are many people on this island who don't. Follow me – we can talk in my office."

O'Reilly struggled to keep up with her. He reckoned that even if his leg had been fully functional, he would have found it hard to match her pace. By the time they'd walked the fifty metres or so to the office, he was exhausted. He was glad when Maureen told him to take a seat. It was good to take the weight off his leg.

"Problems?" Maureen nodded to it.
"Bike accident," O'Reilly said.
He didn't feel like elaborating.
"Do you have any news for us?" he asked.
"That depends on what news you're looking for," Maureen said.
"I believe there were more than a dozen people brought in during the night."
"Nine," Maureen corrected. "I've since learned that four more people ended up at College Hospital complaining of the same symptoms."
"How many fatalities?" O'Reilly said.
"Three," Maureen said. "Five if we include the two men who were dead on arrival."
"Do we have any idea what killed them?" DC Owen said.
"That's going to take time. Is there something I need to be aware of? Is there something you're not telling me?"
"We're just following protocol," O'Reilly said. "When we have something like this, the police have to get involved. Five sudden deaths is suspicious."

Maureen nodded and rubbed her eyes. Her attempt to suppress a yawn failed miserably.

"Excuse me. I've been here since eight last night."

"We won't take up too much more of your time," O'Reilly said. "What do you think happened to these people?"

"Like I said, the exact cause of the sickness is going to take time to determine. There are tests that need to be carried out and it's not a quick process."

"Would you care to hazard a guess?"

"I'm a medical professional, detective," Maureen said. "I don't work on guesswork."

"Me neither," O'Reilly said. "I prefer to look at hard facts, but it doesn't hurt to take a wild stab in the dark once in a while, especially when those facts are proving to be elusive. Come on, humour me."

Maureen didn't even try to disguise the next yawn.

"A wild stab in the dark?" she said.

"Please," O'Reilly said. "Give me something to think about."

"If I were to guess," Maureen said. "Going on the symptoms alone, and not taking patient history into account, I'd surmise that these people were victims of some kind of poisoning."

CHAPTER FIVE

"Poisoning?"

DCI Fish didn't look convinced.

"It's all just speculation at this stage," O'Reilly said. "But from what I witnessed in the Red Snapper last night and what the senior staff nurse at the Princess Elizabeth told me, it's worth considering."

"What did the nurse say?"

"The symptoms were similar in all the people who were hospitalised," O'Reilly said. "Nausea, vomiting, excessive perspiration and difficulty breathing. The effects appeared quickly and without warning, and for five of the casualties it was fatal."

DCI Fish nodded. "How soon before we have something concrete?"

"Not anytime soon," O'Reilly said. "There are numerous tests that need to be done and it's not a quick process. In the meantime, I want to take a look into the lives of the victims."

"We'll refrain from using that term," DCI Fish said. "We don't know that they are victims."

"Come on, Tom," O'Reilly said. "A dozen people started to feel ill at roughly the same time. Nearly half of them were dead within a couple of hours. This isn't a few cases of Delhi belly caused by some dodgy curries. The poor bastard in the Red Snapper was in agony. He looked like he'd been infected with the Plague. We need to investigate this."

"Where do things stand with the series of break-ins?" DCI Fish said.

"We've got nothing," O'Reilly said. "And I've got a feeling that that's not going to change anytime soon. But I'm not particularly perturbed about it. A few broken windows and damaged locks are a minor inconvenience. As far as we're aware, nothing was taken during any of the break-ins. It can be put on the back burner for a while. We need to look into these suspicious deaths. I was under the impression that protocol dictated it."

"Very well," DCI Fish said. "Do you get the feeling that this is the start of something?"

"I don't know," O'Reilly said. "But I sincerely hope not."

After a quick briefing to bring the rest of the team up to speed, O'Reilly and DC Owen were on the road again. They had a name for the man who collapsed and died in the Red Snapper and O'Reilly wanted to know more about him. Because he was there when he died, he felt some kind of obligation to the man's widow.

John Moody was forty-six. That was as much as they'd been able to find out from the hospital. O'Reilly hoped that his wife, Vera would be able to give them a bit more than that. The Moody's lived in one of the apartment complexes adjacent to Fort Road. O'Reilly had called ahead, and Vera was expecting them.

After explaining who they were to the man whose job it was to raise the boom gate they drove up to the parking area. The Moody's lived in apartment number 3. It was a neat, two-bedroom property with a view of an identical apartment across the courtyard. O'Reilly didn't miss his old apartment. He'd grown accustomed to the freedom of a freestanding house and he couldn't imagine moving back to one of these complexes.

Vera Moody wasn't alone when the door to number 3 opened. A woman who looked to be in her early twenties was standing next to her.
Vera looked directly at O'Reilly. "You?"

"I should have mentioned it when I called," O'Reilly said. "This is DC Owen. Can we come in?"

Vera nodded and suggested they sit outside. It was a warm day, and O'Reilly wondered if his internal barometer was somewhat deficient.

They sat on a covered veranda. Vera offered them something to drink but O'Reilly declined. The other woman was Vera's daughter, Jane. She insisted on being there while they spoke to her mother and O'Reilly had no objections.

"We're very sorry about your husband," DC Owen said.

"It still hasn't hit home," Vera said. "Aren't the police supposed to provide support at times like these. Some kind of liaising officer."

"Family liaison officer," O'Reilly corrected. "Unfortunately, a FLO is only assigned after a crime has been committed."

"I told you that already, mother," Jane said.

O'Reilly observed her. She didn't look like a woman who had recently lost her father, but he didn't dwell on it.

"Do you believe that my father was a victim of a crime?" she asked.

"That's what we're trying to find out," O'Reilly said.

"You must suspect something. You wouldn't be here otherwise. My boyfriend's father's shop was broken into the other day, and the Island Police are doing nothing about it."

"Sometimes, our hands are tied. Can you tell us a bit about John?"

The question was addressed to Vera.

"He was as fit as a fiddle," she said. "Never had a day off sick in his life."

"Where did he work?" DC Owen said.

"He was the manager of the Barclays in St Julians," Vera said.

"What has his place of employment got to do with his death?" It was Jane.

"I wouldn't mind something to drink actually," O'Reilly said. "If it's not too much trouble."

He kept his eyes on Jane when he said this.

"Please, love," Vera said. "There's some fresh lemonade in the fridge."

"That would be grand," O'Reilly said. "It looks like it's going to be a scorcher today."

Jane got up and marched inside.

"We're going to find out what happened to your husband," O'Reilly said. "It might take some time, but we will have some answers for you. You said John was healthy?"

"He took care of himself," Vera said. "He didn't smoke, he stopped drinking years ago, and he ate the right foods. He was a fit man."

"Can you run through what you did yesterday?" O'Reilly said.

"What for?"

O'Reilly didn't answer her. "What time did you arrive at the Red Snapper?"

"Just after six," Vera said.

"And was John feeling fine when you set off?" DC Owen said.

"He was as he always is."

"Would he tell you if he was feeling a bit off colour?" O'Reilly said.

"What's that supposed to mean?"

"Men of our generation tend to ignore slight niggles and other symptoms that could be signs of something more serious," O'Reilly elaborated. "Blokes are just like that."

"No," Vera said. "If John wasn't feeling well, he would have told me."

Jane returned with the lemonade. It was clear that she wasn't happy about it. She dumped the tray on the table and informed them that she had to make a phone call.

"Please excuse Jane," Vera said. "This has hit her harder than she's letting on."

"It's fine," O'Reilly said. "Does she live on the island?"

"Only in the holidays. She's studying law in Newcastle. Help yourselves to some lemonade. It might be a bit tart. I made it yesterday, but I can add some sugar if you like."

"There's no need for that," DC Owen said.

O'Reilly poured them each a glass. He took a sip and grimaced. He wondered if there was any skin left on the roof of his mouth. His tongue felt like it had been instantly desiccated.

"It's lovely," he said.

He licked his lips and put down the glass.

"What did John eat yesterday?"

"Excuse me?" Vera said.

"It's possible that his sudden sickness was caused by something he ingested," DC Owen said.

"I can't really remember," Vera said.

"Did you go out at all?" O'Reilly said. "Before you went to the Red Snapper, I mean."

"John had the day off work, and we were both home all day. I made lunch – I remember now. It was a simple Ploughman's with cheese, pickle, salad and a pork pie."

"And you both ate the same thing?" DC Owen said.

"John had half of my pork pie, but we ate the same food."

"Is it possible that John could be allergic to seafood?" O'Reilly said.

This resulted in a smile from Vera. "If he was, he's defied science for two decades. John loves seafood. In fact, I can't recall him ordering anything else in all the years we've been married."

"So, neither of you left the house yesterday until you set off for the Red Snapper. What did you occupy your time with?"

"I had some emails I needed to reply to," Vera said. "I was busy with them most of the day. John was reading a book out here. He likes to unwind with a book when he gets the chance."

"Did you have any visitors?" DC Owen said.

"Not that I recall. Jane may have had some friends round. She's a popular woman."

This surprised O'Reilly, but he didn't bring it up.

"When did John first start feeling ill?" he asked instead.

"We'd been at the restaurant for roughly thirty minutes, and he said he wasn't feeling well."

"Did he elaborate?" DC Owen said. "Was he feeling sick? Did he feel faint?"

"He just said that something was wrong. He never complains about feeling ill, so I suggested we leave. I was about to get the bill when he suddenly stood up and said he had to go to the toilet."

O'Reilly knew how this story had ended, but it didn't help. He wasn't going to get any more answers from Vera Moody. He would have to wait and see what the postmortem turned up. He thanked Vera for her time and promised her he would find some answers for her. He would keep that promise.

CHAPTER SIX

The rest of the team came back with similar tales to tell. None of the family or friends of the people who had suddenly dropped down dead could shed any light on why they'd perished. O'Reilly wasn't deterred and he wrote each of the names on the whiteboard in the briefing room, nevertheless. He was confident that he would get some answers before the end of the day.

He shared his thoughts with his colleagues and tapped on the first name on the list. Felicity Green was at the top for the simple reason that hers was the first name, alphabetically. Until they had more information at their disposal this would be how they would proceed.

"Felicity was seventeen," O'Reilly said. "She was due to return to sixth-form college next week. Andy?"

"Her parents are devastated, sir," DC Stone said. "Understandably. Mr and Mrs Green hadn't seen Felicity since Saturday. She was spending time with some friends over in Cobo. I spoke to one of them. David Sharp was with Felicity when she died. According to him, she started complaining of stomach cramps and rushed to the bathroom. When she didn't return for a while David went to check on her. She was vomiting and sweating profusely. She kept saying she wanted to die."

"She got her wish," O'Reilly said. "Did you ask the friend about what they did in the preceding hours?"

"I did, sir," DC Stone said. "They were planning on spending the evening watching movies. They got a fish and chip takeaway, and I think alcohol was involved too. David Sharp was a bit sheepish about that."

"It doesn't matter, Andy. Did they all eat?"

"All three of them finished their fish and chips."

"But only Felicity became ill?" DS Skinner said.

"That's right, Sarge. The other two suffered no ill effects."

"It wasn't the fish and chips," O'Reilly said. "The symptoms you've described are identical to the ones John Moody displayed."

"Steven Quinn's wife also told me the same thing, sir," DS Skinner said. Steven's was the next name on the list.

"He was twenty-six, and according to the wife he was in good health. He too started feeling sick and it escalated quickly. Mrs Quinn phoned an ambulance when she realised there was something very wrong – he was taken to hospital, but he died shortly afterwards. Mrs Quinn couldn't think of anything Steven had eaten that she hadn't, and the sudden sickness couldn't be explained."

And so it went on. Arthur Williams told his wife that he was feeling a bit peaky at around seven yesterday evening. He said he was going to have a lie down and Mary Williams didn't give it another thought until a few hours later. She went up to check on him, and he was already dead. The bed sheets were soiled with vomit and faeces, and Arthur was on the floor next to the bed. Arthur was fifty years old.

The last few hours of Kirsty York's life were spent in agony while she waited for an ambulance. Her fiancé said the delay with the ambulance was because of a high number of callouts that evening. George Dunn could do nothing but comfort his fiancé in her final hours. Kirsty's heart stopped beating two minutes before the ambulance finally arrived, and George promised to take the matter further. He claimed that it was the fault of the emergency services, and he was going to make them pay. Soon George would learn that even if the ambulance had got there sooner, Kirsty would still have died. The toxins she ingested had already entered her bloodstream, and she was beyond saving. Kirsty was forty-one.

"Five victims," O'Reilly said. "Men and women of all ages and various levels of fitness. Does anybody have any theories about what the devil happened last night?"

"I suggest we avoid speculation until we have more data at our disposal." It was DCI Fish. O'Reilly had forgotten he was there. It wasn't the first time. Even though DCI Fish held a higher rank, he was happy to allow O'Reilly to take the helm in certain investigations. He was a fair boss – he didn't bark out orders, and usually he would offer suggestions instead.

O'Reilly took this particular suggestion on board.
"I agree. We've had no news about the other victims of this mystery sickness, and at this stage no news is good news. It means that they're probably still alive. Something strange is going on and the answers we seek lie in the results of the postmortems on the five people who perished last night. Guthrie has promised to make that a priority."

"In the meantime," DCI Fish said. "I suggest we occupy our time on the recent break-ins."
O'Reilly didn't think this was a great idea, but he kept it to himself.
"So far," DCI Fish said. "We've only completed a perfunctory investigation into the bizarre break-ins, and we need to dig deeper."
"The way I see it," O'Reilly said. "We've dug as deep as we can. The person or people who carried out the break-ins were aware of the cameras. They were in and out before the security companies arrived, and we don't even know if they actually set foot inside the shops."
"Are you suggesting that they simply broke the locks, activated the alarms and scarpered?" DC Stone asked.
"Who knows, Andy?" O'Reilly said. "There is no evidence to suggest they were ever inside the establishments. Nothing was taken, and I'm finding it hard to understand why we're even wasting time on it. The shops affected are all insured. The locks and broken glass will be replaced, and it'll be business as usual in no time. What else can we do?"
DCI Fish's silence told him that it was a question he didn't have an answer for.

None of the team knew then that the mystery break-ins were soon going to be the central focus of the investigation into the sudden deaths last night. And none of them could have expected what form that involvement would take. The sickness on the island was going to escalate, and the five recent fatalities were just the start of something nastier than anyone on the island could have ever predicted.

CHAPTER SEVEN

O'Reilly wasn't particularly au fait with the workings of the Internet, but he was browsing the web now. He'd made a cup of tea, and he was searching the world wide web to see if there were any answers in the millions of pages in cyberspace. He didn't expect it to be simple, but he didn't anticipate the sheer volume of information at his disposal. He keyed *types of poisoning* into the task bar and was rewarded with hundreds of options. He narrowed down the search by adding the symptoms he'd seen firsthand but there was still too much to consider.

"Toxic gases," he read.

He decided he could rule that out straight away. It was impossible for five random islanders to have been the victims of poisonous gases on the same evening.

"Chemical poisoning."

He didn't think this was the cause of the sudden sickness either.

He also ruled out misuse of medication and animal bites and stings. He didn't think the victims had taken the same medication and there were no animals or insects on the island with the potential to kill a human being.

He narrowed down the search further and the only conclusion he could come to was the people who'd died last night were victims of some sort of food poisoning. It didn't really help. There were hundreds of possible toxins that could be present in food. There were subcategories, and sub-subcategories. Bacterial examples such as salmonella, E. coli, listeria and campylobacter were familiar to O'Reilly but there were many others that weren't. He hadn't realised how many potentially lethal bacteria existed.

The list of viral toxins was shorter, but it was a long list, nevertheless. O'Reilly hadn't realised that norovirus and hepatitis could be spread through contaminated food and water. He discounted parasitic infections and his eyes rested on something interesting.

"Toxins that occur naturally in certain foods."

This was worth looking into. O'Reilly was shocked to discover how many potentially lethal toxins existed in seemingly innocuous food. Many species of fish contained toxins capable of causing discomfort and death, as did a whole host of mushroom species.

After an hour of intensive research O'Reilly gave up. His head was throbbing, and he was suffering from information overload. He wasn't going to get any answers from the Internet. There was simply too much data available, and he wasn't in a position to organise it into some semblance of order. He resigned himself to the waiting game. He would have to wait and see what the postmortems uncovered.

His phone started to ring, and when he glanced at the screen he sighed deeply. He could do without this right now, but he had no option but to take the call.

"Sir. What can I do for you?"

Chief Officer Robert Johnson cleared his throat. "Have you got a minute?" It was a rhetorical question.

"I'll be right up, sir," O'Reilly said.

That was the extent of the phone call. O'Reilly drained the last of his tea and left the office.

His leg started to ache again when he reached the top of the stairs to the row of offices occupied by the *important* people of the Island Police. CO Johnson had the office at the very end. It wasn't the most spacious, but it had the best view by far and O'Reilly guessed the man at the helm of the Island Police had chosen it for this reason only.

He was intercepted halfway down the corridor by a man in his early fifties.

"Morning, Liam," DCO Callum Dove said. "What brings you up here?"

O'Reilly liked Callum. The deputy chief officer was a good man, and O'Reilly had a lot of respect for him. Early on in his time on the island, O'Reilly had rescued the DCO from a potentially embarrassing situation and the second in charge of the Island Police had never forgotten it.

"I've been summoned by the big boss, sir," O'Reilly said. "And I have no idea what it's about."

"That's CO Johnson for you," DCO Dove said. "Better not keep him waiting. I trust you're well?"

"Grand, sir. Good to see you again."

O'Reilly carried on down the corridor and knocked on the door. He was surprised when CO Johnson opened it for him.

"Come in. Take a seat."

O'Reilly took a seat at CO Johnson's desk.

The CO sat down opposite him. "Can I offer you something to drink?"

"I've not long had a cup of tea, sir. What can I do for you?"

"What's the progress with these suspicious deaths?"

O'Reilly wasn't expecting this. In all his time with the Island Police he'd never known CO Johnson to take much interest in the early stages of an investigation.

"It's too early to say, sir. Everything rests on the results of the postmortems."

"How long are we talking about?" CO Johnson asked.

He coughed and took a tissue from a box on the desk. He blew his nose and coughed again. "Damn cold. How long are we talking about?"

"These things take time," O'Reilly said. "Five unexplained deaths in such a short space of time are unprecedented, and it's something Pathology has never had to deal with before."

"That's all very well, Liam," CO Johnson said. "But we need answers now."

"My hands are tied, sir. Until what we know what killed those people, we won't have a starting point in the investigation."

"You are investigating it then?"

"Of course, sir," O'Reilly said. "Protocol dictates it."

"Are you working on any theories?" CO Johnson said.

"Once again, until we know how the people died, we can't begin to start working on leads. May I ask why you're so keen to know what happened?"

"No," CO Johnson said. "You may not. Put pressure on Pathology. And I want a detailed progress report every day. We need a quick resolution here, Liam."

"I can only work with the data I have at my disposal, sir, and as of now that data is extremely limited."

"Then do something about it. That will be all. Keep me updated. I want to know about any progress, no matter how insignificant it may seem."

"I'll make sure you get it," O'Reilly said.

"That will be all," CO Johnson said once more.

What the hell was that all about? O'Reilly wondered as he made his way back down the stairs. He didn't get the chance to dwell on it when his phone started to ring. This time the screen made him smile. It was someone he never tired of talking to.

Victoria's first five words caused the smile to vanish from his face in an instant.

I'm feeling really sick, Liam.

CHAPTER EIGHT

O'Reilly made it to the Princess Elizabeth hospital in record time. He wasn't aware that no fewer than six speed cameras had flashed when he sped by, but he wouldn't have cared anyway. Victoria's brother Tommy had informed him that he'd driven her to the hospital and O'Reilly promised to meet him there.

He parked his car in the car park, got out and walked towards the entrance without bothering to lock the car. He found Tommy in the seating section by the reception area. Tommy stood up and they shook hands.
"How is she?" O'Reilly asked.
Tommy shook his head. "They haven't told me."
"What's wrong with her?" O'Reilly said. "Has she been sick? Was she sweating? Did she have a fever?"
"Slow down, Liam," Tommy said. "All she told me was she was feeling like shit, and she thought she should go to hospital. I drove her myself because I thought it would be quicker than waiting for an ambulance."
"You did the right thing. What symptoms did she have?"
"I'm not a bloody doctor."
"Was she having trouble breathing?" O'Reilly said.
"Liam," Tommy said. "I'm just as worried as you are."
"I'm sorry. I'm going to find someone who can give us some answers."

After speaking to Harry behind the reception desk, O'Reilly was told to take a seat. Someone would be along to speak to him shortly. He told Tommy as much.
"That's what they said to me half an hour ago," Victoria's brother said.
"They've got a lot on their plates right now," O'Reilly said.
"Do you think she's got the same thing as that man at the Red Snapper?" Tommy asked.

O'Reilly wished he hadn't. He'd thought the same thing as soon as he got the phone call from Victoria.

"She told you about that?" he said.

Tommy nodded. "She said it was horrible. He just dropped down dead next to your table."

"I'm sure it's something else," O'Reilly said. "You did the right thing bringing her straight here."

A tall man in a white coat approached them. He introduced himself as Dr David Newton.

"Is she going to be OK?" O'Reilly said.

"She is," Dr Newton confirmed.

"What's wrong with her?" Tommy said.

"It looks like a chest infection. Her temperature was dangerously high, but we've managed to get that down. We're giving her fluids, and we'll keep her in overnight to monitor her condition, but I don't see any reason why she shouldn't be allowed to go home tomorrow."

"What caused it?" O'Reilly said.

"Any number of things. Her immune system still hasn't fully recovered after her radiation treatment and unfortunately, she's more susceptible to these things, but there's no need to worry. She'll be right as rain after a few days of rest."

O'Reilly felt like hugging him, but he didn't think it would be appreciated. "Thank you so much," he said instead. "Thank you."

"Like I said," Dr Newton said. "She'll be fine."

"Can we go and see her?" Tommy said.

"Of course. Is there anything else I can help you with?"

"That's all," O'Reilly said. "Thanks again."

Victoria was in bed in one of the general wards. A tube was feeding a saline solution into her arm. Her eyes were closed and O'Reilly wondered if she'd been given something to sedate her. He coughed and her eyes opened.

"You scared the bejesus out of me," O'Reilly said.

Victoria managed a smile. "It wasn't much fun for me either."

"Sorry," O'Reilly said. "How are you feeling?"

"A bit better. They gave me something to get the fever down. Apparently, that's why I felt so terrible."

"The doctor said it's a chest infection," Tommy said.

"It happens," Victoria said. "I've been careful, but sometimes there's nothing you can do about these things. I'm going to need some time off work."

"Take as much time as you need," Tommy said. "And speaking of which, I really should get back. I'm not sure if I really trust that new guy."

"Simon? He seems OK to me."

"We'll see," Tommy said. "I'll come and see you after work."

"What was that all about?" O'Reilly asked when Tommy had left.

"My brother doesn't trust anyone," Victoria said. "You of all people ought to know that."

O'Reilly knew all too well. He and Tommy Radcliffe hadn't got off to the greatest of starts. Tommy was a typical big brother, and O'Reilly was never going to be good enough for his little sister. Their relationship had improved since, but O'Reilly and Tommy were never going to be close friends – that's just the way it was.

"I was so scared, Liam," Victoria said. "I thought I was going to die."

"Not on my watch, Mrs O'Reilly. I'd better be getting back too."

"Do you know anything more about how those people died?"

"Not yet," O'Reilly said. "But I'm going to find out."

"I know you are."

Victoria yawned a gaping yawn.

"Am I boring you?" O'Reilly said.

"Sorry. I feel drained."

"I'll let you get some rest. I'll be back to visit you later."

He leaned in to kiss her and stopped halfway.

"This chest infection isn't contagious, is it?"

"Don't be daft," Victoria said.

O'Reilly kissed her cheek. "See you later."

He was halfway to the exit when an idea came to him. He turned around and walked back down the corridor. He didn't need to ask for directions – he knew exactly where he was going.

CHAPTER NINE

He found Guthrie Lille in his office. The Head of Pathology was eating a sandwich at his desk.
"I was wondering when you would show up."
O'Reilly sat down without being asked.
"I was in the neighbourhood," he said. "And I thought I'd pop by."
"Nothing serious I hope."
"Victoria was rushed in with a chest infection," O'Reilly said. "She's going to be fine."
Dr Lille took a bite of his sandwich and held it out to O'Reilly.
"Want a bite?"
"Jesus," O'Reilly said. "That smells worse than my feet in the middle of summer. What the hell is in it?"
"It's smoked ham with parmesan crusted pesto."
"It stinks like socks."
"Heathen," Dr Lille said. "I don't have any answers for you yet, if that's what this impromptu visit is all about."
"When can I expect some?"
"We've done the PM on your Red Snapper man," Dr Lille said. "The others are scheduled for this afternoon and tomorrow."
"And?"
"And," Dr Lille said. "We've managed to ascertain that cause of death was probably due to organ failure."
"Probably?" O'Reilly repeated.
"There are still some tests that need to be carried out, but I can tell you that Snapper guy's organs were severely damaged."
"Would you not call him that please?"
"His liver, kidneys and spleen showed signs of long-term damage."

"His symptoms came on rapidly," O'Reilly said.

"And I've taken that into account. That's all I've got for you at this stage."

"Fair enough."

"Are you sure you don't want to finish the sandwich?" Dr Lille said. "I'm quite full."

"I'd rather eat the stuff I find between my toes," O'Reilly said. "I hope you're planning on brushing your teeth."

"The dead have no cause to complain about bad breath. When I have anything for you, you'll be the first to know."

"Grand," O'Reilly said. "Only, the big chief is breathing down my neck."

"Since when?"

"Since now," O'Reilly said. "He's never shown any interest before, and I don't know why he's so keen to get some answers now."

"Don't try to understand the reasoning of the people who hold the power, Liam. It'll drive you insane. Will there be anything else?"

"Just one more thing?"

"Make it quick."

"Who the devil came up with the idea of making a sandwich containing parmesan cheese?" O'Reilly asked.

"Goodbye, Liam," Dr Lille said.

"I know when I'm not wanted. You'll call me..."

"As soon as I know anything," Dr Lille interrupted.

O'Reilly left the hospital and got into his car. He wasn't sure what to do next. Everything rested on the tests that Dr Lille had mentioned. O'Reilly took out his phone and found DC Owen's number. She answered straight away.

"Katie," O'Reilly said. "I've just spoken to Guthrie at the hospital, and the test results are going to take time."

"How is Victoria?" DC Owen said.

"She's going to be fine. It was a chest infection, but they've managed to sort it out. I want to speak to the families of the other people who became ill last night. I'll pick you up outside the station."

"I'll wait for you."

The phone started to ring again as soon as he ended the call with DC Owen.

"What the hell do you want now?" O'Reilly asked the screen.

It was CO Johnson again.

O'Reilly let it ring a few times and took the call. "Sir?"

"Have you managed to get anything from Pathology?" CO Johnson didn't beat about the bush.

"I've just this minute spoken to Dr Lille," O'Reilly told him.

CO Johnson cleared his throat. "And?"

"He's done the postmortem on John Moody, and he found evidence of extensive organ damage. His kidneys, liver and spleen showed signs of long-term deterioration, but that doesn't add up with what I saw at the Red Snapper yesterday. Mr Moody would have noticed that something was wrong a long time ago. His organs were damaged rapidly, and that's given Dr Lille something to go on. He's run some tests and he's waiting on the results."

"How long are we talking about?"

"It'll take as long as it takes, sir," O'Reilly said.

"That's not good enough. I presume Dr Lille is aware of the urgency involved?"

"Of course, sir, but these things take time. Our hands are tied."

"I suggest you find a way to untie them. This is not good enough. Do you understand me?"

O'Reilly didn't really, but he didn't tell the chief officer this.

"You'll be the first to know when we have something concrete, sir," he said.

"Make sure of it. Preferably before the end of the day."

"As soon as the results are in, I'll report to you. Why is this so important to you, sir?"

"That's none of your damn business, O'Reilly. I expect you to do the job you're paid to do and from what I've seen so far, you're not doing it. Get it done, Detective Inspector."

The dial tone told O'Reilly that the conversation was over. He made a mental note to speak to DCO Callum Dove when he got the chance. CO Johnson's behaviour was out of character, and he wondered what was going on. He started the engine and drove out of the hospital car park.

CHAPTER TEN

O'Reilly was surprised to hear that Gordon Bell had been discharged from hospital. Gordon's husband, Charles invited them in and told them to make themselves comfortable in the sitting room while he made some refreshments.

"Nice place," DC Owen commented.

That was an understatement. The five-bedroom property was situated in one of the more affluent areas of Vazon on the west of the island. O'Reilly knew that these places cost well over a million, and he wondered what Gordon and Charles did for a living.

Charles came in with a tray of coffee and biscuits.

"Help yourself," he said. "It's Colombian coffee. One of only two good things to come out of Colombia. The godforsaken country would be nothing without its coffee and cocaine, would it? Although I suppose I shouldn't be having this conversation with a couple of police officers. Forgive me – Gordon says I talk too much."

Gordon isn't wrong, O'Reilly thought.

"How is he?" he asked. "I understand he was discharged from hospital."

"Not quite," Charles said. "He insisted on coming home. Gordon isn't a big fan of hospitals. Then again, who is? Nurses waking you up at all hours to ask how you're feeling. And don't get me started on the food."

"I won't," O'Reilly said without thinking. "Can you talk us through yesterday? When did Gordon start feeling ill?"

"I knew something was wrong when he refused a glass of wine," Charles said. "That's unheard of. We usually crack open a bottle of red and watch the sunset. It's a ritual I suppose. It all started when we came back from a wine tasting holiday…"

"May I interrupt you there?" O'Reilly said.

"Sorry," Charles said. "I'm doing it again, aren't I? I do ramble on sometimes."

"What time was this?" DC Owen said. "When did you realise that Gordon wasn't well?"

"About eight."

"Can you recall if Gordon had eaten anything shortly before that?" O'Reilly said.

"We had a spag bol."

"And both of you ate it?"

"We did. It wasn't my best effort, but I couldn't get the mince I usually use, so I put it down to that."

O'Reilly didn't think Gordon's sudden illness was caused by a spaghetti bolognaise.

"Did the doctors at the hospital carry out tests?" he asked.

"A few. They said Gordon was dehydrated, and they put that down to the vomiting and diarrhoea. You do not want to know what the bathroom looked like afterwards. God, and the smell. I haven't been able to go in there since. Luckily, we have three bathrooms. I imagine that's a bit too much information."

"It certainly is," O'Reilly confirmed. "Were the medical staff able to diagnose the cause of Gordon's sudden sickness?"

"It could have been any number of things," Charles said. "But it was almost definitely something he'd eaten."

"Do you remember what Gordon did eat yesterday?" DC Owen said.

"We had a toasted sandwich for lunch."

"Both of you ate the same thing?" O'Reilly said.

"That's right. Cheese and ham – nothing exotic, and we snacked off and on on crisps and dip. We both ate the same things."

"What do you and Gordon do for a living?" O'Reilly said.

"Nothing."

Charles said this like O'Reilly had asked a stupid question.

"Nothing?" the Irishman repeated.

"Oh," Charles said. "You're referring to this place. How did we afford it? Gordon inherited the house from his father, together with a disgusting amount of cash. You must have heard of the Bells."

"I can't say I have," O'Reilly said. "I've only been on the island a couple of years."

"They built up an empire of sorts. Finance, property – you name it. Gordon was the sole heir, and before you say what I know you're thinking, I did not marry him for his money."

"I wasn't thinking any such thing," O'Reilly said. "It's a beautiful house."

"It's a bit over the top for my liking," Charles said. "I mean, it's not like we're ever going to fill the place with children one day, is it?"

"You say that Gordon discharged himself," O'Reilly said. "What did the doctors have to say about that?"

"They advised against it," Charles said. "They recommended he stay in for a few more days so they could monitor his condition, but Gordon insisted on leaving. He felt well enough to go home."

O'Reilly reached inside his jacket and took out a sheet of paper. He handed it to Charles.

"Do you recognise any of the people on this list?"

It was the names of the victims of the sudden sickness last night.

"None of them rings any bells," Charles said. "Who are they?"

"All of them became ill at roughly the same time yesterday," O'Reilly said. "We're looking for possible connections. They all complained of similar symptoms and we're trying to find a common denominator. Something that might lead us to the cause of the sickness."

Charles scanned the list again. "No, I don't know any of these people. Are they going to be alright?"

O'Reilly didn't think telling him that five of them were no longer breathing would achieve anything.

"Would it be possible to have a chat with Gordon?" he asked instead. "I'll try and keep it brief."

"I suppose so," Charles said. "I'll show you to his room. I insisted he use one of the spare rooms – the linen in the main bedroom is satin and it's impossible to clean at the best of times. I didn't want to take the risk of a repeat of the gruesome artwork in the toilet yesterday. That's too much information again, isn't it?"

"It is," O'Reilly said. "If you could just point me in the direction of the spare room, I'm sure I'll find it."

He left DC Owen with Charles and went upstairs. According to the talkative husband, Gordon was in the third room on the right. O'Reilly stopped outside the door and the smell hit him immediately. It was something rancid and there was a metallic tang to it. It became more apparent when he pushed open the door.

The first thing that occurred to O'Reilly was that Gordon Bell really shouldn't have discharged himself from hospital. The man on the bed was clearly dead. The source of the stench was spread all over the sheets. Blood and vomit had coated the duvet and splashed onto the carpet. The second thought that entered O'Reilly's head was Charles's decision to keep Gordon away from the main bedroom and its satin sheets was a wise one. This was a mess that was not going to be easily cleaned up.

CHAPTER ELEVEN

"Is the hospital going to be in trouble for this?" DC Stone wondered.

"No, Andy," O'Reilly said. "Gordon Bell signed discharge forms that confirmed that he was going against the advice of the medical professionals, and he acknowledged all potential risks. The disclaimer puts all responsibility on Mr Bell alone."

"Katie said the husband squealed like a little girl," DC Stone said.

"It was more like the whinny of a horse," O'Reilly said. "I tried to stop him from going inside the bedroom, but he pushed past me. And I'm still not sure if his reaction was because of his husband's demise or if it was due to the state of the bed sheets. I don't envy the person who has to clean up the filth in there."

"We've had reports that two more people have died, sir," DS Skinner said. "Two women who were rushed to hospital last night didn't make it."

"What the devil are we dealing with here?" O'Reilly said.

"I've never seen anything like it before," DC Stone said. "Do you think it could be some kind of pandemic?"

"Perhaps it's something in the water on the island," DC Owen put forward.

"How long before we get the test results back?" DCI Fish asked.

"Soon," O'Reilly said. "As soon as Pathology have something for us, we'll know a bit more."

"The Chief Officer called me into his office earlier," DCI Fish said.

"Me too," O'Reilly told him. "He's acting really odd, and if I didn't know any better, I would swear he knows more than he's letting on."

"He's getting pressure from higher up," DCI Fish said.

"I thought he was as high up as they came."

"Anyway," DCI Fish said. "Chief Officer Johnson is keen to get to the bottom of this."

"All of us want to get to the bottom of it, Tom," O'Reilly said.

He got up and limped towards the whiteboard at the back of the room. He added three more names to the list.

"Eight people. This time yesterday, they were alive and well. As far as we know, they weren't acquainted so something else has to connect them. Any thoughts?"

"It has to be something they all ate," DC Owen said. "But we've got a problem with that. The families and friends of the victims couldn't tell us anything specific that the dead people consumed."

"The spouses of most of the fatalities ate the same things," O'Reilly said. "We're missing something."

"What are we missing?" DC Stone said. "More than a dozen people started complaining of feeling ill at roughly the same time. Most of them are now dead."

"The test results are key," O'Reilly said. "There will be a common denominator in those results. Science does not lie."

"I hope to God you're right, Liam," DCI Fish said. "Because this is bad. People are already panicking, and CO Johnson isn't the only one who wants answers."

O'Reilly took a long look at the names on the board. He knew there had to be a connection somewhere, but for the life of him, he couldn't find one. These were men and women of all ages and from various socio-economic groups. They were from all corners of the island, and they didn't know one another. Why had they suddenly developed symptoms of a sickness that had resulted in their deaths? O'Reilly really had no idea.

"Five people are still alive," he said.

"For now," DC Stone said.

"We have to stay optimistic, Andy. Their symptoms were similar, but they're still breathing. Why is that?"

"I presume they're still in hospital?" DS Skinner said.

"As far as I'm aware," O'Reily said. "Three out of the four who were taken to College Hospital are still alive as are two people who were rushed to the Princess Elizabeth. I suggest we speak to them all and see if they can give us some more answers."

"It's worth a shot," DC Stone said.

"Andy," O'Reilly said. "You and Will can take the ones at the College Hospital. Me and Katie will deal with the survivors at the Princess Elizabeth. I presume you don't have a problem with that, Tom?"

"No problem at all," DCI Fish said. "I've got another meeting with the CO and DCO Dove in thirty minutes. We have to come up with something to alleviate the growing panic on the island."

"Will we be issuing a press release?"

"It's inevitable," DCI Fish said. "Right now, it's all about damage control. The people of the island deserve answers, but the CO is adamant that we don't cause any further panic."

O'Reilly nodded. "We'll give the islanders some answers, but those answers don't necessarily have to be the truth."

"Something like that."

"Rather you than me," O'Reilly said. "Katie, give me twenty minutes. I need a cup of tea – my mouth is as dry as a camel's scrotum, and I need to rectify that."

"Liam," DCI Fish warned.

"Sorry, Tom," O'Reilly said. "I have no idea where that came from."

He got to his feet and left the room. He was halfway to his office when his phone started to ring. It was CO Johnson again and he decided to ignore it. He wondered if he should assign the big chief a ringtone. He would give it some thought later.

He made some tea and sat down at his desk. He'd barely taken a sip when his phone started to ring again. A glance at the screen told him it wasn't CO Johnson this time. It was a name that caused him to put down the tea and take a few deep breaths. It was Guthrie Lille and the brief conversation that followed made O'Reilly feel sick.

CHAPTER TWELVE

"This is deeply concerning, Liam."

Dr Lille's expression was grim. O'Reilly and DC Owen were sitting opposite the Head of Pathology in his office. They were planning on making a trip to the hospital anyway, but they didn't expect to be sitting where there were now.

Dr Lille opened up a file in front of him. "Amanitin toxin. We found traces of it in all of the people who died last night and this morning. The man who died at the Red Snapper had large quantities in his system, and once we understood what we were dealing with we could carry out tests on the others relatively quickly. All of these people died as a result of organ failure due to the toxin."

"Never heard of it," O'Reilly said. "How did this ama thingy get into their systems?"

"Amanitin toxin is present in the common Amanita Phalloides," Dr Lille explained. "Otherwise known as the Death Cap mushroom."

"I've heard of that one. Jesus."

"Indeed. Symptoms caused by the ingestion of the amanitin toxin include abdominal pain, vomiting, bloody diarrhoea, rapid fluid loss and damage to the central nervous system. Massive organ failure occurs within hours of eating the mushroom and this is followed by coma and death."

O'Reilly was finding this hard to process.

"Are you telling me that all these people ate poisonous mushrooms?"

"I'm telling you what the tests results revealed, Liam."

"Where did they even get these deadly fungi?"

"They grow wild on the island, sir," DC Owen informed him. "Usually on oak trees, but they're adaptable."

"DC Owen is correct," Dr Lille said. "They've been known to attach themselves to a wide variety of trees. Beech, chestnut and birch to name a few."

"Why the devil would someone eat one of these things?" O'Reilly said.

"I'm no expert, but I suggest you ask yourself how these people managed to ingest a mushroom that only appears on the island in Autumn?"

"Are you implying they were unaware they were eating it?" O'Reilly said.

"He's right, sir," DC Owen said. "I know a bit about mushrooms. My uncle is a keen forager, and the majority of fungi are seasonal. It's been a long, hot summer and I very much doubt there will be death caps around yet."

O'Reilly considered this for a moment.

"If there's none on the island yet, how did these people get hold of them?"

"That's a question you'll have to put to the ones who are on the mend," Dr Lille said.

"Are they going to be alright?" DC Owen said.

"One of them definitely is. I've spoken to the doctor who treated a man by the name of Jimmy Lloyd. Mr Lloyd happens to be a vet, and his training is probably what saved his life. He started to feel ill yesterday evening, and he realised that the symptoms were caused by some kind of poisoning. He induced vomiting and he managed to expel the majority of the toxins before they had a chance to get to work on his vital organs. Mr Lloyd is a very lucky man."

"We'll speak to him shortly," O'Reilly said. "Death Cap mushrooms. Who would have thought it?"

"It happens," Dr Lille said. "They look perfectly innocuous and apparently, they're not unpleasant to eat. It's this palatability and their slight nutty flavour that makes them so dangerous."

O'Reilly thanked him and he and DC Owen made their way to the private room where Jimmy Lloyd was being treated.

"What do you think, Katie?"

"I don't understand it," she said. "I still can't figure out where they got the mushrooms from. They won't be found on the island for at least another month."

"You said your uncle is a forager?" O'Reilly said.

"It's getting more popular these days. And it's not something you do without extensive knowledge of the fungi on offer. Delicious mushrooms can look like deadly ones and vice versa. You have to know your fungi."

"So I'm beginning to understand. We've cleared up one mystery, and we've been gifted with another, much bigger one in its place. How on earth did more than a dozen people manage to eat a toxic mushroom that won't be found on the island for another month?"

Jimmy Lloyd was sitting on the chair next to the bed in his private room. Jimmy was in his mid-twenties and O'Reilly didn't think he was going to be another fatality of the mystery fungi poisoning. His face was pale, and his eyes were bloodshot, but he didn't look like a man on death's door. O'Reilly introduced himself and DC Owen and told him they needed to ask him a few questions.

Jimmy put down the book he was reading. "What's going on?"

There was only one chair in the room and Jimmy Lloyd was sitting on it. O'Reilly asked DC Owen if she could find a couple more from somewhere. She left the room and returned with a single chair.

"I don't mind standing," she said.

O'Reilly placed the chair opposite Jimmy and sat down. "I do. This leg is giving me trouble again. How are you feeling, Mr Lloyd."

"Please, call me Jimmy. I'm feeling a lot better than I did yesterday. I wouldn't want to go through that again."

"When did you start feeling ill?" DC Owen said.

"Around seven yesterday evening," Jimmy said. "It came on all of a sudden."

"I believe you're a vet," O'Reilly said.

"That's right."

"And that's why you knew to induce vomiting?"

"I suspected that I'd eaten something nasty," Jimmy said. "There was no way to be sure, but I wasn't taking any chances."

"How did you do it?" O'Reilly said.

"A couple of fingers down the throat. It triggers the gag reflex. It wasn't as easy as I thought. I've done it countless times with dogs and cats, but never on myself."

"You stick your fingers in the mouths of dogs and cats?" O'Reilly said.

"It's not common practice, but I've found it to be effective. It was a lot harder to use the procedure on myself."

"But you managed?"

Jimmy nodded. "I waited until there was nothing left in my stomach then I managed to keep down a couple of activated charcoal tablets. They're designed to absorb toxins. I found the strength to make it downstairs, and I called an ambulance."

"That's quite a story to tell," O'Reilly said. "Do you live alone?"

"I'm married," Jimmy said. "But Debbie is visiting her sister in France at the moment."

"Can you remember what you had to eat yesterday?" O'Reilly said.

He wasn't expecting what Jimmy Lloyd did next. He reached inside the pocket of the jacket on the back of the chair and pulled out a piece of paper.

"It's all on there."

He handed it to O'Reilly.

"You documented everything you ate and drank?"

"It was bothering me," Jimmy said. "I knew it was something I'd ingested, and I wanted to see if I could narrow it down. I deal with a lot of dogs and cats brought in with signs of poisoning, and it helps to know what they could have eaten. There's nothing on there that explains the symptoms I experienced though."

O'Reilly debated whether to inform him what had caused his sickness. It didn't take long to make up his mind. The source of the amanitin toxin was key to the investigation.

"Are you familiar with the death cap mushroom?"

"Of course," Jimmy said.

"The tests that were carried out found traces of amanitin toxin in your system."

"What? Impossible."

"The tests don't lie, Jimmy."

"There must be some kind of mistake. Firstly, I can't stand mushrooms, so there's no way I would even be in the position to eat a deadly one and secondly, there won't be death caps on the island for at least another month."

"I'm aware of that," O'Reilly said. "But as I said, the tests don't lie."

CHAPTER THIRTEEN

"Amanita Phalloides." O'Reilly wrote it on the whiteboard opposite the names of the people who had succumbed to its toxins.

"A pleasant-sounding name, but it is definitely not a pleasant mushroom. The death cap is one of the deadliest fungi out there, and we have eight corpses as a result of it. Any thoughts?"

DC Owen had already touched on the fact that the fungus only appeared on the island at certain times of year, but she brought it up anyway for the benefit of the rest of the team.

"That confuses things," DS Skinner said.

"You can say that again, Will," O'Reilly agreed. "We have a bunch of people who somehow managed to ingest fatal quantities of a mushroom that isn't found on the island yet."

"How is that even possible?" DC Stone said.

"What else do we know about this deadly fungus?" DS Skinner said.

"I did a bit more research," DC Owen said. "And this might be something to consider. The amanitin toxin is unusual in that its lethal properties are not inactivated by cooking, freezing or drying."

"Which means it can be stored," O'Reilly said.

"Exactly, sir. In theory, you can keep a load of death cap mushrooms in the freezer for months and when you take them out again, they'll still be deadly."

"It still doesn't explain how more than a dozen people ended up eating it," DS Skinner said.

"Unless they didn't know they were eating it, Sarge," DC Owen said.

"Are you suggesting that this was intentional?"

"It's worth thinking about."

"The thought had crossed my mind," O'Reilly said. "But it was a thought so abhorrent I pushed it to the sidelines for a bit."

"Are you saying that these people could have been intentionally poisoned?" DS Skinner said.

"That's exactly what I'm saying," O'Reilly said. "And if that's the case, we're looking at eight premeditated murders. So far."

The briefing room was silent for a while and O'Reilly made no effort to break it.

"If what you suspect is true," DC Stone said after a brief pause. "We need to be looking at how they did it."

"We need to be looking at a lot more than that, Andy," O'Reilly said. "But that's as good a place as any to start. How did so many people end up ingesting a potentially lethal toxin?"

"How did they not taste it?" DS Skinner wondered.

"Death cap mushrooms don't taste bad, Sarge," DC Owen said. "In fact, from the reports I've read the taste is described as nutty and rather pleasant. That's what makes the mushrooms so dangerous."

"None of the families and friends of the victims mentioned anything about them eating anything out of the ordinary," DS Skinner said.

"Then we look for something ordinary," O'Reilly said.

"I'm not following you," DS Skinner said.

"All of the victims fell ill at roughly the same time. That means they probably ingested the toxin at around the same time. Give or take a few hours, I'd say. This wasn't a case of random poisoning – all of these people were exposed to the toxin in the past few days. We need to complete a thorough audit of everything they stuffed into their mouths."

"Before we do that," DS Skinner said. "Do we know if there's any other way the toxins can enter the bloodstream? Can they be transferred via the air or through the skin perhaps?"

"I'd have to double check," DC Owen said. "But I don't think so. The only way for the amanitin toxin to cause so much damage is if it's ingested. I suppose it would be possible for a concentrated amount to be dissolved into a solution and injected, but injecting over a dozen people would be impossible."

"It would," O'Reilly agreed. "This is the plan of action – we need to examine every aspect of the victims' lives. Where did they go in the hours leading up to them taking ill? What did they eat and what did they drink?"

"I suggest we look at the survivors too," DC Owen said. "I get the feeling that there's a reason why they made it, and the others didn't. Perhaps they ingested the toxins later on – they made it to hospital in time, and that's why they were able to survive it."

"If that's the case," O'Reilly said. "The timeline should give us some answers. If we can narrow down the time frame involved, we'll have a more accurate idea about the source of this cursed toxin. It's a hell of a lot of work, but it's doable if we work smart."

His phone started to ring and when he saw who was trying to get hold of him, he decided that he would definitely assign a ringtone for the chief officer. He didn't bother to answer the call. Instead, he informed the team that he was wanted elsewhere and left the briefing room with no further explanation.

CO Johnson's door was wide open, and O'Reilly could hear a voice from within, so he went inside the office and took a seat opposite the boss of the Island Police. CO Johnson was talking to someone on the phone. He didn't make eye contact with O'Reilly as he hastily brought an end to the phone conversation.

"I've been trying to get hold of you," he said when he'd put down the phone.

"That's why I'm here, sir," O'Reilly said.

"Have we had any developments?"

"We might have something to consider."

"Spit it out then."

"We've managed to identify the exact toxin the victims ingested," O'Reilly said. "It comes from the death cap mushroom and there is no way more than a dozen people accidentally ate some."

CO Johnson reaction suggested he already knew this.

"I see. Anything else?"

"This particular mushroom grows on the island," O'Reilly said. "But there won't be any around for at least another month which leads us to believe that the toxins were stored somewhere and released, which in turn leads us to the conclusion that the victims were targeted."

CO Johnson merely nodded. O'Reilly knew there was something terribly wrong.

The chief officer got up from his chair and walked over to the window.

"You probably think I was given this position on a plate."

O'Reilly wasn't expecting this.

"I don't think that at all, sir."

"This wasn't a fast-track thing," CO Johnson said. "I fought every single day for thirty years to be where I am now."

"Is there something on your mind, sir?"

CO Johnson turned to face him. "Can I trust you?"

"Implicitly," O'Reilly said.

"What I'm about to tell you will go no further."

O'Reilly didn't think this was a question.

"Go on."

CO Johnson sat back down.

"You're absolutely right, Liam. The victims of the death cap toxins were targeted, but not in the way you think."

"I'm afraid you've lost me there, sir," O'Reilly said.

"Yesterday afternoon, I received an email," CO Johnson said. "It was a rather disturbing email and at first I believed it to be a hoax."

"What was in the email?"

"I'm coming to that. I dismissed it from my thoughts, but earlier today another email arrived, and this one left no doubt about the sender's intentions. This can't go any further. Interpret that as a direct order, if you wish."

"What's going on, sir?"

"In a nutshell, I'm being blackmailed."

"Blackmailed," O'Reilly repeated. "By who?"

"I don't know, but I do know that the threat is serious. Do you have skeletons from your past that you'd prefer to keep buried?"

"I think we all do, sir. Does this have something to do with the recent deaths?"

"It does. All of these people were poisoned."

"We've already figured that out, sir," O'Reilly said. "What else? What was in the email?"

"It's confidential."

"If it's connected to my investigation, I want to know about it."

"It's connected to the investigation," CO Johnson confirmed. "We all have secrets, but some secrets are worse than others. The secret I'm referring to cannot see the light of day. The consequences of that don't bear thinking about."

It took a while for O'Reilly to connect the dots but when the realisation dawned on him, he felt the skin on his face heat up. He looked the CO in the eye.

"Are you telling me that you knew these people were at risk?"

"Not immediately," CO Johnson said. "The gist of the first email was so far-fetched I didn't give it another thought, but when people started to die it all became clearer."

"What the fuck are they threatening to expose?" O'Reilly couldn't help himself.

"I can't tell you, Liam – I really can't."

"You knew those people were going to die," O'Reilly said. "You knew about it, and you did nothing. You need to get the emails examined. We have to stop this."

"I can't do that."

"Then I'll take it further. I'll go to the fecking home secretary if I have to. You could have stopped this."

"You repeat a word of what was spoken within these four walls, and your career is over. I will personally see to it."

"Are you even listening to yourself?" O'Reilly said. "Eight people are dead because of some seedy little secret you want to keep buried. You're supposed to be in charge of law and order on this island. I very much doubt the backlash from this little secret of yours can be any worse than what's going to happen when the truth about this gets out."

"This conversation is over," CO Johnson said.

"It's far from over."

 CO Johnson rubbed his eyes and O'Reilly thought he detected a tear in the corner of one of them.

"Please, Liam. Just give me some time to work something out."

"Are more people in danger?" O'Reilly said.

He received a subtle nod in reply.

"Then we don't have time. I want to see those emails."

"No."

"Then I'll report you to someone who can access them."

"The emails have been forwarded to my private email, and I've deleted them from my work account. Give me some time to figure out a solution to this."

O'Reilly considered this, and it didn't take long.

"No," he said. "Fuck that. I'm taking this higher up. I'll take it to the press if I have to. Fuck my job – if I can save just one more life then it'll be worth it."

He stood up.

"Don't do this, Liam," CO Johnson warned.

"You don't know me, sir," O'Reilly said. "You really don't know me at all. I'm prepared to do everything I've told you, but first I'm going to have a quick chat to DCO Dove. Callum will back me up."

"I very much doubt that, Liam."

"We'll see."

O'Reilly turned to leave.

"DCO Dove doesn't know anything about this," CO Johnson said.

"I'm going to do something about that," O'Reilly said without turning around.

"The secret I'm protecting isn't mine, Liam."

This time O'Reilly did turn around.

"And if it gets out," CO Johnson said. "DCO Dove's life is over. His career, his marriage and his freedom will vanish in a heartbeat."

CHAPTER FOURTEEN

O'Reilly sat back down.

"Tell me what you know."

"There are more than one of them," CO Johnson said. "In the email they refer to themselves in the plural. They know a lot more about the recent sickness than they should, so there's little doubt that they're involved."

"What have they threatened?"

"More sickness."

"You're going to have to give me more than that, sir," O'Reilly said. "Firstly, how did they do it? Do you know that at least?"

"I do," CO Johnson said. "They didn't offer specifics, but somehow they managed to contaminate certain foodstuffs and drinks."

"How?"

"The recent break-ins."

The light bulb inside O'Reilly's head was burning brightly now. Things were starting to make sense.

"They broke into the shops and contaminated the products?"

"That's exactly what they did, Liam," CO Johnson said.

"Do we know which products are affected?"

"Therein lies the problem. As I said, I'm not aware of the specifics."

The severity of the situation was starting to hit home. CO Johnson read O'Reilly's mind.

"It's a logistical nightmare," he said. "The right thing to do would be to remove everything from the shelves of the establishments involved, but we can't afford to create the kind of panic that would entail. The contamination was random – not every product was tarnished, and without testing everything on those shelves, we have no clue as to which ones are potentially lethal. The logistics involved in a job like that would be horrific.

The operation would take weeks, if not months and we simply do not have the manpower or the budget to undertake it."

"Let me get this straight," O'Reilly said. "These people are willing to murder at random because of something that DCO Dove did. You need to tell me what that is, sir."

"I've already told you I can't do that."

"You're going to have to reconsider. We're now aware of the motive behind the recent murders, but if I'm to proceed I'm going to need details."

"Let's not be too hasty."

"This isn't going to go away, sir," O'Reilly said. "More people are going to die, and I can't stand by and let that happen. I wasn't bluffing when I said I would go to the press."

"You do that, and you'll be in the dole queue before you know it. You'll have plenty of time to visit DCO Dove in jail, because that's where he's going if this sees the light of day. This does not just affect one man – the reputation of the Island Police will be shattered. This is something we won't recover from."

"So be it," O'Reilly said. "I'll take my chances. I will not be responsible for more deaths."

"Think about the consequences before you do anything rash, Liam."

"I will go to the press, sir."

"And what will you give them?" CO Johnson asked. "All you have is speculation at this time, and I can tell you this for nothing – a detective inspector blowing the whistle on the establishment that pays his salary will not end well for you. Think about that. You'll be unemployable if you go this route."

"Then I'll ask DCO Dove for the details," O'Reilly said. "Callum and I have an understanding and I'm sure he'll back me up."

"Give me some more time before you do that," CO Johnson said. "We now know how they're doing it, so that's something at least."

"You've got until the end of the day," O'Reilly said.

"I need more than that. Give me until the end of the week. Please, Liam. We can fix this."

"Tell that to the families of the eight fresh corpses."

He got up to let Chief Officer Johnson think about this.

He didn't go back to the briefing room. Instead, he walked down the corridor past the front desk and left the station. His leg was playing up again, but he walked towards the esplanade anyway. He sat down on the nearest bench and gazed out to sea. The beach was deserted, and the sea was choppy. A couple of sailing boats were braving the brisk breeze close to the shore. A passenger ferry was motoring further out.

Usually, the sea air and the tranquillity of the boats on the water helped to clear O'Reilly's head but it didn't work now. His mind was muddied with too many conflicting thoughts. The conversation with CO Johnson had come as a shock and O'Reilly was finding it difficult to rationalise his decision. Surely the life of one man wasn't worth the lives of countless islanders. Eight people were already dead, and the potential for more fatalities was endless, given what they now knew. O'Reilly was faced with a moral dilemma, and he wasn't sure how to handle it.

He breathed in a few lungful's of sea air and tried to formulate a plan of action. Firstly, they needed to take a close look at the shops where the break-ins occurred. It was possible the perpetrators had left something behind. There was no detailed forensic analysis carried out initially, and they needed to do something about that.

The next step would be to follow up on what was discussed in the latest briefing. Everything that the victims of the poisoning ate and drank needed to be put under the microscope. They would need to look at everything they'd purchased from the shops that had recently been targeted and that would give them more to go on.

O'Reilly was still in two minds about taking this to the press, but he knew that CO Johnson was right. Until he had more information at his disposal he didn't really have anything newsworthy, and neither of the island's two main newspapers would print anything without proof. Even Fred *the Ed* Viking would be reluctant to put out something based on the word of one man, and he had no moral compass whatsoever.

O'Reilly decided that the only way forward was to carry on with the investigation taking the new information into account. He would continue to put pressure on CO Johnson but in the meantime, he would go through the motions. He got up off the bench and something out to sea caught his eye. One of the yachts had broached in a spectacular manner. O'Reilly observed it as the boat righted itself and the mainsail fell flat in the water on the opposite side.

"I know exactly how you feel," O'Reilly said and headed back to the station.

CHAPTER FIFTEEN

O'Reilly had asked DI Peters to meet him at Freshlife Supermarket on Victoria Street. The shop was the first one to be broken into and O'Reilly decided to start there. It wasn't a big shop and O'Reilly wondered if it had been chosen at random.

"What exactly are we looking for?" the Head of Forensics asked outside. He was accompanied by one of his technicians. DC Glenda Taylor was an experienced forensics officer and O'Reilly liked her.

"It's come to our attention that the recent deaths were the result of random contamination of certain foods and drinks," he told DI Peters. "We couldn't understand why the shops were broken into and nothing was taken and now we know. Whoever did this had no intention of stealing anything – their sole purpose was to poison certain products in various shops."

DC Taylor froze. "I buy my groceries from this shop sometime."

"When was the last time you were in here?" O'Reilly asked her.

"Not for a week or two."

"The break-in occurred on Saturday night," O'Reilly said. "It's safe to assume that was when the products were contaminated."

"How sure are you about this, Liam?" DI Peters asked.

"As sure as I can be, Jim. The rest of the team are busy speaking with the families of the victims to see if they can produce receipts from the shops they recently visited, and if any of them correspond to the shops that were broken into we'll be a step closer but we need to look more closely at them to see if we can see any evidence of tampering."

"Saturday night, you say?"

"The alarm was activated just before midnight," O'Reilly said.

"That was over two days ago," DI Peters said. "Who knows how many customers have been through the doors since then. From a forensic perspective, it's not ideal."

"I'm aware of that, but it can't be helped."

"How are we going to explain this to the owners? We've never had to deal with anything even close to this before."

"I'm aware of that too," O'Reilly said. "You leave that up to me."

In truth, O'Reilly had no idea how he was going to approach the owners of the shops. He couldn't tell them the truth. If it got out that certain products from the shops carried a potential death sentence the backlash would be huge. Panic would spread and it was possible that it would hinder the investigation. No, O'Reilly needed to come up with another explanation.

The owner of Freshlife Supermarket was a woman who looked to be in her fifties. She was a short woman with bright eyes. She introduced herself as Brenda North. O'Reilly explained the reason for the visit and asked if he could speak to her in private. She led him to an office at the back of the shop.

"I'm going to have to ask you to close the shop for a while," he said.

"What?" Brenda said. "What on earth for?"

"Our forensics officers need to take a closer look," O'Reilly said. "And they can't do that with customers coming in and out."

"Why the sudden interest?" Brenda said. "You didn't seem too bothered before."

"I apologise for that. Unfortunately, we're stretched to the limit, and that means it takes longer to get round to things like this. Budget cuts have hit us hard. We'll try to be as quick as we can."

It was a weak explanation, but it seemed to have the desired effect. Brenda informed the staff in the shop what was going on and soon, all the customers were gone. Brenda flipped the closed sign on the door and locked it.

"Thank you," O'Reilly said. "Like I said, we'll try to be quick. I'm going to have to ask you to stay in the office. That goes for the members of staff too."

"I'll give them an early break," Brenda said. "Is there something I ought to be aware of?"

"Nothing at all," O'Reilly lied. "I'll let you know when we're finished."

He went back to the main section of the shop. DI Peters and DC Taylor were already going through the motions. DC Taylor was snapping photographs of the products on the shelves.

"Prints are going to be a waste of time," DI Peters said. "Who knows how many hands have touched the shelves since the break-in. I want to see if there's any evidence of tampering instead. Glenda isn't being shy with the photos, and we'll analyse them in more detail when we get back to the lab. It's a shame we don't know what it was the victims ate or drank."

They were about to get a clue. The screen on O'Reilly's phone told him DS Skinner was calling.

"Will," he answered it. "Please tell me you have something for me."

"I think I do, sir," DS Skinner said. "We've spoken to the families of three of the victims so far, and we might have a link. Arthur Williams, John Moody and Felicity Green all drank apple juice shortly before they started feeling ill."

"Apple juice?" O'Reilly said.

"There's more. The apple juice was bought from Freshlife Supermarket on Victoria Street."

"We're there now," O'Reilly said. "What are the odds?"

"Arthur Williams' wife told us that she can't stand the stuff."

"That's why she didn't get sick."

"It is sir. Same goes for John Moody's wife. Only John drank the juice, and I'm sure we'll see the same thing with Felicity Green. Andy and I have managed to get the empty carton from Arthur's house. Andy's still moaning about having to rummage through the bin."

"What about John and Felicity?" O'Reilly said.

"Unfortunately, not. The refuse collection was yesterday, and the empty carton is long gone."

"That's fine," O'Reilly said. "Good work."

"The empty carton has been put into evidence," DS Skinner said. "It's a brand called *Cloudy Jack*."

"Never heard of it. Thanks, Will."

He ended the call and told DI Peters what DS Skinner had informed him.

"*Cloudy Jack*," DI Peters said. "Let's have a look, shall we."

It wasn't difficult to find it. The apple juice was in the middle of the shelf displaying the drinks. O'Reilly counted sixteen cartons of *Cloudy Jack*. DC Taylor photographed every one of them.

"How do we do this, sir?" she asked DI Peters.

"Bag them all," the Head of Forensics said. "And be careful. Make sure the cartons remain upright. There's a chance we might get possible leakage."

O'Reilly left them to it. He made his way to the front of the shop. Someone was banging on the door. An elderly man had his face pressed to the window in the door. He spotted O'Reilly and waved. The Irishman waved back. He turned around and made his way to the office at the back of the shop.

"Almost done," he told Brenda.

"Did you find anything?" she said.

"I believe we did. I need to ask you about one of your products. *Cloudy Jack* apple juice."

"It's a popular brand. What do you need to know?"

"Could you find out when the apple juice was put on the shelves?" O'Reilly said.

"What on earth for?"

"Could you just find out please. Our Forensic team may have found something relating to the break-in and all the evidence is centred on the *Cloudy Jack*."

Brenda woke up a laptop and tapped the keypad.

"The *Cloudy Jack* was delivered last week, Thursday. It was put on the shelf the same day."

"Do you know how many cartons were delivered?" O'Reilly said.

"Two cases of twelve. And according to the records there are sixteen cartons left."

"Correct," O'Reilly said. "Thank you."

He left the office. The elderly man was still outside. He wasn't giving up and now he was hammering his fist on the door so hard O'Reilly thought he might break the glass. His phone started to ring again, and this time it was DC Owen.

"I think we might have found the source of the toxins," she said.

"I've already spoken to Will," O'Reilly said. "*Cloudy Jack* apple juice."

"No, sir."

"What?" O'Reilly said.

"Two of the victims ate bananas from Freshlife Supermarket on Victoria Street," DC Owen said. "According to the families it was the only thing they could think of that the victims ate, and they didn't."

CHAPTER SIXTEEN

"This is worse than we thought," O'Reilly said.

It was almost five and the team were gathered for a final briefing of the day. "We've done a thorough investigation into what the victims of the poisoning ate and drank in the hours before the sickness appeared, and it appears that there isn't one specific product involved. Three of them drank *Cloudy Jack* apple juice, two more ate bananas and we now know that three more of them helped themselves to a few spoons of mayonnaise."

"They contaminated random products," DS Skinner said.

"They certainly did," O'Reilly said. "And there's more. Every one of those products came from Freshlife Supermarket on Victoria Street. As far as we're aware there haven't been any more reports of sudden sicknesses and that leads me to believe that the other break-ins were decoys."

"Smokescreens?" DCI Fish said.

"It appears so," O'Reilly said. "All of the people who died consumed products from Freshlife."

"That's good news though, isn't it?" DC Stone said.

"I suppose it is," O'Reilly said. "For what it's worth. Bananas, apple juice and mayonnaise."

"How did they do it?" DC Owen asked. "How did they get the toxins into the products?"

"Jim Peters suspects they used a syringe," O'Reilly said. "Probably one with an extremely thin needle. The resulting hole would be barely visible to the naked eye. Forensics have the remaining bananas, juice and mayonnaise from the shop, and there will be a thorough examination."

"Do you think this is the end of it?" DS Skinner said. "Do you think the people responsible are going to strike again?"

O'Reilly didn't know what to tell him. The conversation with CO Johnson was still fresh in his head, but he didn't think sharing it with the rest of the team would be a good idea just yet.

"I really don't know, Will," he said. "We have a lot more information than we did earlier. We know how the victims died, and we know how the toxins got into the products. I'm of the opinion that not all of the juice, bananas and mayonnaise was contaminated. The people responsible had a very short window of time to carry out the sabotage – the security company arrived within minutes, so I don't think they had time to taint all of the products. It will have been a swift operation."

"Let's hope that's the case," DCI Fish said.

"We still haven't considered why these people did this, sir," DC Owen said.

"No, Katie, we haven't," O'Reilly said. "We haven't touched on the motive yet, and I'm open to any suggestions."

"It's clear they meant to kill the victims," DS Skinner said. "You don't inject toxins from death cap mushrooms otherwise."

"The people who died weren't selected though," DC Owen said. "It could have been anybody who ended up buying the products and ingesting the toxins. This is tantamount to a terrorist attack."

"And I'm worried that's how the press is going to portray it," O'Reilly said. "The victims were random and when that happens emotions tend to run high."

"Do you think we could be dealing with a terrorist faction?" DCI Fish said. "Because, if that's the case we're not equipped to deal with it. We're going to need outside help."

"Let's not get carried away," O'Reilly said.

"What would someone possibly stand to gain from this?" DC Owen said. "There's no feasible motivation behind it. They're not gaining financially - the victims were chosen at random so there's no revenge angle there, and unless these people are planning on holding the island to ransom, I can't figure out why they're doing it. What are they getting out of it?"

"Sick, twisted pleasure?" DC Stone suggested.

"Nobody is that warped," DS Skinner said. "No, there's something else behind this."

"There is."

Everyone turned to look at O'Reilly. He was probably going to regret what he was planning on saying next, but he couldn't lie to his colleagues. In the two years they'd worked together they'd proven themselves to be extremely competent detectives, and O'Reilly had a lot of respect for every one of them, even Andy Stone. It didn't feel right to keep them in the dark.

"What is it, Liam?" DCI Fish said.

"Before I open this particular can of worms," O'Reilly said. "You need to be aware that it cannot be closed again. Once those worms are out, they're out for good."

"Worms?" It was DC Stone.

"It's an analogy, Andy. I want you to listen to what I'm about to tell you, and I want you to hear me out. The recent sickness on the island is all about blackmail."

"Blackmail?" DC Stone said.

"Is there an echo in here?" O'Reilly said. "I've been communicating with CO Johnson and there's a reason for his keen interest in the case. Yesterday, the chief officer received an email warning him about a threat to the people on the island. He pushed it aside. He suspected it was some kind of hoax, but another email arrived and this one left little doubt about the intentions of these people. They promised to carry on contaminating food and drink until their demands were met."

"What are these demands?" DCI Fish said.

"I don't know, Tom. CO Johnson wouldn't elaborate, but he did go so far as to tell me it's something that was covered up. Something that involved a senior officer. It's also something that could have grave consequences should it ever see the light of day. Whatever this secret is, that's why these people are poisoning people on the island. They want the person responsible to tell the truth, otherwise they've promised to keep on with their campaign of sickness and death."

"We need to find out exactly what the secret is," DC Owen said.
"I'm aware of that, Katie," O'Reilly said. "Once we know what we're dealing with, we'll be a step closer to figuring out who's doing it, but the big chief is keeping it quiet. He believes the secret will destroy the person involved, and it'll also crucify the Island Police as a whole."
"Why are you only bringing this to our attention now, Liam?" DCI Fish said.
"Because CO Johnson threatened me. That's why. He made it very clear that if I mentioned a word of it to anyone, I would no longer have a job."
"And yet you're telling us?" DCI Fish said.
"It's the right thing to do."
"How do we go about this, sir?" DC Stone said.
"You tell me, Andy?" O'Reilly said.

"What about the press?" DCI Fish said.
This surprised O'Reilly. He didn't think DCI Fish had it in him.
"I thought about that, Tom, but what exactly do we have to offer them? We don't yet know what this big secret is, and we can hardly speak without concrete proof."
"Then we fabricate something," DCI Fish said. "We call in with an anonymous tip-off and cause a bit of speculation."
"No respectable newspaper will print something based on speculation."
"Fred Viking will," DS Skinner joined in. "This sounds right up his alley."
"It's risky," O'Reilly said. "And what is it actually going to achieve?"

"It may just put enough pressure on the person at the heart of the secret to have no choice but to come clean," DCI Fish. "Especially if we word the tip-off correctly. Is one man's life more valuable than that of dozens of islanders just because he happens to hold a position of power?"

"CO Johnson isn't stupid, Tom. He's going to know where the tip-off came from immediately."

"He can't prove it though. If we all stick together with this, it's going to put him in a very delicate position."

"Since when did you become so radical?"

"Sometimes desperate times call for desperate measures. Give it some thought."

"I'll do that," O'Reilly said.

He hadn't expected this kind of reaction from his team, but when he looked at them sitting around the table, he knew he shouldn't really be surprised. They were exceptional police officers and all of them were good human beings, and it gave him a glimmer of hope.

"Right," he said. "I think that's as good a place as any to call it a day."

"I'm going to have to inform Anne about this," DCI Fish said.

"Of course," O'Reilly said. "She needs to be kept in the loop."

Superintendent Anne Hayes was DCI Fish's wife. She was still on maternity leave after the birth of their daughter, but the DCI made sure to keep her up to date on the developments in the investigations they were working on.

"How's the little one doing?" O'Reilly said.

"Already running rings around me," DCI Fish said. "Hannah and Anne are definitely the bosses in our house – there's no doubt about that."

"Girls," O'Reilly said. "Just you wait until the boys start sniffing around."

"She's not yet a year old, Liam."

"It happens sooner than you think," O'Reilly said. "Take my advice – as soon as Hannah hits her teens, invest in a decent shotgun."

"You can't be serious, sir?" DC Stone said.

"I'm deadly serious, Andy. It's not like he'll ever have to use it – all he needs to do is make sure the pimply bastards after little Hannah are aware that he has one. Word will soon get round."

DCI Fish smiled. "I'll bear it in mind."

"Let's wrap things up there," O'Reilly said. "We will get to the heart of this, with or without CO Johnson's blessing."

He left the briefing room and made a beeline for the exit. DC Stone caught up with him halfway.

"What is it, Andy?" O'Reilly said.

"You haven't forgotten about this evening, have you?"

"I haven't a clue what you're on about, so apparently I have."

"Assumpta and I invited you round for your birthday."

"That was yesterday," O'Reilly said.

"And it wasn't exactly a brilliant night," DC Stone said. "I thought we could make it an Irish themed evening."

"I'd rather not. Besides, I've promised to go and visit Victoria in hospital."

"Assumpta has already spoken to her, sir," DC Stone said. "Victoria is exhausted, and she doesn't want you ending up the same way. You can stay over at our place if you want. That way you don't have to worry about driving back to Vazon tonight."

"I have cats to look after," O'Reilly said.

"That's taken care of too. Tommy has offered to pop round and feed them in the morning."

"Am I being manipulated?"

"Not at all, sir. We've invited Katie too. It'll do you good to forget about things for a while."

"How am I supposed to do that with half the team there?"

"Assumpta is cooking her Irish stew with dumplings. She said it was your favourite."

"Now you've got my attention. Alright, you win - what time is this thing?"

"Six."

O'Reilly checked his watch. That was in less than an hour.

"I suppose I'll be there then," he said. "I just need to pop home to pick up a change of clothing for tomorrow. But if you think I'm going to wear something green, you're going to be sorely disappointed."

"Of course not, sir," DC Stone said. "I'll see you later."

CHAPTER SEVENTEEN

"Who knew how many lethal toxins could be found in your backyard."
The woman wasn't taking any chances. Her assistant thought she was taking things a bit far with her makeshift hazmat suit. The facemask and the thick goggles she was wearing were a bit over the top too. There was nothing contained in the jars on the bench that could cause any problems that way. None of the toxins they'd cultured had the capabilities of causing any damage via the air. The three pairs of gloves were excessive too.

"Oleandrin."

The woman spoke the word as though she were addressing a lover. There was tenderness in her voice and when she tapped out a small quantity of the black powder onto the glass dish she gazed at it lovingly. The pinkish-purple oleander flowers had been discarded and only the leaves were retained. First, they were dried and ground into fine powder. The second stage involved extracting the oleandrin from the leaves. This was done by mixing the powdered leaves with a solvent, in this case ethyl alcohol was used. After blending together, the active compounds were extracted and that was what the woman was admiring on the tray in front of her.

"It's supposed to taste like shit."

Her assistant definitely had a way with words.

"The bitter flavour can be masked," the woman said. "Don't worry about that. There are many products on offer to hide this beauty in. I can dye it too, so it'll blend into anything I want it to."

With a glass dropper she squeezed a few drops of water onto the dish and stirred the paste. She repeated the procedure until the mixture was the perfect consistency then she drew the lethal mix into a syringe. There was only enough for one syringeful but that was plenty. The innocuous looking liquid inside the syringe was enough to stop the hearts of fifty healthy human beings. Of course, that wasn't the plan – that would be taking things to the extreme.

"Have you had any word from *you know who*?"
The woman looked into the eyes of her assistant and sighed.
"What do you think? He's a coward and a fool. And he's all about self-preservation – most men in his position are. They only care about number one, but we'll see how he reacts when we introduce the oleandrin onto the island. We'll build up the pressure until he pops like the cork in a bottle of champagne."
"What then?"
"We apply more pressure. Justice will be served."
"But this isn't about justice, is it?"
The woman smiled. "No. No, this is not about justice at all."

* * *

"Sorry I'm a bit late," O'Reilly said.
Assumpta shrugged her shoulders. "Andy told me it was a long day. Come in. The stew still has another thirty minutes to cook."
O'Reilly followed her inside the apartment. Music was playing from somewhere. It was a familiar song, but O'Reilly couldn't recall the artist.

DC Stone was in the kitchen preparing some drinks. O'Reilly recognised the familiar pop of the widget in a can of Guinness as the rat-faced detective cracked it open. He poured it badly and the result was a glass filled with foam.

"You're having that one," O'Reilly said. "Let me show you how it's done."
He demonstrated by popping the ring pull, waiting a few seconds and flipping the can so the liquid was drained quickly. His effort was considerably better than DC Stone's.

He raised the glass. "Cheers. This is just what the doctor ordered. You might want to pour yourself another – that foam is going to take all night to settle."

DC Stone opened a bottle of wine and poured Assumpta a glass. DC Owen came into the kitchen.

"Sir," she said to O'Reilly.

"We'll have none of that nonsense this evening, Katie," he told her.

"Can I get you a drink?" DC Stone asked DC Owen.

"A beer if you've got one," she said.

"Coming up."

"Happy birthday, Dad," Assumpta said. "Again. Tonight can't be any more eventful than last night. Is there any news about the others?"

"My daughter, the journalist," O'Reilly said.

"Your daughter, the concerned island resident," she corrected. "I heard that seven people died."

"Eight," DC Stone said. "Of the thirteen who became sick, eight of them didn't make it."

"Do you know what caused the sickness?" Assumpta said.

"We do," O'Reilly said. "But I'm not going to discuss it now."

"Come on, Dad," Assumpta said. "It's already common knowledge and sooner or later the reason for the fatalities is going to get out."

"I didn't mean that, Summi," O'Reilly said. "I meant, I don't feel like talking about it right now. I thought this was supposed to be an Irish themed evening anyway."

"Irish stew, Guinness and traditional Irish music," DC Stone said. "What more could you ask for?"

"Traditional Irish music? Since when?"

A song by The Cranberries was playing now.

"I've got U2, The Cranberries and some Script."

"That is not traditional Irish music, Andy. I can't stand U2."

"I like them," DC Owen said.

"Well, I don't. The lead singer is an arrogant twit. He thinks that because he was born in Ireland, it gives him a God given right to force everybody to listen to what he has to say."

"He's got a point," DC Owen said. "It's an Irish trait. I've seen it in action."

"Don't you start," O'Reilly said and held up his Guinness. "And what is this shite, Andy? Summi could have told you I prefer Murphy's."

"I couldn't find any on the island," DC Stone said.

"Dad."

The fire in his daughter's eyes told him to quit while he was ahead.

"I'm sorry. I'm an ungrateful idiot. It's been a rough few days. Can we start again?"

"You're going to enjoy your Guinness," Assumpta ordered. "You're going to tolerate Bono and U2, and if you have any further opinions to share, I suggest you share them with yourself. Understood?"

"Loud and clear," O'Reilly said. "Is that Irish stew ready yet?"

CHAPTER EIGHTEEN

"So, there I was with one hand on the neck of Declan O'Leary and the other trying to get his brother to drop the knife he was holding in front of my face."

"Is this really the sort of story we want to hear at the dinner table, Dad?" Assumpta said.

"You asked me to tell you a few stories about life in the Gardai."

"I did not," Assumpta said. "Andy wanted to hear them."

"Do you want to hear it or not?"

"I do," DC Stone said.

"Anyway. Now Declan was a slippery bastard. Neck as thin as an eel and just as slimy. I knew I couldn't hold him much longer and the tip of the knife was getting closer."

"What did you do?" DC Stone said.

"I did the only thing I could do, Andy. I kicked Sean O'Leary in the knackers as hard as I could. Sean screamed, I let go of the two of them at the same time and Sean did what any self-respecting male would do after being kicked in the nads."

"What's that?" DC Stone said.

"After composing himself, he saw red, Andy. Took it out on the nearest thing, which at that time happened to be his little brother, Declan. Dec got a stab in the cheek for his efforts, and that's when things got ugly."

"What happened?"

"If you'd let me finish the story without interrupting me every five seconds you'll find out. By the time the other guards arrived the two brothers had pretty much kicked the living shite of each other. I sat back and watched."

"You're making this up," DC Owen said.

"He's not," Assumpta said. "I'm surprised he hasn't told you this one already. There was even talk of it making the latest Garda training manual."
"The O'Reilly manoeuvre," O'Reilly elaborated. "It never got that far though – some cube dweller in a suit probably thought it was inappropriate behaviour for a police officer."
"Brilliant," DC Stone said. "Tell us another one."
"Please don't." It was Assumpta.
"I'll make you a deal," O'Reilly said. "You get me some more of that trifle and I'll keep my gob shut."
Assumpta was on her feet in a flash. "Deal."

After polishing off his third bowl of trifle, O'Reilly was feeling content. He'd offered to wash the dishes, and he hadn't argued when DC Stone had told him he would do it. The rat-faced DC came back into the room, and the smell of cigarette smoke came with him.
"I thought you'd quit," O'Reilly said.
"I've cut down," DC Stone said. "I'll quit one day. How about a drop of this?" He held out a bottle of whiskey.
"Now you're talking, Andy."
It was a litre bottle of Jameson's.
"Where did you get the big bottle from?" O'Reilly asked him.
"I asked my brother to get it from duty free. He hopped over to France a few weeks ago."
"Irish whiskey from France," O'Reilly said. "The world's gone mad. Are you going to stand and stare at it, or are we going to drink the stuff?"

As he drained his second glass of Jameson's and the smooth, spicy flavour gave way to the burn in his throat O'Reilly's thoughts turned to the investigation. He knew it would. Assumpta was showing DC Owen something on her tablet at the table in the living room and DC Stone was sitting opposite O'Reilly. The shifty-eyed detective was adamant he was going to match O'Reilly drink for drink, and he was looking the worse for wear for it. His piggy eyes were mere slits in his face and there was an inane grin on his face.

"If we look at the facts," O'Reilly said. "There are a number of obvious deductions we can make."
DC Stone observed him as though he was speaking Japanese.
O'Reilly wasn't bothered. "Don't worry, Andy – I can have this conversation with myself. CO Johnson has given us enough information to come to the only logical conclusion we can come to. The poisonings are the result of something that happened in the past – something involving someone high up in the Island Police. And to use the CO's exact words if this secret ever sees the light of day, the reputation of the Island Police will be shattered. It's centred on one man but the position he holds will ensure that the Island Police will go down with him. What does that tell us?"
DC Stone gave him a toothy grin in reply.

"Never mind," O'Reilly said. "It tells us that this isn't something that happened in the man's private life. It's something connected to the job, and it was something that was covered up. Now, I don't know about you but in my experience, it is impossible to bury something entirely. There will always be bits that rise to the surface eventually and it's these pieces of the puzzle we need to unearth. Once we get a grip on the outer pieces, the rest of the picture will become clearer in time."

"Can I stop you there?" It was Assumpta.
O'Reilly wasn't even aware that she was listening in.
"Am I rambling?" he said.
"Not only that," she said. "But your analogies are all over the place. How much of that whiskey have you had?"
"It made perfect sense to me."
"It usually does after the third glass."

"Do you have a better way of putting it?" O'Reilly said.

"You're going to have to give me a bit more before I can offer an opinion on it. I need a bit of context."

"Off the record?"

"Dad," Assumpta said. "How many times…"

"Sorry, Summi. OK, this is what we know. Eight people died in the space of twenty-four-hours. They were killed by the toxins from the death cap mushroom. We're now aware how they were poisoned – various foods and drinks were contaminated, and the fatalities were simply unlucky. They weren't targeted personally."

"Good Lord."

"You can say that again. Katie, do you want to take it from here? I'm in possession of an empty glass and, seeing as your man there can't even keep his eyes open, I doubt he'll be capable of filling it for me."

DC Stone was snoring quietly on the sofa. The grin on his face was still there.

"He's going to have a thick head in the morning," O'Reilly said.

He got up and went to the kitchen.

"We thought you'd got lost," Assumpta said when he came back five minutes later.

"Five pints of Guinness and three Jameson's have to go somewhere, Summi."

"Too much information, Dad."

"What have I missed?"

"Katie told me that all the contaminated products came from one place."

"Freshlife Supermarket," O'Reilly said. "On Victoria Street. Three other places were broken into but so far, nothing anyone bought from them has caused any ill effects."

"Is it possible there's a link there?" Assumpta said. "Why was that the only place where the products were tainted?"

"I can't see how," O'Reilly said. "I get the impression that the other shops were decoys. Smokescreens to throw us off the scent for a while."

"From what I can gather," Assumpta said. "There's only one possible direction the investigation can go in."

"I'm of that opinion too," O'Reilly said.

"Find out what the terrible secret is," DC Owen joined in. "That secret lies at the heart of this."

"CO Johnson isn't going to budge," O'Reilly said. "But I'm not perturbed about that. We will dredge up whatever it is – it's what all of us does best, and when we do get it to the surface it's going to lead us straight to the bastards who think they can go around poisoning the people of my island."

CHAPTER NINETEEN

O'Reilly was no stranger to waking up in unfamiliar beds but each time he did it always took him a while to orientate himself. This time was no different. The blackout curtains in Assumpta's spare room were doing exactly what they were supposed to do, and only a thin gap in the middle let in a sliver of sunlight to tell him it was daytime. A quick glance at his phone told him it was just after seven and he could hear noises somewhere close by in the apartment. He shifted the covers to the side and sat up with his legs over the edge of the bed. He put some weight on his gammy leg and nodded. The twinge from yesterday was gone.

After using the bathroom, he headed straight for the kitchen. His belly was crying out for a cup of tea. Assumpta was tapping away on the keyboard of her laptop at the table.
"You're up early," O'Reilly said.
"I've been up since half-five," she said. "I've got a piece I need to get to Fiona before lunchtime, and I write better in the morning. The kettle's just boiled. The tea and sugar are next to it, and there's milk in the fridge."
"I have to make my own tea?"
"I'm sure you'll manage."
"I don't suppose there's any breakfast on offer?"
Assumpta fixed her eyes on his. "I need to finish this, Dad."
"I can take a hint."

He made the tea and sat down opposite Assumpta.
"What are you working on?"
"It's an historical piece on the tomato crash in the late 70s."
"What the devil is a tomato crash?" O'Reilly said.

"For more than a century, Guernsey was a major player in the tomato export industry. At one stage the island was shipping out more than five-hundred million of them."

"Five-hundred-million tomatoes?"

"I know," Assumpta said. "But in the late 70s it all came to an end. The Dutch took advantage of the cheap North Sea fuel, and it meant that their growers could undercut the price of Guernsey tomatoes. The entire industry collapsed overnight."

"And this is what people want to read about," O'Reilly said. "Tomatoes?"

"It's part of the heritage of the island," Assumpta said. "We like to have something as a backup for when the news dries up."

"I would have thought the recent poisonings would keep you going for a while."

"The content has already been done to death. It's old news now."

"It only happened in the past couple of days," O'Reilly said.

"That's the speed that journalism travels at these days. Now, if you were to give me something fresh – something nobody else knows about, that might make me think about ditching the tomatoes."

"Not going to happen, Summi."

"Not even a snippet about this secret?"

"Where's Andy?" O'Reilly changed the subject.

"I left him where he was last night," Assumpta said. "Snoring on the sofa."

"There might be something I can do for you."

"Go on."

"But I need something in return."

"I can live with that."

"I want to do some digging into this mystery secret," O'Reilly said. "Obviously I can't let it be known that I'm doing that, not with the big chief watching my every move. We're going to have to conduct a parallel investigation with the deadly secret stuff done off the record."

"You want me to some digging too?" Assumpta said.

"Got it in one."

"And you'll let me run with what I find?"

"That depends on what you unearth."

"That's not fair," Assumpta said. "And as far as I'm aware, anything I dig up independently is fair game if I think there's a story in it."

"I understand that, Summi," O'Reilly said. "But if you do discover something significant, I want you to promise to run it by me first. I know you have a job to do, but so do I and I've got a terrible feeling that once this secret is public knowledge, my life and the lives of everybody I work with is going to get extremely unpleasant."

"Do you think it's really that bad?"

"It's bad enough for some psychopathic poisoners to justify killing total strangers for."

"Fair enough. I'll let you see what I find before I do anything with it."

    DC Stone came in, and O'Reilly caught a whiff of something unpleasant. It was a blend of stale whiskey and a sour odour he didn't want to guess the source of.

"Morning, Andy," O'Reilly said. "I hope you're feeling better than you smell."

"My head hurts," DC Stone said.

"Grand. I was planning on having breakfast at your fine establishment, but I think I'll find something to fill my belly with elsewhere. That stench has put me off a bit."

    His phone beeped to tell him he'd received a message. He swiped the screen and saw that it was from Victoria. He read the words and frowned. "Where the devil am I supposed to get turmeric, ginger root and honey on the island?"

"Loads of places," Assumpta said.

"What about this one?" O'Reilly showed her the phone. "I don't even know how to pronounce it."

"Echinacea," Assumpta read. "It's a herb. I think it's a good immune booster. Is this for Victoria?"

O'Reilly nodded. "Apparently her doctor has suggested she go the herbal route in treating her chest infection, given her history."

"There's a health shop on La Grange," Assumpta said. "It sells all sorts of that stuff. I'm sure you'll get all of that there."

"What does a person even do with all of this weird stuff?"

"It's not weird stuff, Dad. You boil it up and make tea out of it. It's supposed to be a lot better for you than pharmaceutical drugs."

"I'll pick it up after I've found somewhere to get some breakfast."

"I'll see you at work, sir," DC Stone said.

"Don't be late," O'Reilly said. "Have a shower and brush your teeth. Brush them twice."

CHAPTER TWENTY

Nature's Gifts stood on the corner of La Grange and Doyle Road. O'Reilly was suitably fed and ready for whatever the day had to throw his way. He didn't think one bacon and egg roll would be enough to fill the gap in his belly, so he'd ordered two and asked for one of them to take away. The second roll was tucked away in his jacket pocket for later. As he pushed open the door of the shop, he noticed that one of the panes of glass was smashed. He went inside and was suddenly bombarded with a sensory overload. The smell was like nothing he'd ever experienced before. It wasn't entirely unpleasant, but he wasn't expecting it.

He took a look around and it didn't take him long to work out he was going to need some help. Packets of products of all colours and sizes were stacked neatly in rows on floor to ceiling shelves. A quick glance at some of them reinforced the fact that he was completely out of his depth. Some of the herbs and spices were familiar but the majority of them most definitely were not.

An entire shelf was dedicated to women's health. There were boxes and packets and tubs with names O'Reilly didn't even attempt to pronounce. He hadn't realised that this was such big business. A stroll across the shop led him to products designed for men and a strange thought occurred to him. He wondered if there was anything on the shelf that would improve DC Stone at all. He doubted whether there was – that man was beyond help.

There were creams and lotions and sticks of things O'Reilly never knew existed. He picked up one of the sticks and tapped it on the side of the shelf. The name on the label was something unpronounceable. O'Reilly wondered what the root was used for. He really was in a different world.

"First time?"

It was a woman who looked to be in her early twenties.

"Is it that obvious?" O'Reilly said.

"A bit."

"I have to admit, I never knew that most of this stuff even existed. You must have half the plants in the Amazon rainforest in here."

The woman laughed. "What can I help you with?"

The name on her badge was Jane. That was it.

"I've got a list," O'Reilly said.

He took out his phone and found Victoria's message.

"Ginger, turmeric, honey and echidna."

Jane laughed again. "I think you mean echinacea. An echidna is an antipodean spiny anteater. It's sort of a cross between a porcupine and an aardvark."

"I definitely don't want one of those." O'Reilly took a closer look at Victoria's message. "You're right – it's what you said. My eyes are not what they used to be. Can you help me?"

"Of course," Jane said.

A young woman came into the shop. She was dressed in gym attire, and it was clear that she was a keen fitness fanatic. Her hair was tied back in a tight ponytail and O'Reilly found himself staring at her for longer than he should.

"I'll be with you in a second, Paula," Jane said.

The woman was obviously a regular.

"It's fine," she said. "I know what I'm looking for."

None of them knew then that this would be one of the last conversations Paula would ever have.

Jane led O'Reilly to a shelf on the other side of the shop. She picked up a small basket on the way.

"Turmeric," she said. "50mg or 100mg?"

"Give me the bigger one please," O'Reilly said.

The packet was placed in the basket. "Ginger – do you want the root or the powder?"

"What's the difference?"

"The powder is quicker to dissolve. The root takes much longer."

"Powder it is then. Honey?"

"Next to the counter," Jane said. "And here's your echidna."

She gave him a cheeky grin.

"I'll know better next time," O'Reilly said. "This is all new to me."

"I imagine it could be overwhelming. Is your chest giving you problems?"

"Not mine," O'Reilly said. "My wife's. She was rushed to hospital yesterday and her doctor advised her to go the herbal route."

"That's very refreshing."

"She had cancer a while ago," O'Reilly said. "She's all clear now, but her immune system isn't quite back to normal yet."

"I can recommend garlic too," Jane said. "It's an amazing immune booster."

"We've got that at home. I think that's everything. I'll grab the honey before I pay."

Jane walked away and returned with two bottles.

"What are they?" O'Reilly said.

"Ginko Biloba," jane said. "It aids blood flow to the eyes. And the other one is a blend of Lutein and Zeaxanthin. It's incredible for eye health."

"There's nothing wrong with my wife's eyes."

"They're not for your wife."

"Ah, right," O'Reilly said. "I suppose it can't hurt to give them a bash."

Jane smiled. "I've seen you somewhere before."

"I get that a lot," O'Reilly said. "I have one of those faces. How much do I owe you?"

"Let's go and see, shall we? And don't forget your honey. Will you be making the tea yourself?"

"Is that a problem?"

"Not at all," Jane said. "Only we have some fantastic recipes. They're free, and there's a good one for chest infections. Ginger, turmeric and honey – that's it. Or you can add some chopped onion if you're feeling adventurous."

"I don't think so," O'Reilly said. "I have to sleep next to her. Did you know that one of the panes of glass in your door is broken?"

"I saw that when I arrived this morning," Jane said. "Probably kids."

"Probably," O'Reilly said.

Five minutes later he was on his way to the station. The herbs and spices had cost him more than he expected but who was he to argue? It had been an eye-opening experience. He'd never considered natural remedies for ailments before but the more he thought about it, he came to the conclusion that all medications had to start somewhere, and it was realistic to assume that most of them had their origins in plants and trees. He wondered what it was like during the trial-and-error stage. He was now fully aware that, just as natural products had the power to cure, there were things that grew wild that had the potential to end life in an instant.

CHAPTER TWENTY ONE

O'Reilly began the morning briefing by suggesting a plan of action that involved conducting two separate investigations concurrently. They would continue to dig deeper into the recent death cap murders, but it was imperative that they got to the heart of the motivation behind the poisonings.

"Something happened somewhere down the line," he said. "Something that involved a high-ranking officer of the Island Police. CO Johnson knows what it is, but he's not sharing it, so we have no option but to find out without his input."

"Can I ask something?" DC Stone said.

A shower and a couple of squirts of deodorant had helped, but O'Reilly could smell stale alcohol when he got close enough to the man.

"You're not in junior school, Andy," he said. "What's on your mind?"

"Are we assuming from Chief Officer Johnson's refusal to talk that he's the high-ranking officer in question?"

"It's not CO Johnson."

"Are you saying it's someone who no longer works here?" DC Stone said.

"For Pete's sake, Andy. Why would the people responsible bother to threaten someone who doesn't work for the Island Police?"

"DCO Dove?" DCI Fish guessed.

O'Reilly's silence answered the question.

"But he's a good bloke," DS Skinner said. "He's been here for almost as long as me, and I've never once seen him lose his cool. There must be some kind of mistake."

"There's no mistake, Will," O'Reilly said. "I got it straight from the CO's mouth. DCO Dove was involved in something, whatever that was never saw the light of day, and now someone has found out about it, and they want the whole world to know about it."

"Have you brought it up with him?" DC Owen said.

"I was ordered not to," O'Reilly said. "CO Johnson made it abundantly clear what would happen if I did. I'm not normally one to back down when I'm threatened but until I have more information, I'm not going to rock an already shaky boat."

"Did you get a book of famous analogies for your birthday, sir?" DC Owen said.

"I'm Irish, Katie," O'Reilly said. "We're full of them."

"Where do you suggest we start, sir?" DC Stone said.

"Andy," O'Reilly said. "I think I saw a small bottle of mouthwash in the staff bathroom. I suggest *you* start with that. You smell like a brewery that hasn't cleaned its pipes for a while."

"I brushed my teeth twice this morning, just like you said."

"As for the rest of us," O'Reilly said. "We'll make a start on unearthing what this blasted secret is."

"What about the eight deaths?" DS Skinner said. "We can't just forget about them."

"We're not forgetting about them. We're simply focusing our attention elsewhere while we wait for the results from Forensics and Pathology."

"That'll work," DCI Fish agreed. "If anybody enquires about our progress, we're following up a number of leads while we await further test results. It'll buy us some time to get stuck into the reason behind it all in the first place."

"On we go then," O'Reilly said. "And I don't have to tell you to stay away from the internal browsers. Until I know who we can trust, I don't want anyone apart from the people inside this room to know what we're up to."

Everybody got up and left apart from DC Owen.

"What's on your mind, Katie?" O'Reilly asked.

"I wanted to ask you something."

"I figured that out by myself."

"We don't know how long we're going to need to go back," DC Owen said. "But it might be worth getting my dad involved."

O'Reilly nodded. "That's a damn fine idea. Tony goes way back in the Island Police and if anyone can shed any light on this cursed secret it's him. Why didn't you want to bring this up in front of the rest of the team?"

"I'm not worried about the rest of the team, sir," DC Owen said. "It's DCI Fish I'm not sure about. He likes to play by the rules, and I wasn't sure if he would approve."

"DCI Fish has surprised me so far during the course of the investigation. He's been more than willing to bend the rules when necessary. He was the one who suggested making something up to give to the press. I don't know what's got into him, but it's clear that fatherhood has changed him. Little Hannah has made him almost human. Speak to your dad, by all means. I trust Tony and he's proven himself to be an asset in the past. And before you say it, I don't give two hoots that he's no longer a serving police officer. Once a detective, always a detective in my book."

"Thanks, sir. I'll give him a call now."

She left O'Reilly alone in the room. He got up and walked over to the whiteboard. He picked up the marker pen and his hand hovered over the surface of the board. He realised that anyone could walk into the room and take a look at the words written on the whiteboard, but he decided that he didn't really care. In big bold letters he wrote one word:

SECRET.

He underlined it and circled it a few times for good measure.

"I'm going to find out," he told the word. "I will find out what happened if it's the last thing I do."

His phone beeped to tell him he'd received a message. It was from

Victoria's brother, and it surprised him. Tommy rarely communicated with him. The message was brief. Tommy was informing him that he was waiting by the front desk. Victoria was to be discharged from hospital and Tommy was going to pick her up. She'd asked him to pick up the herbs and spices that O'Reilly had bought for her. O'Reilly replied with a short message telling Tommy that he would be right there. He left the briefing room and went to his office to fetch the goods from *Nature's Gifts* and made his way to the front desk. He made up his mind. He would give Tommy the weird stuff for Victoria's tea and then he would pay a visit to the man he needed to speak to more than anyone else. He couldn't care less what CO Johnson did to him, he was going to talk to Callum Dove, and he was going to do that now.

CHAPTER TWENTY TWO

O'Reilly didn't think it was a good idea to go and see DCO Dove in his office on the top floor. Chief Officer Johnson's office was right next door, and he didn't want to risk the big boss getting wind of what he was up to. Instead, he stepped outside and brought up DCO Dove's number. The second in charge of the Island Police answered straight away.

"Liam, what can I do for you?"

"Have you got a minute, sir?" O'Reilly said.

"Of course. What's on your mind?"

"I'd prefer to discuss this face to face."

"Come on up."

"And I'd prefer to do it away from the station."

"I'm intrigued. Where did you have in mind?"

O'Reilly told him. DCO Dove promised to meet him in ten minutes.

"I have to admit," DCO Dove said, fifteen minutes later. "I'm curious. Why all the cloak and dagger antics?"

They were sitting on O'Reilly's favourite bench looking out to sea. The esplanade was busier than it was yesterday, and O'Reilly assumed the weather had played a part in that. It was warm and there was barely a puff of breeze in the air. The yachts out to sea were hardly moving.

"This is difficult to talk about," O'Reilly said. "But I need to ask you something."

"Ask away," DCO Dove said.

"I know why those people were poisoned, sir."

"That's good, isn't it?"

"Yes and no," O'Reilly said. "I don't know if you've discussed the matter with Chief Officer Johnson."

"I haven't."

"I thought so. CO Johnson received an email shortly before the victims became sick. In the email there were some veiled threats. The sender claimed to have contaminated certain foods and drinks, and they implied that they would continue to do so unless their demands were met."

"This is serious, Liam. Why was I not made aware of this?"

"I'm coming to that, sir. Another email was sent to CO Johnson, and this one left little doubt that these people are deadly serious. Eight people have died, and these *terrorists* threatened to carry on."

"I was under the impression that the poisonings were random."

"That's true. There were no specific targets."

"Has CO Johnson handed the emails over?" DCO Dove said. "We have a team of experts trained for matters like these."

"Can I trust you?" O'Reilly said.

DCO Dove eyed him with suspicion. "What's that supposed to mean? Of course you can trust me."

They were interrupted by a scruffy man in a jacket three sizes too big for him. O'Reilly smelled him before he saw him.

"Spare some change for a bit of breakfast?"

"I left my wallet at work," O'Reilly told him.

"Get lost," DCO Dove said.

"Miserable git. You have a good day now."

The man doffed an imaginary cap and made to leave.

"Hold on," O'Reilly said.

He remembered the egg and bacon roll he'd bought earlier. He took it out of his pocket and held it out to the man.

"It's not warm, but it's fresh."

The man took it and gave O'Reilly a warm smile.

"God bless you, sir. You're going straight to heaven."

O'Reilly very much doubted that.

"Where were we?" he said.

"You were questioning my integrity," DCO Dove reminded him.

"Hear me out," O'Reilly said. "CO Johnson deleted both emails from his work account. He forwarded them to his personal email and deleted them from his work email."

"Why would he do that?"

"He's keeping something to himself. Something that could blow this entire investigation wide open."

"I'm still not following this," DCO Dove said. "Why would CO Johnson delete potential evidence? What do these people have on him?"

"Now you've hit on the crux of the matter, sir," O'Reilly said. "What do they have on him? He's being blackmailed. CO Johnson is in possession of a secret that cannot see the light of day. It's a secret so big that not even eight deaths are enough to make him reveal it."

"Do you know what this secret is?"

"I was hoping you would tell me, sir."

It took DCO Dove a moment to understand what O'Reilly was getting at. "Me?" he said. "What are you trying to say, Liam?"

"Before I tell you," O'Reilly said. "I want you to know that I'm only going on what CO Johnson has told me. He said the secret is not his – it's yours. Does that ring any bells?"

"No," DCO Dove said. "It does not."

"It was implied that it's something that could bring the Island Police into disrepute."

"That makes it no clearer. I really have no idea what you're talking about." O'Reilly believed him. He prided himself on being an astute judge of character and he sensed that DCO Dove was telling the truth.

He told him as much.

"But it still doesn't explain why CO Johnson would make this up," he added.

"I can't believe you even doubted me," DCO Dove said.

"It was necessary, sir," O'Reilly said. "In order to dismiss it, I needed to consider it."

"Fair enough. Do you know, in all my twenty years in the Island Police, I have not got one blot on my record. Nothing. I'm a spectacularly boring man, and I most certainly didn't get involved in something that would result in the deaths of eight innocent people."

"I believe you, sir. I really do, but this only muddies the waters further. If this isn't about something you did, what is it about? And why would CO Johnson lie about it?"

"There's only one logical explanation for that, Liam," DCO Dove said. "And I suspect you already know what it is."

It wasn't rocket science. O'Reilly knew that the investigation had just got a whole lot more complicated and he was struggling to come up with a strategy to move them forwards. The yachts out to sea had given up and dropped their sails. They weren't going to make any progress until the wind picked up a bit. O'Reilly knew exactly how they felt.

CHAPTER TWENTY THREE

O'Reilly needed a cup of tea, but he was intercepted before he'd even made it halfway to his office. DC Stone was animated, and it was clear that something had happened.
"What's with the ants in your pants, Andy?" O'Reilly said.
"We've had a report of another fatality, sir."
"Go on."
"A woman was rushed to hospital complaining of stomach pains," DC Stone said. "She'd been vomiting and she had a fever. She died fifteen minutes after arriving at hospital. Cardiac arrest."
"That doesn't tie in with the symptoms of the death cap victims," O'Reilly said. "Do we know anything else?"
"I'm just telling you what the hospital told PC London, sir."
"Come on then," O'Reilly said. "Grab your car keys – we're going back to the hospital."

They arrived at the Princess Elizabeth ten minutes later. O'Reilly had spent far too much time here recently and he didn't like it. After speaking to a woman at reception they were told to take a seat. Someone would be along to help them soon.
"What else do we know about the dead woman?" O'Reilly said.
"She was twenty-one," DC Stone said. "That's about it."
"And she suffered a cardiac arrest."
"A bit young to have a heart attack, don't you think?"
"That's what's bothering me. The other victims died due to massive organ failure. Their hearts gave up eventually, but this feels different."
"We meet again."
It was the same doctor who'd treated Victoria when she'd been brought in with her chest infection.

"Dr Newton," O'Reilly remembered.

The two men shook hands.

"This is my colleague, DC Stone," O'Reilly said.

Dr Newton didn't shake DC Stone's hand and O'Reilly didn't blame him.

"What do we know?" he asked.

"I don't know what to tell you," Dr Newton said. "Her symptoms are peculiar. According to her boyfriend she started complaining of stomach ache and she was violently sick. Her temperature soared and this was accompanied by heart palpitations. Her heart rate became dangerously high, and she arrested shortly after she arrived. We tried everything but there was nothing we could do for her."

"What do you think caused it?" DC Stone said.

"I really don't know."

"Could it have been some kind of toxin?" O'Reilly said.

"It's possible, but if you're wondering if it's amanitin poisoning, I can tell you that the symptoms don't fit. This wasn't the result of death cap mushrooms."

"Is the boyfriend still here?" O'Reilly asked.

"I think so," Dr Newton said.

"Could you find out please? It's important that we speak to him."

Dr Newton told them he had patients to see, but he would find someone to help them.

"I don't like this, sir," DC Stone said. "If the young woman died from something other than death cap mushrooms it means that they've diversified."

"Let's not jump to conclusions, Andy," O'Reilly said. "This may be unconnected to the other deaths."

"Is that what you really think?"

"No. I don't think that at all."

A man in a nurse's uniform approached.

"I was told you wanted to speak to the man who came in with the woman who died."

O'Reilly introduced himself and DC Stone.

"Is he still here?"

"He is. He's in one of the private family rooms. I'll show you the way."

The man's name was Gordon King. He was home with his girlfriend, Paula, when she became ill. O'Reilly explained who they were and offered his condolences.

"It still hasn't sunk in," Gordon said. "It happened so quick."

"I know this is hard," O'Reilly said. "But we need to ask you a few questions. How long have you and Paula been together?"

"Just over a year. We moved into the apartment last month. I don't know what I'm going to do now – I won't be able to afford the rent without Paula's salary. God, that sounds so cold, doesn't it?"

"It's OK, Gordon," O'Reilly said. "You're still in shock. Would you consider Paula healthy?"

This resulted in a smile from Gordon.

"Sorry," he said. "Healthy doesn't even come close. She was a health nut."

"She kept herself in shape?" DC Stone said.

Gordon nodded. "She went to the gym four times a week. She didn't drink or smoke and her diet consisted of nothing but good food."

"Can we talk about that?" O'Reilly said. "Is it possible that she ate something she wouldn't normally eat shortly before she became ill?"

"I can't think of anything," Gordon said.

"OK," O'Reilly said. "Talk us through the hours before Paula fell ill. What did she do this morning?"

"She hit the gym at around seven."

"Did she eat breakfast before she left?" DC Stone said.

"She made a smoothie," Gordon said.

"Do you know what was in the smoothie?" O'Reilly said.

"Nothing but good stuff. Blueberries, Kiwi fruit. Super fruits."

"What about when she finished at the gym?" DC Stone said.

"She picked up a few things from the shops, and she came home. She did mention something about a cold."

"She had a cold?" O'Reilly said.

"Not really," Gordon said. "But she could feel the start of one. She had a bit of a chesty cough. She made some lung juice."

"Lung juice?" DC Stone repeated.

"That's what she calls it. It tastes terrible, but it's supposed to be really good for the lungs."

"What's in this *lung juice*?" O'Reilly said.

"I'm not quite sure," Gordon said. "I think it's got honey and turmeric."

It was familiar to O'Reilly. He'd bought these ingredients for Victoria that morning.

"It's also got ginger in it," he said.

"That's right," Gordon said. "In fact, I think Paula had to get some on her way back from the gym – we'd run out."

"She bought ginger?"

"She got the powdered stuff," Gordon said. "It's quicker to boil than the root."

O'Reilly was starting to feel a bit ill.

"Where did she get the ginger powder from?"

"She's got a favourite health shop she goes to," Gordon said.

"I need the name."

"I'm not sure."

"Think." O'Reilly said this louder than he meant to and both Gordon and DC Stone stared at him.

"Please," O'Reilly said. "What's the name of the shop?"

"It was on the label on the packet of ginger," Gordon said. "I remember now – it was *Nature's Gifts*."

O'Reilly shot up from the chair.

"We need to go," he told DC Stone.

"Sir?"

"Now, Andy. We need to go now."

CHAPTER TWENTY FOUR

O'Reilly was out of the car before DC Stone had even come to a complete halt. He'd tried phoning Victoria on the way, but she hadn't answered. His thoughts were running through his head at breakneck speed. Flashes of memories came and went. *Nature's Gifts* featured prominently. He recalled a broken window in the door of the shop. He could see the rows and rows of herbs and spices, and he realised how easy it would be to contaminate them. He also remembered the young woman in the gym attire. Jane had called her Paula, and that had to be more than coincidence.

Paula Troon had died shortly after drinking a concoction she'd prepared. Ginger powder from *Nature's Gifts* was a vital ingredient in the *lung juice* she'd made. It had been the longest drive of his life, and DC Stone hadn't held back. He'd ignored traffic lights, and he'd also disregarded the protests of the angry drivers he'd irritated with his erratic driving. O'Reilly would thank him for it later.

He barged the door open and went inside the house.
"Victoria!" he screamed.
Nothing.
He called her name again with the same result. He raced to the kitchen as fast as his old legs could manage.

Victoria was standing by the sink. The headphones she was wearing explained why she didn't reply when he'd called out. O'Reilly took a step towards her and that's when he noticed the familiar packets on the worktop. They were the products he'd purchased from *Nature's Gifts*, and the packets had been opened.

Victoria still hadn't sensed his presence. O'Reilly saw she was holding something in her hand. It was a coffee cup, and she was raising it to her lips. O'Reilly glanced at the packets on the worktop and rushed towards her.

With a well-aimed swipe, he knocked the cup from Victoria's hand, and it landed with a crash in the sink, spilling its contents in the process.

Victoria turned around and ripped the headphones from her ears. "What the hell is wrong with you?"

"Did you drink any?" O'Reilly nodded to the mess in the sink.

"That took me ages to make," Victoria said.

"Did you drink any?" O'Reilly asked again.

"You didn't give me the chance. What's got into you, Liam?"

O'Reilly put a hand on her arm and suggested they sit down. Victoria reluctantly agreed.

"What's going on, Liam?" she said.

O'Reilly told her.

When he was finished, he rubbed his eyes.

"I thought I was going to lose you. Paula Troon was twenty-one. She was as fit as a fiddle, and she was dead less than an hour after drinking the tea made with ginger from *Nature's Gifts*."

"Who is doing this?"

"We don't know, but I'm going to find out. I'm going to get a forensic team out here. They're busy at the dead woman's house, so they might be a while, but we need to consider the kitchen a crime scene until we know otherwise."

"Are you positive the woman died due to the ginger from *Nature's Gifts*?"

"I am. It's the only thing that makes sense. When I was there earlier, there was a broken glass pane in the door of the shop. We'll do a full forensic on the shop too, but I can't see any other explanation for the young woman's sudden death."

"You've never had to deal with anything like this before, have you?" Victoria said.

"Never," O'Reilly confirmed. "We're fighting against an enemy we can't see. They kill remotely. The victims actually do the killing part for them, and that's going to make them extremely difficult to catch. But I will catch them – this has become personal now, and they've pissed me off. They made a mistake bringing this into my house, and that's going to cost them. I have to go – Andy's waiting in the car outside. Will you be alright on your own?"

"I'm a big girl, Liam."

"Don't touch anything," O'Reilly said. "The forensic team will be here as soon as they can."

Victoria's gaze shifted to the products from *Nature's Gifts*.

"It's rather disturbing, isn't it? That someone on the island is capable of something like this."

"It is," O'Reilly agreed. "And the most unsettling part is the scope involved. The possibilities for poisoning are endless. I'll give you a call later."

He got up and kissed her on the cheek, and something occurred to him.

"I think Summi is working from home today. I could ask her to pop round. She can work just as easily from here."

"I'd like that. I'll call her."

O'Reilly kissed her again and left the kitchen.

DC Stone was talking to someone on his phone when O'Reilly got back to the car and when he got closer, he realised that it wasn't DC Stone's phone. He was holding up O'Reilly's old Nokia. He'd left it in the car in his haste to get to Victoria.

"It's DI Peters, sir," DC Stone said.

O'Reilly took the phone from him. "Jim."

"We're still busy at Paula Troon's apartment," the Head of Forensics said. "But I thought you'd want to know that it was definitely the ginger that caused her death."

"Do you know what it was spiked with?" O'Reilly said.

"That's going to take time," DI Peters said. "We're going to have to carry out tests, but you can see the contaminant in the ginger powder with the naked eye."

"What do you think it is?"

"It's too soon to tell. It's some kind of fine powder, but it's a different consistency to the ginger itself. Same colour, but the powder itself is finer."

"I wonder why she didn't notice it," O'Reilly said.

"Why would she even be looking out for it? She probably spooned the ginger powder into the boiling water without paying it much attention."

"How soon before we know what we're dealing with?"

"Before the end of the day."

O'Reilly told him about the fright he'd had with Victoria, and DI Peters promised to send someone straight there.

"What exactly are we dealing with here, Liam?"

"Something unprecedented," O'Reilly said. "We've got a silent, invisible killer who's indiscriminate. I've never come across such a cold, ruthless murderer before. Let me know as soon as you have any news."

"What now, sir?" DC Stone said.

"What indeed, Andy?" O'Reilly said. "I believe the time has come for drastic measures."

"Fred Viking?"

"As much as it pains me to say this," O'Reilly said. "There are times when Fred *the Ed* can be useful, and this happens to be one of those times."

CHAPTER TWENTY FIVE

The building that housed the offices of The Island Herald appeared to have had a facelift since O'Reilly was last there. The walls had been given a lick of paint, and the windows looked like they'd been replaced with new ones. There was even a new door at the front.
"Looks like business is booming in the world of journalism," O'Reilly said.
"Not according to Assumpta," DC Stone said. "The Gazette is struggling."
"You can't compare the Gazette to the Herald, Andy. But it does seem that the gutter press pays well."
"Is he expecting us?" DC Stone said.
"Viking? Where's the fun in that. And I want to do this alone. You can get back to the station and press on with trying to uncover CO Johnson's precious secret. I'll walk back when I'm finished."
"Don't you want me in there?"
"No," O'Reilly said. "I may be about to make a career ending mistake, and I don't want you involved."
"I'm not scared of CO Johnson. I'm with you all the way."
"And I appreciate that," O'Reilly said. "But it's better if you're don't hear what I'm about to discuss with Fred. On you go."

The interior of the Herald's premises had also had a makeover. O'Reilly wasn't sure what the shade of green on the walls was called but he didn't like it. *Tree frog-green* wouldn't have been his first choice, but he decided there was no accounting for taste. The man behind the desk was familiar but O'Reilly couldn't recall his name. He stood up when he spotted the Irish detective.

"We don't want any trouble," he said.
"Me neither," O'Reilly said. "Is Fred in?"
"Do you have an appointment?"

"Why would I need an appointment?" O'Reilly said. "It's Michael, isn't it?"

"Close. Lewis Michaels. Sub editor."

"Sub editor?" O'Reilly repeated. "I was under the impression that there were only you and Fred working here. Don't be such a pretentious prick. Could you inform Mr Viking of my presence? I haven't got time to fuck around."

"This is outrageous," Lewis said. "You can't just waltz in here like you own the place."

"Could you do it now, please. Or do I have to arrest you for the offensive paint job?"

"That wasn't my idea," Lewis said.

They didn't get the chance to discuss the headache-inducing paint any further. A door opened down the corridor, and the man O'Reilly had come to see walked up to them.

"O'Reilly."

"Viking. It's been a while."

"I won't shake hands if that's alright."

"I wouldn't expect you to. I've got something for you."

"I've heard that one before."

"You're going to want to hear this," O'Reilly said.

"I seem to recollect those words leaving your lips too, not so long ago. I also recall what happened afterwards. I'm not falling for your tricks again, O'Reilly."

"That's a shame," O'Reilly said. "Because you're my last resort. The Gazette won't print what I have to say. They're not big on dirt. I suppose I could approach one of the big dailies in England or France."

"You'd better come through," Fred said. "I won't offer you anything to drink if that's OK."

"I wouldn't accept it if you did," O'Reilly said.

Fred's office hadn't changed. It was clear that the refurbishment budget didn't stretch to the boss's lair.

"Tell me about this dirt," Fred said.

"I assume you've been following the recent deaths," O'Reilly said.

"Poisonings," Fred corrected. "You assume right."

"What's your angle? You'll have to forgive me for not reading the drivel that you put out."

"Eight people have died," Fred said. "All of them were victims of poisoning from the toxins from the death cap mushroom."

"I'm impressed. I won't ask you where you got that information from."

"It wasn't difficult. Now, unless you're here to tell me about a public water contamination scandal, I very much doubt you can give me anything I don't already know."

"You'd be surprised. I'm going out on a limb here, and I need your assurance that I was never here today."

Fred sat up straighter in his chair. "I like where this is going."

The phone on the desk started to ring. Fred lifted the handset and slammed it down again. Then he unplugged the phone jack.

"I'm listening."

"A few days ago," O'Reilly said. "Before this shitstorm hit the island, a high-ranking police officer received a tip-off about a potential terrorist attack."

Fred grabbed his notepad and started scribbling. O'Reilly had forgotten he liked to do that.

"Terrorist attack?"

"Don't quote me on that," O'Reilly said. "In fact, I don't expect you to quote me on any of this."

"I can live with that. Go on."

"When I say terrorist attack," O'Reilly said. "I'm using the term loosely. The threat to the people of the island was implied, nothing more. Another tip-off came shortly afterwards and this one left little doubt as to what these people intended to do. They informed said police officer that they'd contaminated certain products with lethal toxins, and they would continue to do so until their demands were met."

"What exactly were these demands?" Fred said.

"The officer involved was to publicly disclose a scandal that was covered up."

Fred looked across the desk at O'Reilly. "Why are you telling me this?"

"I have my reasons," O'Reilly said. "I take umbrage to one man's self-importance. More islanders are going to die, and it doesn't have to happen. Whatever the secret is, it's a secret that needs to be told. It's a secret that can possibly save lives."

"It must be a juicy one."

"That wouldn't be my choice of words," O'Reilly said. "But yes, I believe it's something big."

"What are you hoping to achieve from this?"

"It's high time the people with the power realise that they're not infallible. They work for the people of the island, and not the other way round."

"I didn't have you pegged for a crusader," Fred said.

"Once this becomes public knowledge," O'Reilly said. "Questions are going to be asked, and I'm hoping we're going to get some answers from it."

Fred put down his pen. "Why are you telling me this? Why not take this information to your daughter at the Gazette?"

"That would be the obvious thing to do," O'Reilly said. "And that's precisely why I'm not doing it."

"You're a shrewd bastard, O'Reilly. You and I are more alike than you think. We could have been friends in another life."

"We're going to have to agree to disagree on that one," O'Reilly said. "I've said all I'm going to say – it's up to you what you want to do with it."

"Oh, I know exactly what I'm going to do with it."

"How long are we talking about?" O'Reilly said.

"I'll have something put together by this afternoon. You realise that your life is going to turn to shit after this? Even though you won't be mentioned by name, your bosses are going to be able to read between the lines."

"So be it," O'Reilly said. "At least I'll be able to close my eyes at night with a clear conscience. You should try it some time."

"A clear conscience is overrated," Fred said. "Watch this space."

"I will. For once, I'll be keeping a close eye on what the Island Herald has to say."

CHAPTER TWENTY SIX

The first thing O'Reilly noticed when he went inside the briefing room was the unfamiliar word on the whiteboard.

"Oleandrin," he read.

"It's been confirmed, sir," DC Stone said. "The ginger that Paula Troon bought from *Nature's Gifts* was laced with oleandrin."

"It comes from the oleander plant," DS Skinner elaborated. "And even in small doses the toxin is lethal. According to DI Peters the concentration of the toxin in the ginger powder indicates that we're dealing with someone with a working knowledge of chemistry."

"This just gets better and better," O'Reilly said. "Would you care to explain?"

"The lethal toxins are found primarily in the leaves of the oleander plant, sir," DS Skinner said. "But if you just ingest them in their raw state, it's not necessarily a death sentence. You'll become extremely sick, but chances are you'll pull through. But if you extract the toxins using an organic solution such as methanol, you're left with pure oleandrin and that is lethal."

"There is one downside, sir," DC Owen said. "Oleandrin poisoning is extremely rare because the leaves are bitter. The taste is enough to alert you that you're eating something bad."

"Why didn't Paula Troon taste it?" O'Reilly said.

"The powder was not only dyed to make it look like ginger," DS Skinner said. "It was slightly sweetened, and the fact that it was disguised in ginger meant that Paula expected it to have a strong flavour."

"And because Paula blended the powder with honey," DC Owen said. "The bitter taste was masked even more."

"There is some good news, sir," DC Stone said.

"What's that, Andy?" O'Reilly said.

"There was no trace of oleandrin in the ginger that you bought for Victoria. Nothing."

"Great. So, I swiped a good cup of lung juice out of her hand for nothing. Do we know how they got the oleandrin into the ginger powder?"

"It looks like the packet was opened, the ginger was spiked, and the packet was resealed. *Nature's Gifts* uses a simple adhesive plastic sleeve. It's airtight but it's designed to be resealable after opening."

"Do we have anything back from the shop itself?" O'Reilly said.

"DI Peters is still there," DS Skinner said. "We do know that they don't have CCTV and the place isn't alarmed. There's never any cash kept on the premises overnight, and I suppose they don't expect anyone to want to steal herbs and spices."

"That shop needs to be closed for business," O'Reilly said. "At least until we know if anything else has been tampered with."

"We can't close every business that sells food and drink, sir," DC Stone pointed out.

"I'm aware of that, Andy. Do you have any better suggestions?"

"No, sir."

"Then I suggest you keep your mouth shut until you do."

"I was just…"

"I don't want to hear it."

The atmosphere inside the room was bleak. Nine people had died in the past few days. Nine unsuspecting islanders had been selected by lottery and the lives of their families and friends had been shattered for no reason other than bad luck. Everyone inside the briefing room was fully aware that this was far from over, but none of them could think of a solution.

"We're dealing with a killer," O'Reilly said. "The likes of which we've never come across before. It's an indiscriminate terminator that doesn't work to any kind of logic. The MO is ingenious when you think about it. With no specific target there are no links to the victims, and all of the murders are carried out without the killer being present for the final act. It's the perfect alibi, and we need to work differently if we're going to stand a chance of stopping it. Any joy with the skeleton in Chief Officer Johnson's closet?"

"According to the records," DC Owen said. "CO Johnson arrived here in 2003 as the new CO."

"I was a PC at the time," DS Skinner said. "I remember when he got here – he was determined to make a name for himself."

"He was ambitious?" O'Reilly said.

"Very. DCO Dove had been here for a few years, and I recall he was sidestepped for the top post. We all thought he was a dead cert for the position but then CO Johnson arrived."

"What did DCO Dove think about that?" O'Reilly said.

"I remember he took it in his stride. He accepted defeat gracefully."

"Sounds like him. Was there anything that jumped out at you? Something that might be worth looking more closely at?"

"I couldn't find anything in the records to suggest that anything was covered up," DC Stone said.

"For Christ's sake, Andy," O'Reilly said. "Isn't that the whole point of a cover-up? It's not going to be in the records, is it?"

"My dad couldn't help either,' DC Owen said. "He was here before CO Johnson arrived and even though he didn't really mix in the same circles, he kept his eyes and ears open. I'm starting to wonder if the secret these people are referring to happened before the CO arrived on the island."

"Do we know where he was before?" O'Reilly said.

"Scotland," DS Skinner said. "He transferred from Edinburgh."

"I didn't know he was Scottish."

"He's not, sir," DS Skinner said. "It seems that he goes where the promotions are."

"If that's the case," O'Reilly said. "Why has he remained in the same job for more than fifteen years? If he's so ambitious, why has been stagnant for so long?"

"Perhaps his career has reached it's pinnacle, sir," DC Owen said.

"Why?" O'Reilly said. "Maybe we should be asking ourselves why that is."

"Are you suggesting his halt on the career ladder could be related to the secret he's protecting?"

"Why not? If it's something that's resulted in nine people dying, it's obviously something huge, and it's very hard to cover up something that big without help. It's possible he was allowed to get away with it, but the price he paid for that was a career freeze."

"With respect, sir," DS Skinner said. "It sounds like you're clutching at straws."

"We're drowning, Will," O'Reilly said. "And sometimes clutching at straws is the only option left."

His phone beeped on the table. The message was short and straight to the point. It was from CO Johnson, and the three words left little room for interpretation.

My office now.

O'Reilly stood up.

"Problems, sir?" DS Skinner said.

"I've got a sinking feeling that the shit is about to hit the fan, Will. I've been summoned by the big chief, and I'm in the mood for a fight. I don't think I'll be able to hold my tongue."

DC Owen got to her feet. DC Stone did the same.

"What now?" O'Reilly said.

DS Skinner followed suit.

"What the devil are you playing at?" O'Reilly said.

"Backing you up, sir," DC Stone said.

"We're coming with you," DC Owen added.

"One for all and all for one, sir." It was DS Skinner.

O'Reilly observed them and smiled.

"You bunch of soft shites."

"You can't stop us," DC Owen said.

"Who said I was going to stop you, Katie. Come on then. And thank you."

CHAPTER TWENTY SEVEN

If Chief Officer Johnson was surprised to see that O'Reilly had come mob handed it didn't show on his face. He told the Irishman to close the door and take a seat. The rest of the team remained standing. There was a tablet on the desk. CO Johnson turned it round so O'Reilly could see what was on the screen.

"Is this your doing?" he asked and coughed loudly.

"What am I looking at, sir?" O'Reilly said.

"Don't take me for a fool, O'Reilly. That has your signature all over it."

O'Reilly glanced at the screen. He was impressed – Fred Viking had worked quickly.

It was the Island Herald's online site. The headline seemed somewhat rushed. O'Reilly had expected Fred *the Ed* to come up with something more eye-catching than this.

Sickness on the Island could have been prevented.

"Well?" CO Johnson said.

"Well, what?"

"Are you going to deny that you had a hand in this?"

"I really have no idea what you're talking about, sir," O'Reilly said.

"What has the Herald written?" DS Skinner asked.

"Some crap about the sickness on the island," O'Reilly said. "They're claiming that someone high up in the Island Police was aware of the threat and they did nothing about it."

"Do you realise the damage you've caused?" CO Johnson said.

"Firstly," O'Reilly said. "This had nothing to do with me. And secondly, this is all true so perhaps you ought to be asking yourself about the damage *you've* caused. Nine people are dead, and you could have prevented it."

CO Johnson's mouth opened but no words came out.

"Will there be anything else?" O'Reilly said. "Because we have a lot of work to do, and this is wasting all of our time."

CO Johnson scanned the people in the room, and his gaze fell on O'Reilly. "How much do they know?"

"As far as I'm aware, they know as much as they need to know, sir. They know about the emails you received and failed to act on, and they know about your sordid little secret."

"Be very careful, Liam," CO Johnson said. "I can make your life extremely uncomfortable."

"With all the respect that's due to you under the present circumstances," O'Reilly said. "My life happens to be rather uncomfortable already. I've not long got back from racing home because I thought my wife had been poisoned. These bastards brought this inside my house and that has made it personal."

"What are we going to do about this?" CO Johnson tapped the screen of the tablet.

"*We're* not going to do anything," O'Reilly said. "This is all on you now. You've only got one option left. You're going to give these terrorists what they want and you're going to do that now."

"I can't do that, Liam."

"That's not your choice to make."

"DCO Dove's life will be over if we go this route."

"Don't talk shite, sir," O'Reilly said. "This has nothing to do with Callum. You know that – I know that and so do the rest of my team. Grow a pair of balls and come clean. It's the only option left for you."

"Are you accusing me of lying?"

"I am, sir. And if there's one thing I despise, it's liars. We will unearth this secret of yours. It may take time, but we will get to the bottom of it eventually. You can speed things up, and perhaps you'll prevent more deaths in the process. I've said all I want to say. I reckon you have an hour, tops before the Herald thing gains momentum and the phone calls start coming."

Right on cue the phone on the desk started to ring. CO Johnson ignored it.

"This isn't about me, Liam," he said when the ringing stopped.

"So you keep saying," O'Reilly said.

"It really isn't."

"It looks like we've reached an impasse," O'Reilly said. "And I really don't have time for it right now. Do the right thing, sir. Do the only thing you can do. We've got work to do."

He got up and left the office. The others followed him out.

"Something doesn't feel right," DS Skinner said when they were away from the offices on the top floor.

"You can say that again," O'Reilly said.

"I didn't get the impression that CO Johnson was lying to us."

"Someone is," O'Reilly said. "And I don't think it's DCO Dove."

"What do we do now, sir?" DC Stone asked.

"We keep digging, Andy," O'Reilly said. "It's not going to be long before the Herald's thing goes viral, and the people of the island are going to want answers. CO Johnson is going to be under pressure, but the man's more stubborn than I am."

"Do you think he kept the emails?" DC Owen said.

"He told me he forwarded them to his personal email and deleted the ones on his work account," O'Reilly said.

"Nothing is ever permanently deleted," DC Owen said. "If you know what you're doing there is always a way to retrieve anything that's been deleted."

"Where are you going with this, Katie."

"As far as I see it, any email that's on the work computer of someone under the employ of the Island Police is police property. We have specialist IT people who will be able to retrieve those emails."

"CO Johnson isn't going to go for that," DC Stone pointed out.

"CO Johnson doesn't have to go for it, Andy. The pressure from the public will leave the powers that be little choice in the matter. Those emails are key pieces of evidence in the investigation and everybody on the island is going to be aware of them soon. CO Johnson will have no choice but to disclose what was said in them."

"Do you think he'll be suspended?" DC Stone said.

"Who knows?" O'Reilly said. "If this secret of his really is so big it'll harm the reputation of the Island Police, the first line of defence will be damage control. And if it comes out that more people other than CO Johnson were involved in the cover up, it's not just Fred Viking and his local rag we'll need to be concerned about. This is going to go global, and whether we like it or not, we're going to be the most famous police force in the world for a while."

CHAPTER TWENTY EIGHT

By four that afternoon emotions on the island were running high. The Island Herald's online piece was the only thing everyone was talking about and confidence in the Island Police had plummeted to an all-time low. Groups of protestors had already taken to the streets, and the general consensus was that CO Johnson should be stripped of his position at the helm.

Shops selling food and drink products had closed their doors. Panic was rife and the owners of the businesses that offered food stuffs were conducting thorough inspections of the products on their shelves. Refuse removal companies were fighting a losing battle with the enormous quantity of discarded food and drink that was piling up outside the properties on the island, and the streets were starting to stink of rotting food. Scavengers had cottoned on to the easy pickings and stray dogs and cats were feasting on the bounty available.

O'Reilly was hiding away in his office. He'd ignored no fewer than a dozen phone calls since the Herald's story went live. The majority of the calls were from foreign numbers, and he assumed they were journalists. He was halfway through his second cup of tea when there was a knock on the door and DC Owen came in.

"It's chaos out there, sir."

"We expected it, didn't we?"

"We didn't expect it to escalate so quickly. Some of the protests are turning violent."

"It's understandable. People are panicking and emotions are running wild."

"Did you know this would happen?" DC Owen said.

"As soon as I left Fred Viking's office, I knew I'd opened Pandora's box, Katie. Things will calm down in a day or two. Unfortunately, this was the only way to back CO Johnson into a corner. He's got no choice but to come clean now."

His phone started to ring again. The screen told him it was his daughter. "Summi," he answered it. "What's it like out there?"

"Hell," she said. "I presume the Herald's scoop came from you?"

"It was necessary," O'Reilly said. "We're going to get some answers out of this."

"That's why I'm phoning. I think I might have something. Can we meet up?"

"Where are you?" O'Reilly said.

"I'm still at your house. I promised to stay with Victoria."

"What have you found?" O'Reilly said.

"I don't want to tell you over the phone, but I'm onto something – I know I am, and it's something you'll want to hear."

"I'll come over now."

"Try to avoid La Villocq Road by Beaucamps," Assumpta said. "There's rumours of rioters there."

"Thanks for the heads-up. I'll see you soon."

"Has Assumpta found something?" DC Owen said.

"She thinks so," O'Reilly said. "Do you feel like a drive?"

"OK. Are you scared?"

"I'm no stranger to protests, Katie."

"I wasn't referring to the rioters. I don't want to eat or drink anything in case it's been poisoned with something. I'm not the only one."

"Look at this taking what we know into account. The only deaths so far have been from the result of toxins found in food and drink from Freshlife supermarket and *Nature's Gifts* health shop. The ginger I bought for Victoria wasn't contaminated."

"But it could have been," DC Owen said. "If you'd have picked up the ginger before Paula Troon did it could have been Victoria that was poisoned."

"We can't afford to think like that."

"The people responsible are ruthless, sir. They're indiscriminate and who knows how many more spiked products there are out there."

"Look at it this way," O'Reilly said. "All of this started two days ago. Nine fatalities are nine too many but when you look at the vast quantities of food and drink available that number is minimal."

"How can you be so calm?"

"Who said I was calm?" O'Reilly said. "But there's enough panic on the island without me adding to it."

A figure in the doorway caught O'Reilly's eye. It was DCO Dove, and O'Reilly was surprised to see him.

"You don't do things by halves, do you, Liam?"

"I'm not following you, sir," O'Reilly said.

"Right. I thought I should be the one to inform you that CO Johnson has been suspended pending an investigation."

"That was quick," O'Reilly said.

"What did you expect?"

"It was nothing to do with me."

"Of course," DCO Dove said. "You need to tread carefully, Liam. Your career is on a knife edge, and I'd advise you to consider your next move very carefully."

"I'm employed by the Island Police to catch criminals," O'Reilly said. "And that's what I intend to do."

"Just take a step back for a moment. I'm advising you to reconsider your methods."

"I'll bear that in mind," O'Reilly said. "We need to let the tech team loose with CO Johnson's computer. They have to retrieve the emails he deleted."

"It's already been set in motion."

"How long are we talking about?"

"No more than a couple of hours."

"Those emails are going to get us a step closer to the fuckers behind this," O'Reilly said.

"And those fuckers, as you call them will pay the highest price for what they've done. You have my word on that. I'll let you get on."

"Thanks for the heads-up, sir."

"I can't protect you, Liam."

"I'm not asking you to."

"I know it was you who leaked the story to the Herald," DCO Dove said. "You can deny it until the cows come home, but I know you were behind it. I hope you know what the hell you're doing."

"Me too, sir," O'Reilly said. "I mean, hypothetically, of course."

DCO Dove sighed. "Of course."

CHAPTER TWENTY NINE

The drive to Vazon passed without incident for the first few miles. There were a lot more people on the streets than there usually were, but the majority of the protests appeared to be peaceful. O'Reilly was glad – the last thing they needed on top of everything else was a bunch of violent islanders to deal with. There didn't seem to be any damage to any of the buildings along the way and O'Reilly was grateful for that too. He'd had plenty of experience with mob mentality and looting and vandalism was common in those instances. He supposed nobody was going to risk looting potentially lethal food and drink.

"I've been thinking," DC Owen said.
They'd just driven through Le Foulon.
"Me too," O'Reilly said. "You go first."
"Do you think this is what the killers wanted? Was it their intention to bring the island to a standstill?"
"I really don't know, Katie. If that is the case, what exactly are they getting out of it?"
"We've experienced something similar before, haven't we? Not so long ago, with the *Fab Four Robbers*. The chaos they created was merely a smokescreen for something else entirely. What if this is what's happening here too?"
"It had crossed my mind," O'Reilly said. "We've got nine dead islanders. Nine unconnected victims who were simply unlucky. The people responsible stand to gain absolutely nothing from the deaths, and it seems to be a lot of trouble to go to for nothing. I do not believe that a human being can kill like this for the fun of it – there has to be something else behind the murders."
"Perhaps that will become clear in time, sir. Maybe this is phase one of their plan, and the real motive will become apparent when they strike again."

"You've got quite an imagination there, Katie Owen," O'Reilly said. "Look at what we have: random food and drink products were contaminated with potentially fatal toxins. CO Johnson received two emails threatening to kill more islanders unless he spoke out about the secret he's been keeping. That in itself has some kind of twisted logic to it. It's an age-old tactic. You issue a threat, and you make your demands. If those demands are not met you carry out those threats, and so it goes on. CO Johnson has made no attempt to rectify the situation by coming clean and we have to work on the assumption that more products will be tainted because of it."

The conversation was cut short by something on the road up ahead. "Damn it," O'Reilly said. "Summi warned me about this. I was driving on autopilot."

He'd taken the same route he drove every day, and they were now fifty metres from La Villocq Road in Beaucamps.

"I think you should turn around, sir," DC Owen said.

A glance in the rearview mirror told O'Reilly that this was no longer an option. He couldn't understand where all the people had suddenly come from. The road behind him was full of bodies too. He slowed down and crawled up to the group of men and women up ahead. Some of them were holding placards but the majority were empty handed.

"This isn't good," DC Owen said. "Look at that placard."

"Island Police," O'Reilly read. "Protectors or murderers?"

"What are we going to do? You're not exactly unknown on the island."

"Let's hope that nobody recognises me," O'Reilly said.

He was forced to stop the car when the mass of bodies made the road impassable. He weighed up his options. The wording on some of the placards left little doubt as to how these people were feeling and he didn't think flashing his police ID would do him any favours. He turned off the engine and opened the door of the car.

He got out and approached the nearest protesters.

"We really need to get through. Could you please move out of the road?"

"You're Island Police," a woman wearing a bandana over her face said.

"And I'm asking you to move on," O'Reilly said.

"He's one of the bastards," a man wearing a baseball cap shouted.

"I understand how you feel, but this isn't helping."

"Fuck you," baseball cap said. "We don't have to listen to you."

"Actually, you do," O'Reilly told him.

This probably wasn't the wisest thing to say given the circumstances, and O'Reilly was forced to back up when a wall of protesters edged closer.

DC Owen got out of the car. "Stop right there."

O'Reilly was surprised when her words had the desired effect.

"We understand your concerns," she added. "We really do, and we're on the same page as you. But this isn't the way to do things. DI O'Reilly and I need to get to Vazon. We will find the people responsible for this, but you're not helping matters. Please, go home and let the Island Police do their jobs."

"The Island Police can't be trusted," bandana woman screamed.

"You're dead right there," O'Reilly joined in. "And the corrupt officers in our ranks will be the next thing on the agenda when we've caught the people responsible for the poisonings and I will make it my life's mission to nail their balls to the wall."

He hoped there were no journalists in the crowd.

"He's all talk," the man in the baseball cap offered.

"Look," O'Reilly said. "From where I'm standing, I can see unlawful protest, obstruction of justice, and a few more infringements but I'm happy to let them slide if you'll just let us get on our way. You really do not want to add assault on a police officer to that list. Come on – let us do our jobs."

A few of the protestors started to disperse and they were left with half a dozen die-hards.

"Please," DC Owen said. "Let us through. This isn't helping anyone."

"What are you going to do about the chief officer?" a man who'd been silent so far asked.

"Chief Officer Johnson will be dealt with accordingly," O'Reilly said. "He's been suspended pending an enquiry and there will be a full investigation into his conduct."

"An internal investigation, no doubt?" baseball cap said. "There'll be another cover-up. We're not stupid."

"Whatever happens is way above my pay grade," O'Reilly said. "I'm asking you one more time to get off the streets and go home."

Later, he would recall the noise the projectile made as it flew towards his head and hit him on the side of the head. The brick connected with his ear and the whooshing sound morphed into a high-pitched scream as the trauma to the cells in the cochlea caused the resulting sound waves to be distorted. O'Reilly's brain registered these waves as a whistle, not unlike that used by the referee in a game of football, and the last thought that entered his head before the lights went out was a strange one. He knew for certain that the pitch of the whistle was C sharp, but he had no idea exactly how he knew this.

CHAPTER THIRTY

By the time the ambulance arrived, it was as if the protestors had never been there. The ones who were present when the brick was thrown had made a sharp exit as soon as they realised what had happened. O'Reilly had been knocked out for a minute or so, and when he regained consciousness the ringing in his right ear was all he could hear. He'd suffered a laceration to the skin over his cheekbone and apart from a serious headache he didn't think he was too badly hurt. DC Owen didn't want to take any chances, and she'd called the ambulance immediately. The person who threw the brick remained a mystery.

"Leave me be."

O'Reilly was sitting up on the road next to the ambulance that had arrived. The paramedics had insisted he didn't get up, and the Irishman wasn't happy about it.

"I'm fine," he said. "There's a tone-deaf leprechaun playing the flute in my head but I'm sure he'll soon shut up."

The shorter of the two paramedics smiled. "Let's check you over, shall we? Are you experiencing any blurred vision?"

"My eyes are no more blurry than usual."

"Headache?"

"A bit," O'Reilly said. "I've had worse."

"There doesn't appear to be any bleeding from the ear," the paramedic said.

"That's good. And the wound to the cheekbone doesn't look too serious. How long were you unconscious for?"

"A couple of seconds," O'Reilly said. "No more than that."

"He was out for almost two minutes," DC Owen corrected.

"I used to like you, Katie. Why did you have to tell him that?"

"Can you walk?" the taller paramedic asked.

"Have been able to for almost fifty years," O'Reilly said.

He was helped to his feet, and his vision abandoned him for a moment. When it returned the throbbing inside his head was more intense and he winced.

"I need to get to Vazon," he managed to say.

"Not happening, sir," the short paramedic informed him. "You don't take any chances with head injuries. You're going to need to be checked over – they'll want to do some scans to make sure everything is as it should be. And you'll be advised to stay in overnight."

"Where are you taking me? Please don't say the Princess Elizabeth."

"The Princess Elizabeth," the paramedic said.

"You could have said it without that dumb grin on your face," O'Reilly said.

"With all respect – you asked for it."

"He's got a point, sir," DC Owen said. "You did ask for it."

"It looks like I don't have much choice," O'Reilly said. "You don't need to come to the hospital. Could you drive my car to Vazon? See what Assumpta has to say."

"Will do, sir. I'll let Victoria and Assumpta know what happened."

"Thanks, Katie. Could you play it down a bit though? I don't want them to worry unnecessarily. I've had worse than a brick to the head – the idiot who hurled the thing threw like a little girl anyway."

* * *

DC Owen parked O'Reilly's car outside Victoria's house in Vazon, and she got out. The sky had darkened, and it looked like there was a storm brewing overhead. DC Owen walked up the path to the house and knocked on the door. Victoria opened it soon afterwards.

"Katie," she said. "Where's Liam?"

"There was a bit of an altercation in Beaucamps," DC Owen said. "A bunch of protestors caused us to stop and one of them threw a brick at DI O'Reilly's head. He was taken to the Princess Elizabeth in an ambulance."

"Oh my God. Is he alright?"

"They want to do some tests, and they'll keep him in overnight, but he was giving the paramedics a hard time, so I'd say he'll be fine."

"Why did they do that?" Victoria said. "Why did they throw a brick at him? Did you catch the person responsible?"

"Unfortunately, not. I didn't see it happen until the brick hit him and whoever threw it was long gone before I knew what was going on. I'm sure he'll be fine. Is Assumpta still here?"

Victoria nodded. "You'd better come in. We're going to get a downpour in a minute."

Assumpta was in the kitchen. DC Owen told her what had happened to O'Reilly.

"He'll be fine," Assumpta said. "Dad has always had a hard head. I did warn him not to go that way."

"We got sidetracked," DC Owen said. "And before we knew where we were it was too late. The Island Police are not popular right now."

"I suppose you could call it poetic justice if you believe in that stuff," Assumpta said. "It was Dad who leaked the CO Johnson thing in the first place – those protesters wouldn't have been there if it wasn't for that."

"You're taking this remarkably well," Victoria said.

"I've become immune to it. Dad will be just fine."

"You said you'd found something." DC Owen got to the reason she was there.

"I think I have," Assumpta said.

She minimised the page she was looking at and clicked on another one.

"This is an article from what was the forerunner of the Island Herald. It was before Fred Viking took the helm and it seems like the paper had integrity back then. We're going back to 2003 now, and very few of the smaller papers had much of an online presence."

"That looks like a page from a newspaper," DC Owen said,

"It is. All the archives were digitalised and put online a few years ago."

"This is a piece on corruption," DC Owen said.

"It's rather vague," Assumpta said. "There were rumours of a cover-up in an investigation in January 2003. It was a rape case, and the main suspect was one of the island's high rollers. Len Hughes was his name. You know the sort – big house, fancy cars and plenty of connections in the right places. Hughes was suspected of raping a seventeen-year-old girl."

"Do we know what evidence they had against him?" DC Owen said.

"According to another report I found on it, the girl reported him shortly after it happened. She did everything right, and I think she was incredibly brave. Hughes was brought in and of course he denied everything. The case was thrown out due to lack of evidence."

"Unfortunately, it happens."

"But if you read between the lines," Assumpta said. "It becomes clear that there was an abundance of evidence. Evidence that never came to light."

"Someone covered it up?" Victoria said.

"The Herald couldn't prove it," Assumpta said. "And you do not accuse an establishment like the Island Police without something to back up the story. Plus, Len Hughes was not a man you went to war against. He had powerful connections. I dug deeper and I found another, independent article touching on the same topic. It was rumoured that Len Hughes had contacts in the police – high ranking contacts, and this is where it gets rather disturbing. The young girl happened to babysit for Hughes, and the alleged rape happened when he came home early without his wife. The girl reported it, and a case was built, but someone high up in the Island Police made damn sure the case never made it to court."

"How is that even possible?" Victoria said.

"It happens more often than you think," DC Owen said. "For a case to even be considered by the crown prosecution service, the evidence has to be watertight. Facts need to be checked and double checked, and sometimes vital pieces of evidence get misplaced."

"Especially if someone helps them to disappear," Assumpta said.

"Do we know who the high-ranking officer was?" DC Owen said.

"I think I do," Assumpta said. "But there's more. Len Hughes was cleared of all charges. He went back to his life of privilege as though nothing had happened."

"Is he still on the island?" Victoria said.

"No," Assumpta said. "He's serving a life sentence in Belmarsh prison in England."

"You're kidding?" DC Owen said.

"It's no joke. Two months after Len Hughes got away with raping a seventeen-year-old he was on the prowl again. This time his victim was fourteen years old. Hughes was caught at the scene, but not before he'd raped and strangled the girl. She died before the ambulance arrived. The bastard was shipped off to England for his own safety; can you believe it? There's only one prison here on the island, and the authorities were concerned that he would be harmed or killed if he served his time on Guernsey."

Neither Victoria nor DC Owen said anything for a while. The story that Assumpta had told them was horrific and it had happened right there on their doorstep.

"I'm sure I know the identity of the officer who covered up the rape of the seventeen-year-old," Assumpta said. "Not only was he a member of the same golf club as Len Hughes but their children attended the same school. And when I looked more closely, I learned that they were good friends."

"Chief Officer Johnson?" DC Owen said.

"This is where the story gets even more interesting," Assumpta said. "According to the Island Police records, CO Johnson didn't arrive on the island until March 2003. Most of what I've just told you happened before he got the CO job. And, this is just guesswork on my part, but if you were to dig a bit deeper, you'll see that the person who was in line for the top job was overlooked because of the part he played in the travesty of justice that resulted in a young girl being murdered in the worst possible way."

"DCO Dove?" DC Owen said.

Assumpta nodded. "I'd say the motive behind the recent poisonings has become a whole lot clearer, wouldn't you?"

"We need to look at the family and friends of the girl that Len Hughes raped and murdered."

CHAPTER THIRTY ONE

"We also have to consider the family of the seventeen-year-old," DS Skinner said.

DCI Fish had been called to an emergency meeting, so DS Skinner was assuming command in O'Reilly's absence. DC Owen had returned to the Island Police HQ armed with the information that Assumpta had managed to dig up.

"Weren't you working here when Hughes was arrested?" DC Stone asked.

"I was," DS Skinner said. "And I remember it well. It was one of the most high-profile cases to date on the island, and there were very few people on the island that didn't get to hear about it."

"Why didn't it ring any bells earlier?" DC Stone said.

"Why would it? Why would I connect a brutal rape and murder from 2003 to a spate of poisonings now? There was nothing to link the two."

"But Hughes was accused of rape earlier that year."

"I seem to recall something about that, Andy, but nothing was proven, and the case was dropped."

"What about afterwards?" DC Owen said. "When the rape and murder of the fourteen-year-old came to light, was anything done about reopening the earlier case?"

"There was no evidence to justify it, Katie."

"Because the evidence was tampered with," DC Stone said. "And now we know who was responsible for that."

"This new information puts a whole new perspective on things," DS Skinner said. "And it complicates matters somewhat. CO Johnson wasn't even on the island when all this happened, and the poor man has been unjustly suspended. Does the DI know about the new developments?"

"I didn't want to worry him with it yet, Sarge," DC Owen said.

"He won't thank you for it."

"He suffered a head injury," DC Owen said. "He needs to rest."

"What are we even going to do with this information?" DC Stone wondered. "After the backlash to O'Reilly's leak to the Herald, we can't go to the press again."

"Especially as the wrong man was punished for it," DC Owen said.

"We'll focus on the families of the two victims of Len Hughes," DS Skinner decided. "The name of the seventeen-year-old was never released to the press, but it should be easy enough to track her down. Len Hughes got away with what he did to her, and that must have caused an awful lot of pain for her family. And when Len Hughes' true colours were shown, the least they could have expected was for the Island Police to take another look at the case, but that didn't happen."

"Something still doesn't feel right," DC Owen said. "It's understandable that the parents of the girl who Len Hughes raped would want justice, but it doesn't explain why they would go about it by poisoning random people all these years later."

"It doesn't seem like something the family of a victim would do," DS Skinner agreed.

"And how did they stumble upon the cover-up?" DC Stone said.

"Assumpta found an earlier article that hinted on some kind of corruption," DC Owen said. "It was all based on supposition and there was no evidence to prove that anything untoward really did take place, but I always say there's no smoke without fire. What if the people responsible for the recent murders took it a step further and found actual proof that a high-ranking officer protected a potential murderer? Not only did he retain his position in the Island Police, but he was also advised to take a few weeks off while the smoke cleared. He was given paid leave which in my book is tantamount to being rewarded for breaking the law."

"Where did you get this information from?" DS Skinner said.

"My dad. When I discussed the timeline with him, something occurred to him. DCO Dove's leave coincided with CO Johnson's arrival on the island, give or take a week or two. DCO Dove's name was all over the CO position, but an outsider was given the post instead."

"That's some coincidence," DC Stone said.

"And it also implies that the big bosses had their suspicions about DCO Dove's dubious behaviour," DS Skinner said. "They just couldn't prove anything. Is it just me who's feeling a bit ill?"

"The whole thing stinks," DC Stone said. "I've a good mind to go up and see DCO Dove right now and give him a piece of my mind."

"You're not going to do that, Andy," DS Skinner said.

"We need some help," DC Stone said. "But who do we go to? The chief officer has been suspended, and his assistant has lied to us from the onset."

"We'll keep this to ourselves for the time being," DS Skinner said. "O'Reilly should be back in action tomorrow, and I know he'll come up with a plan of his own. I suggest we wrap things up for today."

"This isn't going to end well for the Island Police," DC Owen said. "When the truth about what DCO Dove covered up comes out, it's going to be the scandal of the century. I think that's why CO Johnson was so reluctant to spill the beans."

"His silence makes him complicit," DC Stone said. "He could have prevented the deaths of all those people, and even though he wasn't directly involved in the cover-up of the evidence in the rape case, he knew about it and that makes him a part of it in my book."

"We can discuss the morality involved until we're blue in the face, Andy," DS Skinner said. "But it's not going to achieve anything. What's done is done, and we have to move past it and come up with a solution to the here and now."

A massive clap of thunder sounded outside. The rumble shook the windowpane in the briefing room. It was followed by a flash of lightning and then the heavens opened.

"I'll take that as a sign to finish up," DS Skinner said.

"I'm not driving in that weather," DC Stone said.

"It won't last long," DC Owen said. "It's a proper late summer thunderstorm. It'll be over in twenty minutes or so."

"Get yourselves off home," DS Skinner said. "I'm going to find the DCI to bring him up to date."

"I think I'll go and see the DI to do the same," DC Owen said.

"Take him some grapes," DC Stone said.

"DI O'Reilly hates grapes, Andy."

DC Stone grinned a toothy grin. "I know. Take him some grapes."

CHAPTER THIRTY TWO

DC Owen thought O'Reilly looked more irritated than ill. The Irishman was sitting on the bed looking at something on his mobile phone. DC Owen hadn't brought him any grapes, but she hadn't come empty handed. She held out the jumbo packet of Licorice Allsorts and O'Reilly's face lit up.
"You're a lifesaver, Katie. I don't know how they expect anyone to survive on the portions of food they offer up here."
"How are you feeling?"
"Grand," O'Reilly said. "They gave me something for the pain, and the flute-playing idiot has stopped tooting away inside my head. What brings you here?"
"I thought you'd want to know what Assumpta found out."
"Now you're talking," O'Reilly said. "What did Summi dig up?"
DC Owen told him. She told him about DCO Dove's involvement in the cover-up of evidence in the rape case and she told him about the subsequent rape and murder of the fourteen-year-old girl.

It took O'Reilly a while to process it all and he remained silent for a moment.
"Well?" DC Owen said.
"I'm of a mind to kill the bastard," O'Reilly said. "The man fooled us all, didn't he? He pulled the wool over all our eyes. I trusted him – I really did, and this betrayal of my trust will not go unpunished, Katie. This has made me even more determined to finish this. What else have I missed?"
"We discussed the way forwards," DC Owen said. "And it's imperative that we track down the girl who was raped – the seventeen-year-old. She'll be in her early thirties now. It's possible that she's still on the island."
"And we need to look into the family of the young girl who was raped and murdered," O'Reilly said.

"We discussed that too."

"Of course you did."

"Andy thinks we need some help," DC Owen said.

O'Reilly ripped open the bag of Licorice Allsorts and stuffed three in his mouth.

"Ah, this takes me back. We don't need help, Katie – we're more than capable of tackling this. In all my time in law enforcement, I've never worked with such an exceptional team. Even Andy has his strong points. We'll do this as we always have done."

"I still can't believe DCO Dove did what he did."

"Me neither," O'Reilly said. "But then again, nothing surprises me anymore. Do you want one?"

He nodded to the bag of licorice.

"No thanks," DC Owen said. "Has Victoria been in to see you?"

"I told her not to. She's not long left the place herself, and she needs to rest. It's bad enough being stuck in here when there's bugger all wrong with me without having to look at the sympathetic mugs of people coming to visit. Present company excepted of course."

"Of course," DC Owen said. "My dad said CO Johnson's arrival on the island coincided with DCO Dove taking enforced leave. That suggests the people higher up were well aware of DCO Dove's dodgy dealings."

"It doesn't surprise me," O'Reilly said.

"The tech team have managed to retrieve the emails that Chief Officer Johnson deleted," DC Owen said.

"And?"

"We haven't been allowed access to them yet. The DS called me as I was on my way here, and he told me that DCI Fish is pressing the powers that be for access, but they're not playing ball."

"Those emails are key evidence, Katie," O'Reilly said.

"They're also key evidence in the investigation into CO Johnson."

"We need those emails."

"DS Skinner is confident that we'll have them by tomorrow. I'd better go – I'm having dinner with my mum and dad."

"Give them my regards," O'Reilly said.

"I will do."

"And Katie?" O'Reilly said.

"What is it?"

"Not once since you arrived, have you addressed me as sir," O'Reilly said.

"Sorry. I…"

"It's refreshing," O'Reilly interrupted. "I like it."

"Will you be back at work tomorrow?"

"Try and stop me. I need to file a report on the incident, but as far as I can see it's a case of being in the wrong place at the wrong time. The prick who hurled the brick didn't stick around and I'm not particularly perturbed. Shit happens."

"You're a strange man, sir."

"Get out of here," O'Reilly said. "Thanks for the Licorice Allsorts."

"I did check the packet for any evidence of tampering."

"Well, that's just put me off eating them."

"Why don't I believe that?" DC Owen said.

"I didn't mean it anyway."

He demonstrated this by grabbing a handful of licorice.

"I'll see you tomorrow."

O'Reilly stuffed the licorice in his mouth and savoured the familiar taste. Even though he was forced to stay in hospital overnight he was feeling content. The new information that Assumpta had dug up had inspired him and he was feeling confident that this was the breakthrough they'd been waiting for. They were going to make progress in the investigation tomorrow – he could sense it.

Dr Newton came into the room and asked him how he was feeling.

"I don't suppose there's any chance of an early release?" O'Reilly said.

"You're not in prison, Liam," Dr Newton said.

"Is that a no then?"

"It's a no," Dr Newton confirmed. "The tests didn't give us any cause for concern, but we like to monitor head injuries just to be on the safe side."

"I've had worse than a brick to the head," O'Reilly told him.

"I'm sure you have, but I'm not taking any chances. Do you mind?"

He pointed to the bag of Licorice Allsorts.

"Fill your boots," O'Reilly said. "I'm not slavering at the mouth like a rabid dog so it's safe to assume they haven't been contaminated."

Dr Newton helped himself to two.

"You're a strange man, Liam."

"You're the second person to tell me that in the space of ten minutes."

"I'll come and check in on you in the morning," Dr Newton said. "Get some rest, and don't eat all the licorice."

"I'll save you a few. Good night, Doc."

CHAPTER THIRTY THREE

When O'Reilly got to work the next day, he felt like he was in the middle of a war zone. He had to park in the street next to the station – the car park had been cordoned off and there was nobody manning the police tape. A crowd of people had gathered in the street, and it was quite obvious from the vehicles lined up who most of them were. The logos of the various newspapers were a dead giveaway. He'd been discharged from hospital and, after a shower and a change of clothes at home he'd come straight to work.

He was barely out of the car when a barrage of voices bombarded him.
"Do you have any comment on the suspension of CO Johnson?"
O'Reilly didn't reply.
"O'Reilly, what's the big secret?"
He ignored this question too.
"We pay well for decent info."
This didn't interest him either.

He ducked underneath the police tape and came face to face with PC Martin Woodbine. The giant PC looked sheepish, and O'Reilly could smell cigarettes on him. He hadn't realised that he was a smoker.
"Sorry, sir," he said. "Did you have to park outside?"
"There was nobody manning the cordon. I assume that was your responsibility?"
"Sorry, sir," PC Woodbine said once more. "I've been here since first light, and I just popped away for a quick smoke."
"Don't let it happen again," O'Reilly said. "You're not paid to smoke – you can poison your lungs all you like in your own time, not when you're supposed to be working."
"Sorry, sir."

"And if you apologise once more, I won't be responsible for what I might do."

He realised how ridiculous this sounded straight away. PC Woodbine was at least a foot taller than he was and he weighed almost twice as much.

O'Reilly went inside the station and headed straight for his office. In his haste to get straight to work he'd neglected to drink a cup of tea, and he was of the opinion that nobody should have to start the day without a good cup inside them. He closed the office door and switched on the kettle. His mobile phone started to ring before it had finished boiling and the screen told him it was DCI Fish.

"Tom," he answered it. "I'm just getting some tea in my belly, then I'm all yours."

"No rush," DCI Fish said. "How are you feeling?"

"Grand."

"Are you well enough to be back so soon?" DCI Fish asked. "You're entitled to take more time than this."

"I can't afford to take time off, Tom," O'Reilly said.

"I'm relieved to hear that."

"Was there something you wanted me for?"

"I was just checking in to see how you were. Briefing in fifteen?"

"Sounds good. Any joy with the emails?"

"We've got them, and I have to say the content is rather anticlimactic."

"Is there any clue about who sent them?" O'Reilly said.

"The IT guys are working on it, but they're not sounding confident. The mails were probably sent using a VPN and that's untraceable unless you have limitless time and a hefty IT budget – both of which we're seriously lacking, but we'll go through the emails at the briefing to see if we can spot something the tech team missed. It's good to have you back."

"I've only been gone a few hours," O'Reilly said.

"Anyway. Enjoy your tea."

O'Reilly ended the call and made said cup of tea. He took a sip and sat down at his desk. He made a mental to-do list and decided that tracking down the families of Len Hughes' victims was the priority. The emails that CO Johnson kept secret left little doubt as to the reason behind the poisoning. Whoever was responsible wanted the cover-up of the evidence in the rape case made public, and the logical assumption to make was it had to be connected to the families or friends of the two young victims.

O'Reilly was halfway through his tea when his phone started to ring again. The number on the screen was one that he didn't recognise but he answered it anyway.

"O'Reilly."

"Liam," a familiar voice said.

It was Chief Officer Robert Johnson.

"What is it, sir?" O'Reilly said.

"I'm not supposed to be talking to you, but I need you to hear what I have to say."

"I'm listening."

"Not on the phone," CO Johnson said. "Can you get away for an hour?"

"We're snowed under at the moment, sir. Some new evidence has come to light and we're going to be flat out checking it out."

"Please, Liam," CO Johnson said. "I wouldn't ask if it wasn't important."

"Where are you?"

"I'm at home. My wife has a hair appointment at eleven and she'll be gone for a good few hours. It's better that she's not here when you pop round."

"Can't you just tell me over the phone?" O'Reilly said.

"It really is better if we meet."

"OK," O'Reilly found himself saying. "Where exactly is home?"

CO Johnson gave him the address.

"And it goes without saying that you're to tell nobody about this," he added.
"Of course, sir," O'Reilly said. "I'll be there at eleven on the dot."
"Good man," CO Johnson said and rang off.

O'Reilly rubbed his eyes and finished the rest of his tea. He was about to leave the office to make his way to the briefing room when something occurred to him. He'd neglected to pick up the bag of Licorice Allsorts when he was discharged from hospital. He cursed himself – the bag was still half full, and he'd left it on the table in the hospital room.

CHAPTER THIRTY FOUR

O'Reilly was the last to arrive for the morning briefing. The rest of the team were already seated. A projector screen had been set up, and O'Reilly could see the words of the two emails on it. The first thing that occurred to him was both emails were brief. They were concise and straight to the point. "You're in possession of a secret," he read. "It's a secret that needs to be told, and you will tell it. This is your first warning – should you choose to ignore it, the consequences for the people you've sworn to protect will be dire."

"Obviously, that was the first one," DCI Fish said. "The second email goes into more detail about what the threat actually entails."
O'Reilly could see that. This time the sender warned of the contamination of random food and drink products if the chief officer remained silent.
"And they did it, didn't they?" DS Skinner said. "This wasn't an empty threat."
"And still the CO kept the secret to himself," O'Reilly said. "Even after nine islanders lost their lives, he kept his mouth shut. But now the truth is out there, and the man has been suspended."
"The sender is clearly not uneducated," DC Stone pointed out. "The language they use is clear and it leaves little doubt about their intentions."
"I think it's rather dramatic," O'Reilly said. "Anyone who reads a lot of second-rate spy novels could come up with something like that."
"I very much doubt it's worth wasting time on analysing the semantics involved," DCI Fish said.
"Probably not," O'Reilly agreed.
"Something has been bothering me," DC Owen said.
"What's on your mind, Katie?" O'Reilly said.
"Why is CO Johnson so determined to protect DCO Dove?"

"The cover-up at the heart of this occurred before CO Johnson even arrived on the island," DS Skinner said. "Why risk everything to protect a secret that has nothing to do with you?"

"Perhaps he was worried about the reputation of the Island Police," DC Stone suggested.

"Why?" DC Owen said. "Nothing that DCO Dove did can be associated with him. The Len Hughes business was before his time, so why all the secrecy?"

"When exactly did CO Johnson start as Chief Officer?" O'Reilly asked.

"March 2003," DS Skinner said. "He was here when Len Hughes raped and killed the girl."

"But he can't have been involved in the earlier cover up," DC Owen said. "So why is he keeping secrets now?"

"You make a valid point, Katie," O'Reilly said. "And I'll be sure to bring it up when I speak to the man later."

"DCO Dove?" DCI Fish said.

"CO Johnson," O'Reilly said. "He phoned me and asked me to come to his house in St Sampson. He told me to keep it to myself, but he may just as well have asked me not to breathe. There have been too many secrets and lies recently, and I will not keep my team in the dark. I'll speak to the man, and I'll share everything that he has to say with all of you."

"Going back to the emails," DCI Fish said. "As far as I can see, there is nothing in the content that gives us any idea about who sent them. The email address is what the tech team termed a *trash-mail*."

"A burner?" DC Stone said.

"Something like that," DCI Fish said. "It's more than likely protected using a VPN network and the address itself is a temporary one. Nothing in the body of the mail suggests that the sender requires a reply, and even if CO Johnson had done so his mail would have been returned undelivered. In a nutshell, the address the emails were sent from are no longer in existence."

"Dead end then," DC Stone decided.

"And unless anyone here can read anything into the wording used," DCI Fish said. "There is no possible way to identify the sender from the emails."

"Can we get printouts of them?" DC Owen said.

"No problem," DCI Fish said.

"What for?" DC Stone said. "We've already established that there's nothing there to see."

"There might still be," DC Owen said. "I just want to make doubly sure."

"What time is your appointment with CO Johnson?" DCI Fish asked O'Reilly.

"Eleven. Where are we now? I neglected to put on my watch earlier."

"It's just after nine, sir?" DC Stone said.

"Grand. That gives us time to see if we can track down the people connected to the victims of the Hughes monster."

"I got the name of the woman who he raped in 2003," DC Owen said. "Her identity wasn't made public, but it was in the records from when she reported it. Her name is Amy Winter and according to what I could gather from social media she's still Amy Winter. She never married."

"Is she still on the island?" O'Reilly said.

"It looks like it. Most of her Facebook photos were taken at various places on the island."

"It should be easy enough to get an address for her," DS Skinner said.

"I've already got one, Sarge," DC Owen said.

"You're on form this morning, Katie," O'Reilly said.

"I did it all last night, sir. I had too much on my mind, and I couldn't sleep. Amy's Facebook security settings are virtually non-existent and there were a few photos of her daughter's birthday party."

"I thought you said she wasn't married?" DC Stone said.

"Marriage isn't a prerequisite for reproduction, Andy," O'Reilly said.

"I just meant..."

"I don't care what you meant," O'Reilly cut him short. "Go on, Katie."

"Obviously she didn't advertise her address on Facebook," DC Owen continued. "But she might as well have. The party took place in the garden last month, and if you zoom in you can make out the number on the front door."

"But no road name?" DC Stone said.

"That's where Google Street View came in. As the majority of the photos have been location tagged I guessed that she lived somewhere in Delancey Park. It didn't take long to find the house. The Google info was a bit outdated but there's a distinct gargoyle on the wall surrounding the property. Amy Winter lives at number 17 Harrow Road."

"That's some impressive detection, Katie," O'Reilly said. "And it's precisely why I refrain from using social media."

"Most people don't realise how vulnerable they leave themselves," DC Owen said. "They have no idea how easy they're making it for predators. I found out where she lives in the space of an hour. I know she has an eight-year-old daughter called Millie and I also know which school Millie attends."

"Facebook is a dangerous animal," DS Skinner agreed.

"Delancey Park," O'Reilly said. "My geography of the island isn't great, but isn't that close to St Sampson?"

"It is, sir," DC Stone said. "It's a five-minute walk away."

"The big chief just happens to live in St Sampson. I say we kill two birds with one stone. Come on, Katie – let's go and see if Amy Winter is at home."

CHAPTER THIRTY FIVE

Number 17 Harrow Road was an attractive bungalow with a thatched roof. The property looked well maintained and the garden was neat. O'Reilly pulled a face at the solitary gargoyle on the wall post at the front of the house. He was sure that the grotesque figure smiled back. There was a narrow driveway off to the side and there was a small white car parked in it.

"Looks like someone's home," O'Reilly said to DC Owen. "We're in luck." They'd discussed how they were going to proceed with Amy Winter on the short drive north. Amy was a victim of a travesty of justice, and it was likely that she wouldn't have too much faith in law enforcement. The systems put in place to protect her had let her down in a big way and O'Reilly wouldn't blame her if she slammed the door in their faces. She was violated at a very young age, and nobody had been punished for that violation apart from Amy herself. O'Reilly decided that they would play it by ear. If Amy told them to go away, he would respect her wishes. They had no concrete proof that she was involved in the poisoning anyway.

The doorbell didn't appear to be working so O'Reilly knocked hard on the door. It was opened soon afterwards by a young girl whom O'Reilly assumed was Amy's daughter.

"Is your mum in?" he asked her.

"She's baking biscuits."

"We've come at just the right time then," O'Reilly said. "What kind of biscuits?"

"Chocolate."

"My favourite. You're Millie, aren't you?"

A woman appeared behind her. She looked O'Reilly and DC Owen up and down.

"Can I help you?"

"Amy Winter?" O'Reilly said.

"That's me."

O'Reilly took out his ID. "DI O'Reilly and this is DC Owen."

"I know who you are," Amy said.

"Can we have a word?" DC Owen said.

"Of course," Amy said. "I've been half expecting you."

O'Reilly didn't ask her why. Instead, he accepted her offer to come inside and they were asked to take a seat in the living room.

"I just need to check on the biscuits," Amy said. "Can I offer you something to drink?"

"Tea would be grand," O'Reilly said.

She gave him a smile and left the room.

"I didn't anticipate a welcome like this," O'Reilly said. "I thought she would start throwing things at us as soon as she found out who we were."

"Me too," DC Owen said. "Why would she have been expecting us?"

"Beats me. Perhaps she's been following the news, and she's put two and two together."

Amy returned with two cups of tea. She placed them on the coffee table in the middle of the room and sat down.

"I've asked Millie to keep an eye on the biscuits. If you're here for what I think you're here for I don't want her to hear the details."

"Why do you think we're here, Amy?" O'Reilly said.

"Len Hughes."

"Can I ask why you would think that?"

"Simple logic," Amy said. "I've been keeping up with the developments in the poisonings. The Herald reported that a high-ranking police officer knew about the toxins in the food, but he refused to do anything about it. He let all those people die because he was protecting a secret that would bring the police into disrepute. Am I getting warm?"

"You are," O'Reilly confirmed.

"And I suspected the sordid secret had something to do with what happened after I was raped by Len Hughes."

"I'll understand if you don't want to talk about it," O'Reilly said. "But can you tell us what happened?"

"I don't have any problem talking about it," Amy said. "I came to realise a long time ago that it needs to be talked about. I was Len Hughes' babysitter. I used to look after his two children when he and his wife went out. The night it happened started off the same as any other. Mr and Mrs Hughes left at about seven. I read to the children for a bit and put them to bed at eight. It was the beginning of the new term at sixth form, and I'd brought some coursework with me. At about half-eight I heard the door open and Mr Hughes came into the living room. He told me he wasn't feeling well. I knew something was wrong straight away – I could feel it. I asked him where Mrs Hughes was, and he said she'd decided to stay at the restaurant. He started asking me questions about college and what I wanted to study at university, and he came and sat down next to me on the couch."

Millie came in to announce that the biscuits were done.

"I took them out and left them on the metal thing to cool down," she added.

"Good girl," Amy said. "We'll give them ten minutes. Could you go and play in your room for a bit?"

"OK."

Millie left the room without any arguments.

"She's a sweet kid," O'Reilly said. "My daughter was a nightmare at that age."

"We're all each other has at the moment," Amy said. "Have been for quite some time."

"Is her father not on the scene?" O'Reilly asked.

"He left when Millie was two. The gutless bastard didn't even have the balls to let us know."

"I'm sorry."

"I'm not," Amy said. "If he's capable of something like that, we're better off without him, wouldn't you agree?"

"I can't argue with that," O'Reilly said. "Where were we?"

"I was about to tell you about the worst night of my life," Amy said. "And that's no exaggeration."

CHAPTER THIRTY SIX

"I knew he was lying about feeling unwell. He poured himself a drink and asked me if I wanted one. I said no. I didn't drink then. The questions turned from college work to more uncomfortable topics. He asked if I had a boyfriend. I did, but I didn't tell him that – it was none of his business. Then he started asking really personal questions. Was I a virgin? Did I like boys, or perhaps I preferred girls. I told him I had to go home and that's when he started getting nasty. He said I was being paid until eleven and I was damn well going to work until eleven. I said he didn't have to pay me and that's..."
"It's OK," DC Owen said. "You don't have to carry on."

"It's fine," Amy said. "That's when he said it was OK – I could go if I wanted to. I gathered up my books, and I was halfway out of the living room when he grabbed me. He put his stinking hand over my mouth and pulled my hair back. He slapped me twice and forced me onto the couch. He was just too strong."
"I think you've told us enough," O'Reilly said. "I really am sorry that this happened to you."
Amy looked him in the eyes. He'd encountered many victims of sexual assault in his career, but Amy Winter didn't look like any of them. There was real defiance in her eyes.

"When it was over," she said. "He told me to get out. He said if I told anyone what he'd done, nobody would believe me. He reminded me how powerful he was, and it would be my word against his, and I didn't argue with him. I wanted to get as far away from there as possible. I didn't live far from him, and I walked home. When I got there, I told my mum exactly what had happened, and she drove me straight to the police station. There was nothing I wanted more than a shower – I wanted to wash every trace of him off me, but my mum told me not to."

"Your mother did the right thing," O'Reilly said. "Where was your father?"
"Dad died when I was thirteen," Amy said. "Which was just as well. If he'd have been there that night, Len Hughes wouldn't be alive now."
"I can appreciate that."

"The police officers were nice," Amy continued. "I was told that what was about to happen would be unpleasant, but my mum kept me strong. I put what had happened on record and then I was examined. I kept my eyes closed the entire time and I had a picture of Len Hughes in my head throughout. I imagined him in a prison cell. I pictured him spending the rest of his life in jail and that's what kept me going. They told me I had a strong case. And it was strengthened further when Mrs Hughes put it on record that Mr Hughes didn't leave the restaurant because he wasn't feeling well. They'd had a fight, and he left her there. She was told not to bother coming home."
"Surely that would have sounded some warning bells?" DC Owen said.
"You would have thought so," Amy said. "But then she changed her tune and went and stood by him. She knew exactly what he'd done, but she didn't make it known."

"What evidence did they have against him?" O'Reilly said. "I believe it was rather compelling."
"There was no doubt that we'd had sex," Amy said. "His DNA was all over me – it was inside me, and there were indications that it may not have been consensual, but he never denied the sex. He claimed that it was what we both wanted. He regretted it, of course, but he always denied raping me. According to the police doctor the injuries I sustained were consistent with what I claimed, and mum and I both expected him to be punished for it."
"But the case never made it to court," DC Owen said.
"You know it didn't. When we were asked to come to the police station a few weeks later, we imagined it would be about some other formalities we needed to sort out. We assumed it was just a case of going through the

motions. I was ready to stand up in court and tell the world what a monster that man was – I was mentally prepared for it, and then we were told that the case was being dropped. The evidence against him was insufficient."

"I really am sorry about that," O'Reilly said. "And you have my word that we're going to make it right. We suspect that one of our officers was responsible for this miscarriage of justice and he's not going to get away with it. That's a promise."

Amy gave him another smile. "I believe you."

"I must admit," O'Reilly said. "Your outlook on life is admirable. You experienced something abhorrent and the man responsible didn't pay the price for it. You have my utmost respect."

"What happened to me didn't have to define me," Amy said. "It took a very long time to get past it, and it will never be forgotten, but my mum made me see that this is how it had to be. I was raped – it happened but it didn't make me into something you can put into a box. I was still me afterwards, albeit changed somehow, but if I let it destroy me, he would have won twice, wouldn't he?"

"I can understand you having no time for the police after how you were treated," O'Reilly said. "But you don't seem to hold any resentment."

"What would that achieve?" Amy said. "It was one rotten officer. You can't tar them all with the same brush. It's like getting bitten by a dog. Have you ever been bitten by a dog?"

"I've been bitten by a cat," O'Reilly said. "More than once."

Amy laughed. "And do you hate all cats because of that?"

"I don't even hate the free-loading bastard who bit me," O'Reilly said. "But I see what you're getting at. We won't keep you any longer. We've taken up too much of your time already. You really are an extraordinary woman. Millie must be proud to have you as her mum."

"Stay a bit longer. I like talking to you."

"We really need to get going," O'Reilly said. "We have another appointment in thirty minutes."

"At least have a biscuit or two before you leave."

"I suppose we can spare five minutes. Those chocolate biscuits do smell good, and I didn't get the chance to grab some breakfast this morning."

Amy fetched the tray of biscuits from the kitchen and told O'Reilly to help himself. He didn't need to be asked twice. He took a bite and wolfed it down. "These are very good. Just one more question before we leave you in peace. Did you have any contact with the family of the young girl that Len Hughes raped and murdered?"

"I did," Amy said. "I felt some kind of obligation to them. They're good people."

"That must have been difficult," DC Owen said.

"It was, but it was something I needed to do. I attended the sentencing. I watched when him he received his sentence, and I'll never forget the expression on his face."

"It must have come as a shock to him," O'Reilly said. "Men like Len Hughes believe themselves to be invincible – they think they're above the law."

"That's not the impression I got," Amy said. "If anything, he seemed more smug than usual. He looked like a man who thought he was still going to get away with it."

"But he didn't get away with it, did he?" DC Owen said. "He was shipped off to Belmarsh for his own safety, and he's still there. He'll be an old man when he's finally released."

"And Belmarsh is no picnic," O'Reilly said. "Compared to the prison on the island it's akin to a Soviet gulag. Len Hughes' connections won't help him one bit over there. We really have to be going. Thank you for the biscuits."

"Take some with you," Amy said. "I made two batches. I'll ask Millie to pop a few in a bag for you."

"That would be most appreciated," O'Reilly said. "We may need to talk to you again."

"I've got nothing to hide."

"So, I've come to realise. You really are an incredible woman, Amy."

CHAPTER THIRTY SEVEN

"Do you want me to wait in the car?" DC Owen said.

They were almost at the address CO Johnson had given them.

"I think it's for the best, Katie," O'Reilly said. "I suspect that the big chief will be reluctant to open up if you're there. I tell you what – see if you can find somewhere to get some early lunch. Grab me something too."

"Amy Winter gave you a bag of biscuits," DC Owen reminded him.

"And they'll make the perfect accompaniment to whatever lunch you can find."

"I think there's a café on the beachfront. Do you have any preferences?"

"Anything that's not green," O'Reilly said. "And make sure it contains a lot of cheese."

"I don't where you put it all, sir."

"It's one of life's wonderful mysteries, Katie. I'll give you a bell when I'm finished."

 Chief Officer Johnson's house wasn't what O'Reilly was expecting. He'd imagined the man in charge of the Island Police to live in a much grander property than the three-bedroom place on Summerside Road. The house was situated in the north of St Sampson, and the views were spectacular. From the front of the property CO Johnson looked out onto the castle and the sea beyond.

 O'Reilly walked up the path and pressed the buzzer next to the door.

"Liam," CO Johnson's voice came over the intercom. "The door's open – come in."

O'Reilly didn't know how he knew who was at the door. He pushed it open and went inside.

 CO Johnson met him halfway down the corridor. The two men shook hands and CO Johnson suggested they sit outside.

"My wife won't be back for a good few hours. Can I offer you anything to drink?"

"No thanks," O'Reilly said. "You need to tell me everything."

"Straight to the point. I thought I asked you to keep this visit to yourself."

"Sir?"

"DC Owen dropped you off outside," CO Johnson said. "I installed exceptional CCTV cameras. You can't be too careful these days."

"Katie has no idea what I'm doing here, sir," O'Reilly lied. "Can we get straight down to business?"

CO Johnson opened the sliding doors that led outside.

"Take a seat."

There was a wooden pub bench on the patio. O'Reilly sat with his back to the view. CO Johnson sat down opposite him.

"This place isn't much, but the views make up for it. Did you know that you pay more for a view than you do for bricks and mortar these days."

"That's all very well, sir," O'Reilly said. "But I'm not here to discuss the ins and outs of real estate on the island."

CO Johnson took out a packet of cigars and offered one to O'Reilly.

"No thanks," the Irishman said.

"I only smoke them when my wife isn't here," CO Johnson said. "And I make sure not to smoke inside. I really shouldn't smoke with this damn cold, but it helps me to relax. Are you aware of the background behind the Len Hughes business?"

"Len Hughes business?" O'Reilly repeated. "I assume you're referring to the rape of his babysitter and the travesty of justice that followed. Or perhaps you're talking about the subsequent rape and murder of the fourteen-year-old after he was wrongly acquitted of the earlier rape."

"I understand your frustration, but…"

"Frustration?" O'Reilly interrupted, much louder than he intended. "A seventeen-year-old girl was violated and Hughes walked free because of his fucking privilege. That girl went to hell and back, and we let her down. Frustration doesn't even begin to cover it. Ask the family of the fourteen-year-old if they're frustrated. An officer in the Island Police covered up for a murderer, and he needs to be held accountable."

CO Johnson managed to light the cigar on the third attempt. He took a drag, exhaled a cloud of smoke and coughed.

"You shouldn't have gone to Fred Viking," he said.

"I have no idea what you're talking about," O'Reilly said.

"Yes, you do. I know it was you."

"However Viking got his information," O'Reilly said. "It doesn't matter. This is a story that needed to be told. Len Hughes got away with a despicable crime because he had friends in high places, and you of all people should know that secrets like this are never buried forever. Nine more innocent people have lost their lives because of this, and you could have stopped it."

"You're like a stuck record, Liam," CO Johnson said.

"OK," O'Reilly said. "Let's move on to the next track on the record, shall we? We now know that the Len Hughes business, as you chose to term it, happened before your time on the island. As far as I can see, there is nothing tying you to the scandal involving DCO Dove so why are you so determined to protect the man?"

"It's complicated."

"It really isn't sir. It's not complicated at all. The second in charge of the Island Police played a major role in a travesty of justice and you knew about it. May I ask how it even came to your attention? Len Hughes raped Amy Winter in the January of 2003. He was exonerated and he went on to up his game by adding murder to his repertoire. Most of this happened before you even set foot on the island and yet you chose to turn a blind eye to a potential mass poisoning anyway. You said you've got something to tell me, and I'm all ears."

CO Johnson's cigar had gone out and after a few unsuccessful flicks of the lighter it was clear that he wasn't going to get it lit again. He put both down on the table and stared at them.
"Story of my life. You're right of course. I arrived on the island when the damage had already been done, but you have to believe me when I tell you that I had no idea of the scope of Callum's actions. I really didn't know."
"You're not making any sense," O'Reilly said. "If you didn't know what he was complicit in why risk the lives of everybody on the island in order to protect the man? You're going to have to give me a lot more than you already have."

"DCO Dove is not the man you think he is," CO Johnson said.
"So, I'm starting to realise," O'Reilly said.
"The facts surrounding the Len Hughes business only came to my attention very recently. I lied to you about sharing the details of the emails with DCO Dove. He was privy to the information from the onset, and he warned me not to give in to the demands of these people."
"And we now know why. What are you not telling me?"
"I'm telling you that DCO Dove is not a man you go to war against."
"You're his boss, for God's sake," O'Reilly said.
"That makes no difference."

O'Reilly was struggling to make sense of this. He got the impression that CO Johnson was still holding something back.
"What has he got on you?" he said. "What can be any worse than what he helped to cover up? And for that matter, what could possibly be more damaging to you than your decision to ignore the emails you were sent? Nine people are dead and as far as the people on this island are concerned you've got their blood on your hands. What is it you're hiding, Robert?"

The shock of hearing O'Reilly address him this way was apparent. CO Johnson's expression was one of disbelief.

He rubbed his eyes and fixed them on O'Reilly.

"Margaret is my second wife. I moved around a lot, chasing promotion and it took its toll on my first marriage. I met Margaret shortly after I arrived on the island and we were married within a year."

"I'm not in the mood for a tale about happy families," O'Reilly said.

"Hear me out. I played no part in the Len Hughes affair. Like I said, I'd only just arrived on the island when he raped and killed that girl, and I wasn't involved in the investigation, and I had no idea about the earlier cover-up. You have to believe me."

"What is it then?" O'Reilly said. "How else do you explain your behaviour?"

"My wife is a good woman," CO Johnson said. "And a weaker woman would have probably left the island after what happened with Len Hughes, but she didn't. She kept her head held high, and I love her for that."

"What has your wife got to do with Len Hughes?" O'Reilly asked. "Are you about to tell me what I think you're about to tell me?"

CO Johnson sighed deeply and nodded. "I believe I am, Liam."

CHAPTER THIRTY EIGHT

"CO Johnson is Len Hughes' brother-in-law."
O'Reilly didn't waste any time when he gathered the team for an afternoon briefing. The chief officer's revelation needed to be shared, and O'Reilly had no qualms about repeating everything that was spoken about in the meeting with the big boss.

"Why weren't we aware of it?" DCI Fish wondered. "This is a small island, and surely this would have been impossible to keep quiet."

"According to CO Johnson," O'Reilly said. "Margaret and Len were estranged. When he was convicted of the rape/murder they hadn't had any contact for over a decade."

"Was CO Johnson aware of the family connection?" DS Skinner said.

"Not until later. By the time he found out they were already married. Margaret wanted nothing to do with her brother long before he was exposed as a rapist and a murderer, and CO Johnson saw no reason to hold it against her."

"Why would he?" DC Stone said. "It's not her fault that her brother is a sick, depraved pervert."

"It still doesn't explain his actions regarding the emails he received," DCI Fish said. "How does that fit into all of this?"

"It appears that DCO Dove wasn't content with taking the fall alone," O'Reilly said. "Should it ever come to that."

"Are you saying he threatened the chief officer?" DC Stone said.

"DCO Dove is not a stupid man," O'Reilly said. "When he tampered with the evidence in the Amy Winter rape case, he made sure he had a contingency plan in place. His enforced leave coincided with CO Johnson's appointment as Chief Officer, but it appears that DCO Dove wasn't happy to stay away. According to CO Johnson it later transpired that his signature was on certain documents pertaining to the Amy Winter investigation – documents that all but ensured that the case remained closed *in perpetuum*."

"In what?" It was DC Stone.

"It means forever, Andy," O'Reilly told him.

"CO Johnson didn't sign them, did he?" DC Owen guessed.

"No. He did not. But as DCO Dove was absent, and the scribbles were identical to CO Johnson's signature, it looked like he had done. Combine this with the fact that the chief officer happened to be in a relationship with Len Hughes' sister and it's not looking too good for the man. DCO Dove threatened CO Johnson with exposure."

"Even though he'd done nothing wrong?" DC Owen said.

"And he didn't marry Hughes' sister until long after he was sent down for the rape and murder of Vicky Ingram," DC Stone added,

"It doesn't matter, Andy," O'Reilly said. "Everything DCO Dove had on his boss was pretty incriminating, and CO Johnson damn well knew it. On the surface it would appear that he was involved and mud like that is almost impossible to scrape off. For what it's worth, his intentions were honourable. He wanted to spare his wife a repeat of the treatment she received when Len Hughes was convicted. She was persona non grata on the island for a very long time after that."

"Now we know the back story," DCI Fish said. "What is CO Johnson's next move? Are we talking full disclosure now, because as far as I'm aware, it's the only option left for him."

"He's promised to accept what's coming to him," O'Reilly said.

"Do you believe him?" DC Stone said.

"I have no choice, Andy. I explained to him that he's reached the end of the road, and there are no avenues left for him to take. It's a case of damned if you do and damned it you don't. Whatever he does next, the outcome is not going to change."

"It stinks though, doesn't it?" DS Skinner said. "He may have made some bad choices, but he's still not a bad person, deep down."

"When he refused to disclose the threat to the people of the island," O'Reilly said. "He all but dug his own grave. He's big enough and ugly enough to take what's coming to him, and I get the feeling that he's not going to let DCO Dove off the hook so easily. It's highly likely the two top posts in the Island Police will be vacant soon. It's going to be the scandal of the decade, but people will soon forget about it. We need to leave the fate of CO Johnson and his deputy in the hands of the people paid to deal with crap like that and focus on the real issue here. Who are the people who are hell bent on poisoning people on this island, and how the devil do we catch them?"

"What was your impression of Len Hughes' first victim?" DCI Fish said.

"Amy Winter," O'Reilly said. "An extraordinary woman. She was still no more than a child when she was badly let down by the people who should have protected her, but she bears no grudges. She didn't strike me as someone who would exact revenge because of what she had to endure. She's a single mother and she and her daughter seem to be thriving."

"Did she have any contact with the family of Len Hughes' second victim?" DS Skinner asked.

"She did. She felt obliged somehow."

"It wasn't her fault that Len Hughes was allowed back on the streets," DC Stone said.

"I said she felt obliged, Andy," O'Reilly said. "Not responsible. She felt that it was her duty to contact the family of the fourteen-year-old."

"What do we know about them?" DCI Fish said.

"I got their details from the records, sir," DC Owen said. "The girl's name was Vicky Ingram, and her parents are still resident on the island. There's a sister, too. Janet was six when her big sister was murdered."

"Do we have their address?" DS Skinner said.

"It shouldn't be difficult to find them. They'll be on file somewhere."

"We'll speak to them as soon as we have an address," O'Reilly said. "I'm still of the opinion that the emails sent to CO Johnson came from someone connected to the Len Hughes business, as the chief officer put it."

The briefing was interrupted by the door flying open so violently that it slammed against the wall with a crash. It was DCO Callum Dove, and his crimson face and wild eyes told them he was not a happy man. He glanced around the room and his eyes landed on O'Reilly. The Irishman noted the fire in his eyes and got to his feet.

"You bastard," the second in charge in the Island Police said.

"Calm down," O'Reilly said.

"Don't you dare tell me to calm down."

DCO Dove moved surprisingly quickly. He was across the room in an instant, and O'Reilly didn't have time to deflect the blow that was aimed at his face. There was a flash of light before he felt his top lip split in two. The blood came quickly and splashed onto his shirt. He wiped his mouth with his hand and grinned a bloody grin at DCO Dove.

"I believe the appropriate term for what you are right now is *well and truly fucked*, sir," he said. "Does anyone in this room disagree?"

The absence of sound that followed told him that nobody did.

CHAPTER THIRTY NINE

"You're not having a great week, are you, sir?" DC Owen said.
She was sitting opposite O'Reilly in his office.
"I believe that's what is known as litotes."
"Correct, sir," DC Owen said.
"I can understand the brick to the head," O'Reilly said. "But I never in a million years expected the deputy chief officer to give me a fat lip. I didn't think he had it in him. And he's no slouch – that was quite a left hook."
"Is it sore?"
"I'll be fine, Katie," O'Reilly said. "I didn't have him pegged as a south paw – those lefties are tricky to defend against."
"What do you think will happen to him?"
"I wasn't exaggerating when I told him he was well and truly fucked. And that was definitely not litotes – there was no ironic understatement intended there. DCO Dove's career is over."
"I still think you should press charges," DC Owen said.
"What for? The man is going to lose his job, and to be honest I really cannot be doing with the hassle. There will be enough paperwork to deal with without having to go through the rigmarole of a criminal charge. What's done is done."

"I've managed to get an address for Vicky Ingram's parents," DC Owen said. "They've got an apartment here in the capital."
"Let's go then," O'Reilly said. "Is it within walking distance?"
"Are you sure you're up to it?"
"I've got a fat lip, Katie," O'Reilly said. "It's not a gunshot wound."
"Perhaps you should change your shirt though. It's got blood and something that looks like cat vomit all over it."

"That'll be tea," O'Reilly said. "You try to drink a cup of tea with a lip like this. It's worse than after you've had an injection at the dentist. I've got a clean shirt in the cupboard there. And I suggest you leave me in peace to change, unless you want to see the less than impressive physique of a portly Irishman."

"I'll wait for you outside, sir," DC Owen said.

Five minutes later they were on their way to Belmont Road. They'd just passed the impressive Government House when O'Reilly's phone started to ring in his pocket. The screen told him it was Chief Officer Johnson, and he ignored it. He'd had enough of the top brass in the Island Police for one day and he didn't feel like speaking to the man in charge.

The walk was a familiar one for O'Reilly – his old apartment wasn't far from where the family of Vicky Ingram lived.

"I thought I'd miss living in the capital," he said to DC Owen. "But I don't. It was convenient, but these apartment complexes feel claustrophobic now. It's funny how things turn out, isn't it?"

"You never know what life is going to throw at you next," DC Owen said.

"Our entire existence is a lottery, isn't it?"

"Are you sure you don't have any Irish in you somewhere down the line?"

"Not that I'm aware of."

"You have an old head on those young shoulders, Katie Owen."

"So you keep telling me," DC Owen said. "Do you think the Ingrams are involved in the deaths of all those people?"

"I'm convinced the recent poisonings are connected to what happened because of what Len Hughes did in 2003," O'Reilly said. "I don't know what that link is yet, but we need to look at every aspect of what that monster did. What was the address again?"

The apartment was on Belmont Road. Number 6 was in the middle of a row of identical buildings. O'Reilly was glad that they'd gone there on foot.

There were no parking spaces available. He rang the bell on the door, and it was opened shortly afterwards by a man who looked to be in his mid-fifties.

"Mr Ingram?" O'Reilly said.

"That's me. Who are you?"

"DI O'Reilly. Island Police."

He showed his ID and introduced DC Owen.

"What do you want?"

"Just a quick chat," O'Reilly said. "Can we come inside?"

Bert Ingram was a short, stocky man with a thick head of black hair. He asked O'Reilly and DC Owen to make themselves comfortable in the conservatory at the back of the apartment while he went to fetch his wife.

"This is actually quite nice," O'Reilly said.

The conservatory looked out onto the stretch of green that was King's Health Club. It was a cloudless day, and the sky was an unusual shade of blue.

Bert Ingram returned with a woman who looked considerably older than him. She walked with the aid of a stick and O'Reilly sympathised with her.

"This is my wife Tina," Bert said. "Can I offer you something to drink?"

"No thank you," O'Reilly said. "We're here to talk to you about your daughter Vicky."

"Oh my," Tina said.

Bert put a hand on her shoulder. "It's alright, love."

"I apologise if this is dredging up some painful memories," O'Reilly said. "But your daughter's murder has come up in the course of a recent investigation."

"How?" Bert said. "It was more than sixteen years ago."

"I need to take my pills," Tina said. "I forgot earlier."

She eased herself up off the couch with the help of the stick and left the room.

"She's not been well," Bert said. "In fact, she hasn't been herself since Vicky was taken away from us."

"I understand that this is painful," O'Reilly said. "But can I ask you about the day Vicky died?"

Bert's expression darkened. "She didn't die – she was murdered."

"I'm sorry. What happened?"

"Len Hughes killed her," Bert said. "But not before he'd violated her. She was still a baby."

"Did you know Len Hughes?"

"Hardly. We didn't mix in the same circles. He grabbed Vicky when she was on her way back from school. Dragged her to his car and threw her inside."

"He was caught almost straight away, wasn't he?" DC Owen said.

"One of Vicky's friends saw it happen, and she had the presence of mind to take down the registration number of his car. They found Vicky at his house, but by then it was too late."

"That must have been a terrible time for you," O'Reilly said.

"And it didn't have to happen, did it? If your lot had done their jobs properly in the first place, she would still be with us today."

"What do you mean by that?" O'Reilly asked, even though he had a good idea.

"Hughes," Bert said. "He'd done it before, hadn't he? That young babysitter."

"What do you know about that?" DC Owen asked.

"He raped her, and before you get all defensive and tell me the case never made it to court, it doesn't change the facts, does it?"

"No," O'Reilly said. "It doesn't, and for what it's worth, I believe Len Hughes should have been jailed for what he did to that young woman."

"And if he was behind bars, he wouldn't have been able to do what he did to little Vicky. She was an angel, you know."

"I imagine she was," O'Reilly said.

Tina came back and sat down next to her husband.

"What is it you really want from us?" Bert said.

"You must have been angry when it came out that Len Hughes had a previous rape charge against him," O'Reilly said.
"Angry?" Bert said. "What do you think?"
"Do you know the details about his alleged first victim?"
"Alleged?" It was Tina. "There was nothing alleged about it. It bloody happened – Amy came to see us shortly after Vicky passed away."
"We've spoken to her," DC Owen said.
"She was a lovely girl," Bert said. "Strong as an ox, and she wouldn't have lied about what happened."
"I don't believe she lied about it either," O'Reilly said.

"Why are you really bringing all this up so many years after it happened?" Bert said.
"It's only just come to my attention," O'Reilly said. "I've only been on the island for a short time, but when I hear about something like this it makes my blood boil. It shouldn't have happened, and I'm sorry that it did."
"What's changed?" Tina said. "Something must have changed if you're revisiting the case. Hughes was sent down for what he did to our baby girl. I'm just sorry he wasn't banged up here on the island. He'd be dead by now if he was – I know he would."

"You have another daughter, don't you?" O'Reilly said.
"Janet," Bert said. "She doesn't live with us anymore."
"I believe she was a few years younger than Vicky," DC Owen said.
"She was only six when it happened," Tina said.
"Where is she now?" O'Reilly said.
"She's got a place over in Le Foulon," Bert said.
"She's still on the island then?" O'Reilly said.
"Why wouldn't she be?" Tina said. "She's doing well for herself. She's only twenty-two and she owns her own apartment."

"And the business," Bert said. "She started her own business a while ago and it's doing well."

"What does she do?" O'Reilly said.

"Health food stuff," Bert said. "She owns a place that sells all kinds of herbs and strange wonder spices."

O'Reilly was instantly wide awake.

"It's not *Nature's Choice*, is it?"

Bert nodded. "That's the place."

CHAPTER FORTY

By the time they'd walked the half a mile to *Nature's Choice* O'Reilly's gammy leg was screaming at him in protest. It was telling him that he'd definitely overdone it today and he decided he would rest it tomorrow. They'd discussed the likelihood of Janet Ingram being their mystery poisoner on the way.

"It's a coincidence we can't afford to ignore," O'Reilly said. "The woman happens to be the sister of Len Hughes' second victim. And she owns one of the shops where the contaminated products came from. That's suspicious in my book."

"She was only six when Vicky was murdered," DC Owen pointed out.

"Old enough to understand the gist of what happened, and who's to say she didn't dig deeper when she got a bit older?"

"How are we going to play it?" DC Owen said. "We can't simply come out and ask her if she sent the emails to CO Johnson."

"I hadn't thought that far ahead, Katie. Something will come to me."

There were no customers inside the shop when they went in, and O'Reilly wondered if word had got out about the lethal ginger. He walked straight over to the woman sitting behind the counter. She was tapping away on the screen of her phone and O'Reilly wondered if she'd even heard them come in.

"Excuse me," he said. "We're looking for Janet."

The woman looked up. "She's not here."

"Do you know where we can find her?"

"How should I know?"

The name on her badge was Denise.

"Let's start again, shall we?" O'Reilly said. "I'm DI O'Reilly and this is DC Owen. We're from the Island Police and we'd appreciate it if you could be a tad more cooperative. Can you do that for us, Denise?"

"I really don't know where she is," she said. "She only works half day on Thursdays. I can give you her address."

"That's more like it," O'Reilly said.

Denise scribbled the address on a piece of paper and handed it to him.

"What's she done?" she asked.

"We just need to talk to her," DC Owen said.

"How may people work here?" O'Reilly said.

"Just me and Janet," Denise said.

"When I came in earlier in the week," O'Reilly said. "There was another woman who helped me. The name on her badge was Jane."

Denise laughed.

"Did I say something funny?" O'Reilly said.

"No," Denise said. "It's a running joke. The name badge is ancient, and the T has worn off."

O'Reilly cottoned on to what she was telling him.

"Janet. Jane."

"She gets it a lot. I keep telling her to get another badge made."

"It's quiet in here today," O'Reilly said.

"It always is on Thursdays," Denise said. "I don't know why. That's why Janet takes half the day off."

"How long have you worked here?" DC Owen said.

"Since the start."

"When did the shop open?" O'Reilly said.

"Two years ago," Denise said.

"And business is good?" O'Reilly said.

"We do alright. More and more people are switching to natural products. Here at *Nature's Gifts*, we don't only stock healthy foods and drinks, we have alternative medicines and cosmetics made from nothing but natural products. It's a growing industry. People are getting disillusioned with the propaganda they've been fed for decades. The poisons they stick in the majority of the food on the shelves is killing people. The people in charge tell us it's perfectly safe, but it isn't. Did you know that a hundred years ago cancer was virtually unheard of? Why do you think that is?"

"I have no idea," O'Reilly said.

"Because that was before food became such big business. Companies figured out they could increase their profits by doctoring the products. They worked out how to make food last ten-times longer, but at what cost?"

"You're clearly very passionate about your job," DC Owen said.

"It's not just a job," Denise said. "It's a lifestyle choice."

O'Reilly hadn't come here for a lecture on healthy eating. He got the feeling that Denise could wax lyrical on this topic until the cows came home.

"How well do you know Janet?" he asked.

"As well as any employee knows her boss."

"Do you socialise with her outside of work?"

"Very rarely."

"Do you know if she's tech savvy?" O'Reilly said. "Does she know much about computers and the like?"

"As much as she needs to know. Enough to run a business. Why are you asking these questions? Is Janet suspected of something?"

He didn't get the chance to answer her. His phone started to ring. It was DCI Fish and O'Reilly knew he needed to take the call.

He went outside and answered the phone.

"Tom. What can I do for you?"

"CO Johnson received another email," DCI Fish said. "And this time he made us aware of it immediately."

O'Reilly recalled the phone call he'd ignored from the chief officer earlier. "Go on," he said.

"You're not going to believe this," DCI Fish said.

"What do they want now?" O'Reilly said. "They got what they demanded. The truth about Len Hughes is out there for the world to see."

"They've issued more demands."

"What other scandal have they uncovered?" O'Reilly said.

"That's not what they want," DCI Fish said. "They've threatened to up their game and contaminate more products on the island, and this time we're not talking about death caps and oleander. This is something infinitely more lethal."

"What is it they want?" O'Reilly said. "They got what they asked for."

"Apparently the Len Hughes business was just the beginning, Liam. We've been looking at this all wrong from the very start. This has never been about exposing a travesty of justice."

"You've lost me there, Tom," O'Reilly said. "If it's not about that, what is it about?"

"Money," DCI Fish said. "This has been about money all along."

CHAPTER FORTY ONE

O'Reilly decided to put the visit to Janet Ingram's apartment on hold. The phone call with DCI Fish had shocked him and he needed to see the email that was sent to CO Johnson for himself. He would track Janet down later.

The team were gathered once more in the briefing room. The email was staring at them from the big screen at the back of the room. O'Reilly had already read it twice and its content really did beggar belief. It was addressed to CO Johnson personally, and the threats that were issued told them the people responsible were prepared to unleash a toxin so lethal, it had the potential to wipe out half of the population of the island.

There was no beating about the bush.

You are now fully aware of what we're capable of. You've witnessed first hand what we can achieve with very little effort. Now it's time for you to listen carefully. 100g of castor bean seeds will yield enough toxins to terminate over twenty thousand healthy human beings. We are well versed in the extraction of the toxin and we will not hesitate to distribute it randomly throughout the island.

Steps have already been taken to put phase one of the plan into action and we will not hesitate to proceed to phase two should you ignore our demands. You have the power to save thousands of lives. Our demands are simple: 104 million Euros will be transferred to an account. The details of which will follow. You have until this time tomorrow to consider your options.

"What are they planning to use?" DC Stone asked. "What's this business with the beans?"

"Ricin, Andy," O'Reilly said. "One of the nastiest toxins in existence. It's recently been declared a potential biological weapon."

"Even in small quantities it is lethal," DCI Fish said. "After ingestion, it enters the bloodstream and attaches itself to the cells, preventing them from producing the proteins the body needs to survive. There is no antidote, and ninety-nine percent of cases of ricin exposure are fatal."

"It can be deadly even when it's in the air," DC Owen said. "It can be breathed in, or it can enter through the skin."

"Surely you need specialist equipment to produce it?" DC Stone said.

"That's the horrifying part," O'Reilly said. "It's possible to extract the ricin from the seeds with very little scientific background."

"It's a similar process to extracting the oleandrin from the leaves of the plant," DC Owen said. "You can use any one of the solvents you can find in most hardware shops. We have to take this seriously."

"A hundred and four million?" DC Stone said. "They're not playing around. How is CO Johnson supposed to get his hands on so much money?"

"The chief officer is merely a conduit in all of this, Andy," O'Reilly said. "These people don't expect him to pay out of his own pocket."

"Why 104 million?" DC Owen said. "Don't you think that's a strange amount to ask for?"

"They probably plucked a figure out of the air," DC Stone said.

"I don't think they did," DC Owen said. "It's a really bizarre amount to demand."

"I don't think it's worth wasting time on," DS Skinner said.

"I think Katie might have a point," O'Reilly said. "And it's definitely worth looking into."

"Do you think the Len Hughes cover-up was just a smokescreen?" DS Skinner asked.

"I think that somehow these terrorists found out about the Len Hughes travesty," O'Reilly said. "And they used it for the first phase of their plan. They wanted to demonstrate that they're not playing around and when that became apparent, they moved onto phase two. A hundred-odd million Euros is what they really want."

"What are we going to do with this new information?" DCI Fish asked. "We cannot keep a threat like this to ourselves."

"We've got two choices," O'Reilly said. "We either pass the info along to the people who claim to be qualified to deal with it, or we don't."

"Choice two isn't really an option, Liam. When they brought ricin into the equation it became tantamount to a terrorist threat, and none of us is equipped to handle something like that."

"Hear me out," O'Reilly said. "We hold off on passing the recent emails on to an outside department while we focus on finding the people behind them."

"Do you have a plan in mind, sir?" DS Skinner said.

"Not yet, Will," O'Reilly said. "But something will come to me. In the meantime, I suggest we carry on as normal. According to the email, we've got until tomorrow to formulate a way forward, and I suggest we persevere looking into the lives of the people connected to the Len Hughes business."

"I thought we'd established that what happened in 2003 was just misdirection," DC Stone said.

"What if it's not, Andy? What if the people who were somehow involved in the miscarriage of justice are the same people who are demanding a hundred million?"

"It's worth considering," DC Owen said. "There's something about the wording of the email that's bothering me."

"Of course it's bothering you," DC Stone said. "They're threatening to unleash a bacterial weapon."

"I'm not talking about the threat, Andy. This strikes me as something a young person would compose."

"What gives you that impression?" O'Reilly said.

"You don't need to analyse it in too much detail to see that there is virtually no punctuation. They've used full stops, but there are no commas or hyphens. I think this was written by someone who's well-versed in textspeak. They haven't used abbreviations, but the email reads as though they've only thought about the content. This is how the majority of young people communicate on social media."

"Some of the posts I read these days make me cringe," DS Skinner said. "We're skyrocketing towards an era where the English language is set to become bastardised to such an extent that future generations will simply lose the ability to grasp the concept of basic grammar.'

"This is all very well," DC Stone said. "But how exactly does it help?"

"I think Katie is correct," DS Skinner said. "This email is the work of someone young – perhaps late-teens or early twenties."

"Janet Ingram is twenty-two," DC Owen said.

"And we'll continue to try and find her," O'Reilly said.

"Can I say something else?" DC Owen said.

"Of course, Katie," O'Reilly said.

"If you compare the recent email with the first two that were sent to CO Johnson it's quite clear that they were written by different people. I suspect the author of the first email was much older. The language and use of grammar is very different."

"We're not going to achieve anything by analysing the writing styles, Katie," DC Stone insisted.

"Probably not," DC Owen said. "I just thought it was something to think about."

"OK," DCI Fish said. "I'll trust your judgement on this for now. Liam – we'll keep the recent email to ourselves for the time being, but we need to work quickly."

"Do you think the ricin is already in the food and drink?" DC Stone said.

"I don't think it is," O'Reilly said. "Why take the risk of contaminating anything before your demands have been met? They're going to want to wait and see if they can get their hands on the cash before they poison anything else."

"Where are we going to get hold of a hundred-odd million Euros?" DC Stone said.

"Put it out of your mind," O'Reilly said. "Your focus needs to be on working towards finding the people responsible. I'm open to any suggestions you have, no matter how bizarre they might seem."

"I have been wondering about something else." DC Owen said.

"Let's hear it then," O'Reilly said.

"The locations of the tainted products have been bothering me."

"How so?" DS Skinner said.

"A number of businesses were broken into," DC Owen said. "But we've had no reports of any fatalities caused by products that were purchased from most of them."

"The majority of the cases were linked to Freshlife Supermarket," O'Reilly said.

"Eight Islanders died because they shopped there," DC Stone said.

"And we had one fatality caused by poisoned ginger from *Nature's Gifts*," DS Skinner said.

"What are you thinking, Katie?" O'Reilly said.

"I think we need to consider the possibility that the purpose of the break-ins was to throw us off the scent. What if the contamination didn't take place during the break-ins?"

"You've lost me there, Katie," DC Stone said.

"Isn't it entirely possible that the food and drink was contaminated by someone involved in those two businesses?"

CHAPTER FORTY TWO

By three that afternoon O'Reilly was no closer to tracking down Janet Ingram than he had been that morning. The owner of *Nature's Gifts* was proving to be elusive. She wasn't at the address her employee had given them and according to her parents, they hadn't heard from her in two days. O'Reilly decided to turn his attention to Freshlife Supermarket. He believed that DC Owen's suggestion was a valid one. Five businesses that stocked food and drink had been broken into, but they'd only found contaminated products in one of them.

He experienced a strange sense of déjà vu when he and DC Owen went inside Freshlife on Victoria Street. Apart from the bored-looking employees the supermarket was empty, and it put him in mind of the scene that met him in *Nature's Gifts* earlier in the day.

"People are going to be reluctant to shop here for a while," DC Owen said. "Even if they were to discard everything on the shelves and restock the entire shop, it's not going to bring customers back. You can't really blame them – I'm not going to be in a hurry to buy anything from this place anytime soon."

"It looks like the manager is here," O'Reilly said.

He nodded in the direction of the canned food section. The shop manager was speaking to a man who didn't look like he was long out of school, and it was clear that the conversation was not a friendly one.

"What part of new stock is to be placed behind the old stock do you find so difficult to comprehend, Matthew?"

The expression on the youngster's face made O'Reilly suspect that Matthew's time at Freshlife was going to be extremely short. It didn't appear that he'd understood anything of what the manager was trying to tell him.

"Can we have a word?" O'Reilly asked her.

"What now?" the manager said.

"Just a few more routine questions," O'Reilly said. "It's Belinda, isn't it?" She nodded and turned to Matthew. "Can I trust you to get it right this time."

"Of course, Mrs North," he said.

"It makes you wonder what they teach them at school these days, doesn't it?" Belinda said on the way to her office.

O'Reilly didn't comment on this.

"Business seems to have taken a dive," he said instead.

"Tell me about it," Belinda said. "The owner is acting like it's my fault."

"Who owns the place?" DC Owen said.

"Susan Arnold."

Belinda opened the door to her office and told them to take a seat.

"What happened to your face?"

"Occupational hazard," O'Reilly said. "Does Mrs Arnold have much to do with the running of the shop?"

He sat down and stretched out his gammy leg.

"We very rarely see her," Belinda said. "She inherited the supermarket from her parents, and I get the impression that working in a shop is beneath her."

"Does she ever come in?" DC Owen said.

"We communicate mostly via phone calls and emails."

"Does she have keys for the shop?" O'Reilly said.

"What's this all about?" Belinda said.

"Could you just answer the question please."

"Of course she has keys," Belinda said. "She owns the place."

"Have you spoken to her since the food contamination?" O'Reilly said.

"What?" Belinda said. "Of course I have. She wants to know how I'm going to go about getting the customers back."

"That's a bit unfair," O'Reilly said. "It's not like you were the one who contaminated the food and drink with potentially deadly toxins, is it?" He looked at her face and tried to gauge her reaction. Belinda broke eye contact first and her gaze rested on one of the pictures on the walls.
"You don't think I had something to do with it, do you?" she said to the portrait.

O'Reilly skirted this question too.
"Do you know a woman by the name of Janet Ingram?" he said.
"Who's she?"
"You and she are not acquainted then?"
"I don't think so."
"How long have you lived on the island?" O'Reilly said.
"I was born here," Belinda said.
"And you're what now," O'Reilly said. "Mid forties?"
Belinda glared at him. "I'm thirty-nine."
"Please forgive me. Guessing a woman's age has always been one of my failings. That means you'd have been born in 1980."
"That's correct," Belinda said. "What is this? Am I under suspicion of something?"
"DI O'Reilly likes to get all the facts," DC Owen said.

"You will have been in your early twenties in 2003," O'Reilly said. "Do you recall something that happened in that year? Something involving a man by the name of Len Hughes?"
Her reaction to Len Hughes' name was obvious. There was clear recognition in her eyes.
"Why are you asking me about Len Hughes?"
"What do you remember about him?" DC Owen said.
"Only what I read in the papers," Belinda said. "He killed a teenage girl."
"After he raped her," O'Reilly said.

"I remember it. That sort of thing just didn't happen on the island back then, and it was big news at the time."

"What else do you remember about it?" O'Reilly said.

"He abducted the girl, took her back to his house and killed her. What else is there to remember?"

"Do you work here every day?" O'Reilly said.

"Five and a half days a week," Belinda said.

"What days do you have off?"

"It's never the same one and a half days. Sometimes I have to work weekends, and sometimes not."

"When are you off next?" O'Reilly said.

"Tomorrow."

"So, you've been in the shop all week?"

"What aren't you telling me?" Belinda said. "Why all these irrelevant questions?"

"I think we've taken up enough of your time, Belinda," O'Reilly said. "We may need to talk to you again."

"What on earth for?"

"That's just how it is. Thank you for your time. You can get back to supervising the stocking of the shelves."

He got to his feet and rubbed his leg, but he made no effort to leave the office.

"Was there something else you wanted?" Belinda said.

"How long have you worked here?" O'Reilly asked.

"Four years."

"Have you always worked in retail?"

"I was a teacher before."

"What did you teach?"

"History."

"What brought on the career change?" O'Reilly said.

"I taught for over ten years," Belinda said. "But I became disillusioned along the way. Education isn't what it once was."

"What do you mean by that?" DC Owen said.

"Someone your age wouldn't understand," Belinda said. "And I believe my career choices are none of your business."

"You're quite right," O'Reilly said. "Thanks for the chat. We'll find our own way out."

CHAPTER FORTY THREE

O'Reilly was eating a sandwich in his office when DC Owen came in. It was just after five and he wasn't sure when he would get the chance to put something in his belly again. He wiped the crumbs from his mouth and winced when he rubbed his bust lip. He noticed that there was blood on his hand. He asked DC Owen to take a seat.

"I don't know if this is significant," she said. "But I did some digging into Belinda North's teaching career, and I found something interesting. Mrs North taught at the same school that Janet Ingram attended. I appreciate that it's a small island and we can't expect a teacher to remember every student they've ever taught, but I think it's worth looking into."
"What school was it?" O'Reilly said.
"St Sampson High. Belinda taught History there from 2003 until 2015. Janet Ingram attended the school from 2007 until 2012, and she stayed on at the sixth form there for a further two years."
"Perhaps she didn't have Mrs North as a teacher," O'Reilly said.
"I checked that too, sir. She did. Janet took History at GCSE, and she also did History A-level. She will have definitely been taught by Belinda North. And this was the clincher for me – Janet aced her exams. In fact, she was the student with the highest grades in both the GCSE and A-level exams. Any teacher worth their salt will have remembered a student like that."
"She will," O'Reilly agreed. "Why did she lie to us about knowing Janet?"
"And what else has she lied to us about?"

"St Sampson High, you say?" O'Reilly said.
"It's a good school," DC Owen said.
"It'll be closed now, won't it?"

"It is," DC Owen said. "But I managed to track down someone who works there. Eleanor Brown is the head of the school and she's more than happy to speak to us at home."

"What would I do without you, Katie?"

"I'm just doing my job, sir."

"No," O'Reilly said. "You're going the extra mile, as usual. Where does this head of school live?"

"Not far from the school. It's a bit too far to walk."

"I was hoping you would say that," O'Reilly said. "Come on then."

* * *

Eleanor Brown was a petite woman who looked to be in her late forties. She opened the door with a warm smile on her face and invited them in. O'Reilly declined her offer of something to drink but he didn't refuse the freshly baked scones on the table in the kitchen.

"Help yourself," Eleanor said.

O'Reilly did. He cut one in half and spread some butter on both slices. He added a spoon of strawberry jam and took a bite, splitting his lip open again in the process.

"Are you OK?" Eleanor asked.

O'Reilly realised that he must look quite a sight. There was an adhesive dressing over the cut on his cheekbone, and his lips resembled the result of a botched Botox injection.

"It's been an interesting few days," he said.

Eleanor took a tissue from a box on the counter and handed it to him. "You're bleeding."

O'Reilly took it and dabbed his bust lip. "Thank you. You're quite a cook. These are exceptional scones."

"I'm afraid I can't take the credit," Eleanor said. "You have my husband to thank for that. You're not here to discuss scones, are you?"

"Unfortunately, not," O'Reilly said. "You're the head of school at St Sampson High. How long have you worked there?"

"I started there shortly after I graduated. So, mid-nineties. Your colleague told me you were interested in Belinda North when we spoke on the phone."

"That's right. What do you remember about her?"

"She was a good teacher, and the students liked her."

"Do you recall a student by the name of Janet Ingram?" DC Owen said.

"Of course," Eleanor said. "Janet was one of our shining stars. In fact, I was surprised when I learned that she wasn't planning on studying further."

"Do you know why she chose not to?" O'Reilly said.

"I really don't, I'm afraid. She could have taken her pick of universities, but she chose to stay on the island instead."

"She owns a business selling natural products," DC Owen said.

"Are you aware of what happened to Janet's sister?" O'Reilly asked.

"It was hardly a secret," Eleanor said. "I don't think there's anyone who was on the island then who didn't know about what Len Hughes did."

"Janet was only six when her sister was murdered," O'Reilly said. "It must have affected the family terribly."

"I was aware of the family history," Eleanor said. "But I didn't see any evidence of it influencing Janet's schoolwork. As I've already said – she was one of St Sampson's highest achievers. Can I ask why you're so interested in Janet Ingram? I was under the impression you were here to discuss Belinda North."

"Mrs North taught Janet History for a good few years," O'Reilly said. "She was a star student, and it's logical to think that someone like that would stick in the head, but when we asked her about Janet, she insisted that she didn't know her. Can you think of a reason she might lie about it?"

Eleanor shook her head. "I really can't. I've been doing this for more than two decades and I can recall the majority of students I've taught."

"And, as Mrs North is a history teacher, it would be safe to assume that she has a better memory than most."

They were prevented from discussing this further when a bald man came into the kitchen.

"Sorry to interrupt," he said. "I just need to grab my phone. I left it on charge in here."

"Are you the one responsible for the scones there?" O'Reilly pointed to the plate.

"That's me."

"This is my husband, Ian," Eleanor said.

"Best scones I've tasted since I've been on the island," O'Reilly said. "Truly exceptional."

"Glad you approve. I'll leave you to it."

He unplugged his phone from its charger and left the room.

"Sorry about that," Eleanor said.

"Not a problem," O'Reilly said. "Were you surprised when Mrs North decided to turn her back on teaching?"

"Is that what she told you?"

"She claimed that she'd become disillusioned with education," DC Owen said.

"Is that not why she left St Sampson High?" O'Reilly said.

"It was not. Belinda was a good teacher, but she had a habit of overstepping certain boundaries, especially where teacher-student relationships were concerned."

"She got a bit too involved with them?" O'Reilly said.

"Belinda took a somewhat unhealthy interest in some of the students," Eleanor said. "There was nothing sinister involved – it was probably the reason she was such a popular teacher but some of the parents didn't appreciate the interference."

"Do you know if Janet Ingram was one of the students she took an interest in?"

"She was."

"Do you know what form this interest took?" O'Reilly said.

"I don't recall the exact details," Eleanor said. "But it was enough for a formal complaint to be lodged by Janet's parents. I think it had something to do with the murder of Janet's sister."

"And she was asked to leave the school because of it?" DC Owen said.

"She was persuaded to consider the options that were still available to her."

"Leave the school before those options were no longer an option?" O'Reilly said. "If that makes any sense."

"Precisely. And I'm afraid I cannot discuss the details further."

"You don't have to," O'Reilly said. "But can you at least do us the courtesy of confirming whether Belinda North's sudden exit from St Sampson High involved Janet Ingram in any way?"

"I really can't give you anything else," Eleanor said. "I have to consider what's best for the school."

"Your refusal to comment is good enough for me," O'Reilly said. "Thank you – you've been a great help."

CHAPTER FORTY FOUR

"What do you think really happened?" DC Owen asked O'Reilly on the way back to the station.

"When the boss of a school refuses to comment," he said. "It means there's something to look into."

"Why couldn't she just tell us?"

"It's how the world works these days, Katie. She's the head of school, which means she has to be part-teacher, part-politician. I remember my time at school back in Dublin. The teachers there were exactly that – they would educate you about all sorts of pointless things and when they weren't doing that, they were inflicting serious pain. We knew where we stood with them, but nowadays the kids are in charge. And they have their parents behind them. If a teacher gave me a clip round the ear, I kept it to myself. There was no way in hell I was going to make my Mammy aware of it. Good times. Life was a lot simpler then."

"What's the plan of action?" DC Owen said.

"I'm going to drop you off at the station," O'Reilly told her. "And then I'm heading home. There's something connecting Janet Ingram with the ex-History teacher but whatever it is will still be there in the morning. And Katie."

"Sir?"

"Put the investigation out of your mind for tonight. I appreciate the extra work you do, but you need to cool it for one evening. Tomorrow's another day, and we will get to the heart of this. Go home and relax in a hot bath. Have a few beers – that's what I'm planning on doing."

"You shouldn't really be drinking so soon after suffering a head injury."

"Nonsense," O'Reilly said. "In Ireland we drink before, during and after we sustain head injuries with no ill effects whatsoever."

"I give up with you, sir. I don't know how you can just switch off. Time is running out before whoever is behind this is going to release ricin onto the island."

"I don't think they're going to make good on their threat."

"We don't know that," DC Owen said. "They've already caused so much sickness and death, and we have to take them seriously."

"I don't know what it is, Katie," O'Reilly said. "I just get the feeling that they were bluffing. Here we go. I'll see you in the morning. And no work for you this evening."

"Yes, sir."

"Consider that an order," O'Reilly said. "Get some rest."

He was about to drive away when something caught his eye in the rearview mirror. Someone was approaching the car from behind and when the figure got closer O'Reilly realised who it was. He debated whether to drive away but his curiosity was roused so he turned off the engine and waited to see what DCO Callum Dove had to say.

He was surprised when the second in charge of the Island Police got in the passenger side without being invited.

He closed the door. "Can we get away from here?"

"What do you want?" O'Reilly said.

"Please, Liam," DCO Dove said. "I can't be seen with you."

"I fail to see what difference it's going to make now. When you swung a punch at a fellow officer in front of a bunch of witnesses, you kissed your time in the Island Police goodbye. You can tell me what's on your mind right here, and then you can get the fuck out of my car."

DCO Dove took a look around and sighed deeply. "I'm sorry about your lip."

"Is that it?" O'Reilly said. "You could have said that in a text message."

"I really am sorry. When I found out that you and CO Johnson had been in secret talks, I just saw red. I came to find you, and you know the rest. I wasn't thinking straight."

"I'm not in the mood for this. You've apologised, now you can go."

"Not everything is as it seems," DCO Dove said.

"It's pretty cut and dry as far as I'm concerned," O'Reilly said. "You protected a man who'd raped a young woman. You tampered with evidence, and he got away with violating a girl with her whole life ahead of her. Her rapist went on to rape and murder another, much younger girl and you need to take some responsibility for that. You're also partly to blame for CO Johnson's suspension. He might have kept quiet about the impending threat to the people of the island, but why did he do that? I'll tell you why – you were holding him to ransom. I used to like you. I used to respect you, but what you've done cannot be forgiven. You're scum, Callum. You're no better than the toe rags we're employed to bang to rights. Unless you have something to help further the investigation, I suggest you get out and let me go home."

DCO Dove ran his hands through his hair.

"Is it sore?" he said after a while. "The lip, I mean? I've been told I punch like a little girl."

"You and I are not friends, Callum. You've got thirty seconds before I make a phone call that will make your predicament even worse."

"CO Johnson is Len Hughes' brother-in-law."

"Old news," O'Reilly said. "The chief officer has told me everything. Unlike you, CO Johnson has a conscience. I know all about his marriage to Len Hughes' sister. I'm also aware of the way you forged his signature on vital documents in the Amy Winter rape case. Why, Callum? That's the part I'm struggling to get my head around. I've always prided myself on being a shrewd judge of character, but I got you all wrong, didn't I? I never would have had you pegged as a bottom feeder in a million years. Time's up. Fuck off."

DCO Dove opened the car door, but he didn't get out. He turned to O'Reilly and offered him a feeble smile.
"I know who you need to look more closely at, Liam."
"I don't believe you," O'Reilly said.
"Trust me on this," DCO Dove said. "I know who's behind the threats."
"I don't believe you," O'Reilly said again.
He raised his good leg and with as much strength as he could muster, he shoved DCO Dove out of the car and onto the pavement. The second in charge of the Island Police landed on his side and groaned. O'Reilly leaned over to close the door.
"I'd say we're even now, sir."
He turned the key in the ignition, engaged first gear and drove away from the broken man on the ground outside the station.

CHAPTER FORTY FIVE

O'Reilly walked through the doors of the station just before eight the next morning. He'd had an early night, and he felt well rested. He stopped by the front desk and greeted PC London.

"Have we had any interesting developments overnight?" he asked her.

"Not as far as I'm aware, sir. I've not long got here myself. Are you alright – your face looks sore."

"I'm grand, Kim," O'Reilly said. "Never better."

"I saw you shove DCO Dove out of the car yesterday."

"That's not going to be a problem, is it?"

"No, sir," PC London said. "I'm telling you so you're aware of it, but as far as anyone else is concerned, it never happened."

"Thanks, Kim," O'Reilly said. "I appreciate it. If anyone is looking for me, I'll be having a cup of tea in my office. We don't have any drinking straws in this place, do we?"

"Sir?"

"Never mind."

He went to the office and closed the door behind him. He boiled the kettle and made the tea and took it to his desk. He didn't even get the chance to take a sip when there was a knock on the door and DC Stone came in.

"Morning, Andy. What can I do for you?"

"I thought you'd want to know that Janet Ingram has been located," DC Stone said.

"You thought right. Where is she?"

"At work."

"You're kidding me?" O'Reilly said.

"I'm not. I phoned *Nature's Gifts* and Janet was the one who answered."

"Did you tell her who you were?"

"No, sir," DC Stone said. "I didn't want to give her the opportunity to do another runner. I apologised and told her I'd dialled the wrong number."

"Good call. Could you arrange for a car to pick her up?"

"Are we going to formally interview her?"

"No, Andy," O'Reilly said. "We're going to take her on a guided tour of the island in a police car. Sorry, that was uncalled for. Good work."

DC Stone's rat eyes narrowed.

"And while you're at it," O'Reilly said. "I want Belinda North picked up too. Those two have a lot of explaining to do."

"I'll get right onto it, sir."

Something occurred to O'Reilly a couple of minutes after DC Stone had left. He took out his phone and brought up the shifty-eyed DC's number. The call was answered immediately.

"Andy," O'Reilly said. "Janet Ingram and Belinda North must not have access to any mobile devices."

"I've already made that clear to the uniforms, sir," DC Stone said. "If we're to interpret what was said in the email yesterday as fact, another email is going to arrive at midday today. If those two women are behind this, they won't be able to send the email if they're here at the station."

"Sorry I doubted you. How long are we talking about?"

"They'll be brought in within the hour," DC Stone said. "Do you really think they're involved in this?"

"If they are, I'm going to find out."

He ended the call and finished his tea. A quick dab of a tissue to his lips told him they were no longer bleeding and his thoughts turned to Callum Dove. The deputy chief officer's parting words were still niggling away at him. After everything that had happened, he didn't trust him anymore but what if he was telling the truth about knowing who was behind the poisoning on the island? Stranger things had happened recently.

After trying DCO Dove's number three times with the same result O'Reilly admitted defeat. The deputy chief officer wasn't available, and O'Reilly didn't think it was worth leaving a message. He left the office and made his way to the briefing room. Everybody else was already there with the exception of DCI Fish. DS Skinner brought O'Reilly up to date. DCI Fish was going to be tied up in meetings for most of the day. O'Reilly wasn't too bothered. The interviews with Belinda North and Janet Ingram were their main priority and DCI Fish's involvement in them wasn't necessary. He told the detectives in the room as much.

"Katie. You and I will interview Janet Ingram and Will and Andy can tackle Belinda North. They'll probably request legal representation, but they may waive that right. It's important that we keep them here for as long as possible. The people responsible for the poisonings on the island have promised to be in touch by lunchtime today, and if that correspondence isn't forthcoming, we'll have grounds to hold the two women for even longer."
"What if another email does arrive?" DS Skinner said.
"We'll cross that bridge when we come to it. Belinda North lied about knowing Janet Ingram and I want to know why she lied."
"How can you be so sure that she and Janet are acquainted?" DC Stone asked.
"When a student shines as bright as Janet did," O'Reilly said. "You remember them. Belinda taught Janet for her GCSEs and her A-Levels – the girl achieved the highest grades in the school, and you do not forget someone like that."

"Katie reckons that two different people wrote the emails," DC Stone said. "Do you think it could be Belinda and Janet?"

"I don't know, Andy," O'Reilly said. "If that's the case, it feels too easy for my liking. Belinda manages the supermarket where eight of the fatalities purchased contaminated food and drink and Janet owns the shop responsible for the ninth fatality, but something feels a bit *off* about it."

"It does seem rather too obvious," DS Skinner said. "Surely if you're planning on tainting a product with a potentially fatal toxin, you do not do it in a place that can be directly linked to you."

"There's a phrase for it," O'Reilly said. "It's something about shitting in your own backyard. Perhaps it really is that simple. Both women had ample opportunity and from an evidence perspective, it's quite brilliant. Forensically speaking, both women could deny responsibility for the exact reason we're suspecting them. It's unavoidable that there will be evidence of them on the products – they come into contact with them on a daily basis."

"How do we prove it then?" DC Stone said.

"We unearth the motivation behind it."

"I thought we'd already established that the motive is financial gain," DS Skinner said.

"I get the impression that there's a lot more to it than that, Will."

The door to the briefing room opened and PC London came in.

"Janet Ingram and Belinda North have arrived sir."

"That's grand, Kim," O'Reilly said. "Have they asked for legal representation?"

"Mrs North has," PC London said. "But Janet Ingram told us she doesn't need a lawyer."

"Interesting. Could you inform the duty sergeant that we'll be along shortly."

"Will do, sir."

"We're going to get some answers today," O'Reilly said. "I can feel it in my weary Irish bones."

CHAPTER FORTY SIX

O'Reilly didn't think Janet Ingram looked particularly fazed by her predicament. He wondered if she believed her presence in an interview room was related to the fact that somebody had died after consuming a product bought from her shop. He went through the motions for the record and asked Janet if she wished to reconsider her decision to carry on without legal representation.

"I don't have a lawyer," she said.
"We can arrange one for you," O'Reilly explained. "Free of charge."
"It's fine. I have to get back to work. How long is this going to take?"
"You can never tell. Do you understand the reason you're here?"
"I imagine it has something to do with the ginger that Paula bought from *Nature's Gifts*."
"Correct. But we'll come back to that. Where were you yesterday? We couldn't get hold of you."
"I was at my boyfriend's place. You can check with him if you don't believe me."
"That won't be necessary. You attended St Sampson High, is that correct?"
"It is."
"And I believe you did exceptionally well there."
"I've always found schoolwork easy."
"You achieved the highest grades in your year for GCSE and A-level. That's impressive."
"Can I ask what my grades have to do with Paula's death?" Janet said.
"I like to get some background information when I interview someone," O'Reilly said. "You were taught by Mrs North, is that right?"
"She was a great teacher."
"I believe she was more than a simple educator at the school."

Janet looked at her watch, and she did it rather obviously.

"Is there somewhere you have to be?" DC Owen asked.

"I'm needed in the shop. We've got a delivery coming in and I like to be there when it arrives."

"I'm sure your assistant can handle it," O'Reilly said.

"Have you been taking the supplements I recommended?" Janet said.

"It must have slipped my mind. I'll make sure to start soon."

"Can you tell us about Mrs North," DC Owen said.

"She was my history teacher," Janet said. "End of story."

"That's not strictly true, is it?" O'Reilly said. "She was a bit more than that. In fact, I believe your parents lodged a complaint about her because of it. Can you tell us a bit more about what happened?"

"It was a mistake on their part."

"Are you talking about your parents?"

"Belinda did nothing wrong."

"Belinda?" O'Reilly repeated.

"Mrs North."

"You were on first name terms with your teacher?"

"Only outside of school hours."

"You saw her after school?" DC Owen said.

"She was a good listener."

"What did you talk about?" O'Reilly said.

"Mostly family stuff."

"And your family stuff isn't your run of the mill family stuff, is it?"

"You're talking about Vicky?" Janet said.

"You were only six when she was murdered," DC Owen said. "That must have been hard for you."

Janet shrugged her shoulders in response to this.

"Why didn't you carry on with your studies?" O'Reilly said.

"Money," Janet said. "It was as simple as that. My mum and dad didn't have any."

"That's rough," O'Reilly said. "Did you want to go to university?"

"I've done alright for myself here on the island."

"So I can see. But still, it must have stung. You could have had your pick of universities."

"We weren't always poor," Janet said. "But my parents' never-ending quest for justice soon used up everything they had."

"I'm not following you," O'Reilly said.

"They couldn't let it lie. Thay wanted justice for Vicky and justice didn't come cheap, even if nothing was ever achieved. I lost count of how many lawyers and private investigators came to the house over the years. And for what? It didn't bring my sister back, did it?"

"Just now," O'Reilly said. "When my colleague brought up the murder of your sister, your reaction was a curious one."

"What do you want me to say?" Janet said.

"I want you to explain your apparent indifference to the death of a sister."

"I was six years old when Vicky was murdered. I knew she'd died and I was sad, but that sadness soon turned to resentment."

"You resented your sister because she was murdered?" DC Owen said.

"I didn't resent Vicky," Janet said. "I resented what my parents turned her into. I spent what were supposed to be the happiest years of my life living with a ghost that my mother and father revered. Why do you think I threw myself into the books? Vicky was the one who had died, but I was made to feel like I was invisible. Do you know what it's like to live with a shadow like that every second of the day? Vicky was everywhere – she lingered in every room in the house, and my parents made sure she never left. She should have been laid to rest and remembered only in here."

She tapped her head.

"But no, that didn't happen."

"Did you talk to Mrs North about this?" O'Reilly said.

Janet nodded. "She was great. She made me understand it from all perspectives. She was a good listener."

"Is that why your parents lodged a complaint about her with the school?" DC Owen said.

"I was furious. Belinda did nothing wrong. In fact, she was the one who made me see things from my parents' perspective. She helped me to understand that there is possibly nothing more terrible in this world than having to bury your child. She didn't attack them – she empathised with them, and that was the thanks she got. Is this going to take much longer?"

O'Reilly didn't give her an answer.

"How did you feel when you realised that one of your customers had died as a result of something she'd purchased from your shop?"

"How do you think I felt?" Janet said. "Paula was a good customer, and I liked her. I was devastated."

"How do you think the toxins ended up in the ginger?" DC Owen said.

"Someone must have put it there. I've been watching the developments on the news sites. Eight people died due to contaminated products from Freshlife supermarket too."

"A supermarket that just happens to have your old history teacher and mentor as a manager," O'Reilly said. "And on that note, I suggest we take a short break."

"What else do you want me to tell you?" Janet said.

O'Reilly stated the time for the tape and paused it.

"We'll reconvene in an hour," he said.

"An hour?" Janet said. "I have to get back to work."

"I'm afraid it can't be helped. I'll arrange some refreshments for you."

"You can't keep me here without good reason."

"Actually, I can," O'Reilly said.

"Am I suspected of something?" Janet said. "You can't possibly think it was me who put the toxins in the ginger."

"I'll get someone to bring you a sandwich and a cup of tea," O'Reilly said. "Or would you prefer coffee?"

CHAPTER FORTY SEVEN

"I don't think she's involved," DC Owen said.

O'Reilly rubbed his fat lip. "Me neither, Katie, but we can't take any chances. That email is due in just under an hour, and I'm not letting either of those women leave until we have confirmation one way or another."

"I didn't expect her reaction when we brought up her sister's murder."

"It must have been hard for her," O'Reilly said. "Growing up overshadowed by the ghost of a sibling. Who knows what that does to a kid?"

"Is it a motive for murder though?"

"If it is, there's no logic to it. What is she getting out of murdering complete strangers? None of the people who died played any part in what happened to her sister, so why punish them for it? We're missing something here – something vital."

PC London came in and apologised for the interruption.

"No problem, Kim," O'Reilly said. "What's up?"

"Janet London has changed her mind about legal representation. Shall I arrange a duty solicitor?"

"If you could," O'Reilly said. "I wonder what's brought on this change of heart."

"I'll see if I can find someone to come in."

"That'll work in our favour," O'Reilly said. "It's going to take a few hours for the duty solicitor to get here."

"Why do you think she wants a lawyer now?" DC Owen said.

"Who knows. Perhaps she has something to tell us, but she wants a lawyer present when she does. Who knows?"

"I wonder how Andy and the DS are getting on with the ex-History teacher."

"I'm sure we'll soon find out."

* * *

"So far," DS Skinner said. "We've touched on your time at St Sampson High and your relationship with Janet Ingram."

"Is it really necessary to go over topics you've already discussed?"

It was Belinda North's lawyer. Gregory Pontier was a smug looking man wearing a badly fitting wig. They'd been in the interview room for less than fifteen minutes and he'd adjusted it no fewer than a dozen times.

DS Skinner nodded. "Going back to your relationship with Janet Ingram. Can you tell us more about that?"

Gregory opened his mouth to protest but Belinda silenced him by raising her hand.

"My relationship with Janet was a purely professional one," she said. "I was her teacher."

"And you also saw her after hours," DC Stone said. "In a kind of counsellor capacity."

"Janet came to me with her problems," Belinda said. "I wanted to help her. We spoke about the problems she faced at home, and I gave her advice. Whether she took that advice was beyond my control."

"When DI O'Reilly and DC Owen spoke to you earlier," DS Skinner said. "You told them you left the school in St Sampson because you'd become disillusioned with the educational system. That was a lie, wasn't it?"

"It wasn't entirely untrue," Belinda said. "I was given an ultimatum. Either I resign from my post, or I get forced out. That made me realise that it was time to get out anyway. I didn't want to work for an establishment capable of treating one of its employees like that. Especially as I'd done nothing wrong."

"Janet Ingram's parents lodged a complaint against you," DC Stone said.

"As was their right, but it doesn't mean the complaint was justified."

"Why did you lie about Janet Ingram?" DS Skinner said. "When you were asked about her, you denied all knowledge of her."

"I regret that," Belinda said. "It was a mistake. I thought it would make things less complicated if I simply denied knowing her. I apologise."

"OK," DS Skinner said. "Let's move on to Freshlife Supermarket. You're the manager there, is that correct?"

"It is."

"How did you feel when you realised that eight islanders had died as a result of products on your shelves?"

"I was shocked. It didn't seem real."

"How do you think the products were contaminated?" DC Stone said.

"I thought we'd already established that. Someone broke in and tainted them."

"There's something I'm struggling to understand," DS Skinner said. "When our forensic team examined the shop, they reported that there were no fewer than four CCTV cameras inside."

"Five," Belinda corrected.

"Five. Can you explain why none of these cameras caught the culprits in action? Surely one of them would have captured the person responsible for contaminating the products?"

"The cameras weren't working."

"That's rather convenient."

"Detective Sergeant," Gregory said. "Your attitude is bordering on the aggressive."

"Nonsense," DS Skinner said. "I was merely making an observation."

"They've since been fixed," Belinda said.

"Very convenient. Surely, cameras that aren't in operation means you're not covered by insurance."

"I only became aware of it yesterday."

"Why do you keep on lying to us?" DS Skinner said.

"I'm telling the truth."

"You're not. In fact, you explained the situation with the cameras to our forensics officers when they were there three days ago."

"I sometimes get times and dates mixed up."

"It's probably for the best that you're no longer teaching History then, isn't it?"

"Detective Sergeant," Gregory Pontier said. "I'm warning you."

"You're in no position to do that Mr Pontier. When someone lies to me, it tends to make me irritable, and your client has done nothing but since she set foot inside this interview room."

"Who is responsible for the cameras?" DC Stone said.

"I am," Belinda replied. "I made a mistake."

"You seem to be making a lot of them." DS Skinner turned to face Gregory Pontier when he said this.

"Is this going to take much longer?" Belinda said.

"How long is a piece of string?" DS Skinner said. "Is there somewhere you need to be? Perhaps you have pressing matters to attend to."

"I have a lot to do, yes."

"Maybe there's an urgent email you need to send?"

"What?"

"Never mind. Now that we've established that you are aware of Janet Ingram's existence – when was the last time you saw her?"

"Not since I left St Sampson High."

"Are you sure about that?" DC Stone said.

"I'm not an idiot."

"My colleague never implied that you were," DS Skinner said. "So, you haven't seen Janet since she left school. You haven't perhaps bumped into her? This is a small island, after all."

"I haven't seen her since I left St Sampson High."

"Do you own a computer?" DS Skinner asked.

"Of course I own a computer," Belinda said. "Who doesn't?"
"Would you have any objections to us having a look at it?"
"On what grounds?" Gregory chipped in.
"I can't divulge that."
"Then I can't let you anywhere near my client's computer. Unless you have reasonable grounds and a search warrant, the answer is no."
"Is there something on there you'd rather not let us see?" DC Stone said.
"I've got nothing to hide," Belinda said.
"Then you've got nothing to worry about," DS Skinner said. "A search warrant may take time, but there's nothing preventing you from volunteering the computer."
"Not without a warrant," Gregory advised.

DS Skinner's mobile phone started to ring. He looked at the screen and sighed.
"I apologise, but I have to take this."
He left the room and closed the door behind him.
"I presume my client is free to go," Gregory said to DC Stone.
"That's not my decision to make," DC Stone said. "I'm just a lowly detective constable."

DS Skinner came back in.
"Sorry about that. Some new information has come to light. I suggest we take a short break."
"What new information?" Gregory Pontier demanded.
"This isn't a court case," DS Skinner said. "We're not obliged to tell you. We'll reconvene in an hour."
"This is outrageous," Gregory said.
"Belinda, would you like something to eat or drink?"
"I don't want something to eat," she said. "I want to get out of here."

"What about you, Mr Pontier?" DS Skinner said. "Because if you're hungry or thirsty there's a coffee machine by the front desk."

"There's a snack vending machine too," DC Stone added. "I think there's still a couple of packets of salt and vinegar crisps in it."

CHAPTER FORTY EIGHT

DS Skinner wasn't quite telling the truth when he mentioned new information coming to light. It was O'Reilly who'd made the phone call and the excuse about the new info was merely designed to stall the proceedings. O'Reilly also wanted to compare notes. The interview with Janet Ingram hadn't given him what he'd wanted, and he hoped the interrogation of Belinda North had been more productive.

It hadn't.

"The only thing I found suspicious about the manager of Fresh Life supermarket," DS Skinner said. "Is the fact that the CCTV cameras weren't working at the time of the break-in we assumed corresponded with the products being contaminated."

"The cameras are Mrs North's responsibility," DC Stone said. "But there was nothing else that sounded any warning bells about the woman."

"She's a compulsive liar," DS Skinner said. "But that doesn't make her a multiple murderer."

"Katie and I didn't get the impression that Janet Ingram was lying to us," O'Reilly said. "In fact, she was very open about her sister's murder and the hell she went through afterwards. Her parents basically forgot all about her in their quest for justice for Vicky. I can't imagine how awful that must have been for a young girl."

"And she seems to have come out of it relatively unscathed," DC Owen said. "She aced her exams, and she owns a successful business. She's only twenty-two and it's clear that she has her head screwed on."

"Where do we go from here?" DS Skinner asked O'Reilly.

"I want to keep the two women here until we can be certain neither of them is behind the emails. If we don't hear anything from the terrorists responsible for the murders, we'll have more ammunition. We'll have reasonable grounds for warrants to search their properties."

"I asked Belinda for access to her computer," DS Skinner said. "But her lawyer scuppered that immediately."

"I doubt we'll get anything from the computer anyway," DC Stone said. "The email address will be a burner, and they used a VPN to send the emails."

"VPNs can be bypassed," DC Owen pointed out.

"If you've got a team of experts," DC Stone said. "And a whole load of time."

DCI Fish came into the room, and his face told a story that was easily interpreted.

"Rough meeting?" O'Reilly said.

"I need a cigarette," DCI Fish said. "And I quit more than ten years ago."

"Is there anything we need to be aware of?"

"The discussions were centred on the best way to proceed," DCI Fish said. "Do we bow down to the terrorist threat, or do we refuse to be blackmailed?"

"And?" O'Reilly said.

"The debate is still ongoing. The general consensus is that we wait to see what their next move is going to be."

"We're keeping the two suspects waiting," O'Reilly told him. "If another email isn't forthcoming, we'll have grounds to up the ante a bit. Obviously, if we do receive another email while they're enjoying the hospitality of the Island Police, we're going to have to rethink our strategy."

"Do you have a contingency plan?" DCI Fish asked.

"No, Tom. I do not, but something will occur to me."

"There are grave concerns about the possibility of a ricin attack on the island," DCI Fish said. "The Island Police is simply not equipped to deal with a crisis of that magnitude."

"I don't think we have to worry about that," O'Reilly said.

"The threat wasn't veiled, Liam," DCI Fish said. "It was quite clear what these people are willing to unleash on the island if their demands are not met."

"It's just a feeling I get, Tom. Ricin is a far cry from death caps and oleandrin. The simple process of extracting the toxin is risky, and one slip of the hand can be a death sentence. I also believe that the people responsible will be aware of the repercussions of an attack of this nature. As you've pointed out, the Island Police are not in a position to deal with something like this, so assistance will be brought in from agencies you do not want to go to war against. I think they're bluffing. The risks involved are vastly greater than the rewards."

"Are you suggesting we simply ignore the threat?"

"I'm not suggesting anything of the kind," O'Reilly said. "But I don't believe time spent on worrying about a ricin attack will be time well spent. We have other fish to fry, and so far, it looks as if those fish are sweating it out waiting for us to finish interrogating them."

"Did you discuss the possibility of actually handing over the money?" DC Stone said.

"We did," DCI Fish confirmed. "There were numerous suggestions put forward and the most popular one centred on appealing to the people of the island for assistance. A hundred and four million is not loose change, but there are plenty of people on the island with the means to help out. Naturally, giving in to the demands of terrorists is always going to be the last resort, but it needs to be considered, nevertheless."

"How will we know if another email does arrive?" DS Skinner said.

"The tech team are monitoring CO Johnson's email account. As soon as anything comes in, we'll be made aware of it."

"I suggest we don't sit here twiddling our thumbs while we wait for something that may never materialise," O'Reilly said. "Let's look at what we know."

"It all started with a string of break-ins," DC Owen said. "A number of random shops were targeted, and nothing was taken in any of the break-ins."

"No," DC Stone said. "The purpose of them was to poison food and drink."

"And we now know that out of five shops," O'Reilly said. "Only one of them actually ended up with tainted products on its shelves. Freshlife supermarket. Eight people lost their lives because they consumed products bought from Freshlife. Why was that the only one?"

"We also now know that the CCTV cameras were not functioning," DC Owen said. "And the person responsible for the cameras is here at the station."

"As is the woman who owns the business where the ninth victim bought the contaminated ginger from," DS Skinner said. "And we haven't had any news about another email yet. It's past noon, so unless these people are not the best timekeepers, it's looking likely that we have our culprits right here. All we need to do is get them to crack."

When DCI Fish's mobile phone started to ring, all eyes were on him. O'Reilly could feel his heartbeat speeding up. DCI Fish looked at the screen of the phone and his eyes met O'Reilly's. The Irish detective would later describe the sensation he felt right then as something akin to premonition. He knew beyond a shadow of a doubt that the mobile phone was about to give them bad news.

The conversation was short, and DCI Fish's contribution consisted of just a few words. He ended the call and put the phone on the table.

"We've got a problem. Another email has arrived."

CHAPTER FORTY NINE

The language that Derek Nunn was speaking was definitely some form of English, but O'Reilly was only able to understand half of the words that came out of his mouth. The man in charge of the team of IT experts may as well have been speaking Japanese. Terms like virtual private networks were vaguely familiar but the majority of the others weren't.

Derek had joined them in the briefing room to explain some of the aspects of the email that had landed in Chief Officer Johnson's inbox a few minutes ago. The message got straight down to business.

You have precisely 48 hours to comply with the following:
One hundred and four million Euros is to be converted to Litecoin and deposited into the account below. Should you fail to meet these demands 100 grams of Ricinus communis will be distributed across the island and more than 10 thousand islanders WILL die.

Once we have confirmation that the transaction has been completed we will cease operations and you will hear no more from us.

The bizarre account number was written at the bottom, but that was the extent of the email.

"What the devil is Litecoin?" O'Reilly said.

"It's a derivative of Bitcoin," Derek explained. "It is also a decentralised peer-to-peer cryptocurrency, and the only real difference is the main chain, which has a slightly moderated codebase."

O'Reilly looked around the room. "Did anyone else not understand a word of that?"

DS Skinner raised his hand. "I didn't."

"I'm glad it's not just me then."

Derek laughed. "I apologise. I take it for granted that everybody speaks the same language as me. In a nutshell, Litecoin was designed to facilitate faster and smoother payments."

"Can we trace the transaction?" DCI Fish said.

"Not unless we send a bot along for the ride," Derek said. "Sorry, I'm doing it again. We could attach a spyware bot to the Litecoin transaction, but there are a number of reasons I would recommend not doing that. The risks are too great."

"What kind of risks?" O'Reilly said.

"Firstly, the measures these people have put in place thus far suggest a high level of technical expertise and they will pick up the spyware in an instant. And in order to even attempt the spy bot we would need to make the payment, and that would entail handing over more than a hundred million Euros with no chance of recouping it afterwards."

"You're telling us there's nothing we can do to track the people responsible?" DCI Fish said.

"I'm afraid not," Derek said.

"What if you had the computer the emails were sent from?" DC Stone said.

"All three emails were sent from different trash mails," Derek said. "They're no longer in existence, and the private network they were sent from makes it even more difficult to trace. There is a possibility of finding something deep down in the hard drives, but that's hit and miss, and it's also extremely time consuming."

"And we don't even know which computer the emails were sent from," DC Owen said. "So, it would be like looking for a needle in a haystack. Who knows how many computers, laptops and tablets are on the island."

"It definitely wasn't Belinda North or Janet Ingram who sent the email," DS Skinner said. "They were here at the time without any access to their devices."

"That makes no difference," Derek said.

"How could they send an email if they're nowhere near a computer?" O'Reilly said.

"Easily. The mail could have been set to be delivered at a certain time."

"Like on a timer?"

"Precisely," Derek said. "Any one of the people in this room could do it."

"Not me," O'Reilly said.

"You can program an email to be sent out at any time you choose. There have been instances where corpses have sent emails to family members."

"Corpses?" DC Stone said.

"People who have committed suicide."

"That's just sick."

"Isn't technology wonderful?" Derek said. "Sorry, my wife is always moaning about my macabre sense of humour."

"That means we can't discount either of those women yet," DCI Fish said.

"Listening to all this tech talk is making my mouth dry," O'Reilly said. "Would anyone object if I leave you for ten minutes while I drink a cup of tea?"

"No problem, Liam," DCI Fish said. "You can crack on with part two of the interviews when you're finished."

"How can listening to tech talk make your mouth dry?" DC Stone wondered when O'Reilly had gone.

"Perhaps it's an Irish thing," DC Owen said.

"Do you need me for anything else?" Derek asked.

"I don't think so," DCI Fish said.

"I'll keep on chipping away at the emails. Who knows – I might get lucky with something."

"Thanks for your help," DCI Fish said.

"There's more to this than we've touched on," DC Owen said. "Nine people are dead and I don't believe they died just so some greedy blackmailer can get their hands on a hundred and four million."

"If the motivation behind it is financial gain," DS Skinner said. "Surely the drastic measures they used were overkill."

"Unless that was the whole point, Sarge," DC Stone said. "They knew we'd be more inclined to take them seriously with nine fatalities than we would if they'd only killed one islander."

"Perhaps," DS Skinner said. "But I agree with Katie – we've missed something important."

"Everyone who died bought products from only two shops," DC Owen said. "Freshlife supermarket and *Nature's Gifts*. That has to be significant."

"How?" DC Stone said. "We've got the women who run those shops here at the station, and nothing so far has incriminated them in any way."

"We can't ignore the fact that both women are linked to Len Hughes."

"Belinda North isn't," DC Stone argued.

"But she is," DC Owen said. "Albeit, indirectly. Belinda helped Janet Ingram through her problems at home. Janet's sister Vicky was raped and murdered by Hughes, and I know for a fact that there is a reason why Freshlife was targeted. All of this stems from what Len Hughes did in 2003, and I believe that's where our focus should lie."

"Did I just hear you mention Len Hughes?"

Everybody turned to look at O'Reilly in the doorway.

"Katie believes we need to take a much closer look at Len Hughes, sir," DS Skinner said.

"Katie is absolutely right," O'Reilly said. "As usual. While I was grabbing a cup of tea I received a disturbing phone call. The caller had been trying to get hold of me all week, but I've been ignoring unknown numbers, assuming they were journalists. Len Hughes is about to become a free man – the monster who sent shockwaves around the island sixteen years ago will be eligible for parole early next year."

"You're kidding?" DC Stone said.

"I'm not. And that's not the worst of it. I have it on good authority that the parole will be granted."

CHAPTER FIFTY

"How can that even be possible?"

DS Skinner was the first to find his voice after a lengthy silence inside the briefing room.

"He raped and murdered a fourteen-year-old girl," DC Stone added. "How can he be eligible for parole after only sixteen years?"

"We should have examined the details of the case," O'Reilly said. "We were all under the impression that Len Hughes was sent down for rape and murder. In essence, he was but he's always denied the murder charge."

"He was found at his place of residence with her body," DCI Fish said. "The girl had been strangled. Hughes was the only one inside the house, so how could he deny it?"

"The evidence against him was all circumstantial," O'Reilly said. "His DNA was all over the girl – there was no denying that, but as he never denied raping her, that was never in dispute. What was disputed was the evidence of her murder. If we disregard the rape for a moment and focus solely on the murder, nothing at the scene and nothing from the evidence on her body suggested that Hughes was responsible."

"This doesn't make sense," DS Skinner said. "Either he was convicted of rape and murder, or he wasn't."

"I don't know all the details," O'Reilly said. "But if I read between the lines it looks like there was some kind of deal in play. Hughes admitted to the rape, but not once did he take responsibility for the murder, and the evidence substantiated this. I get the impression that the people involved in the investigation at the time wanted a quick result – they wanted Hughes off the island, hence the clandestine deal. He was given a twenty-year stretch with the possibility of parole after sixteen years."

"And those sixteen years are up," DC Owen said.

"According to the man I spoke to," O'Reilly said. "Hughes is a model prisoner. He's kept his nose clean, and there is no reason for the parole board to deny him his early release."

"This is outrageous," DS Skinner said. "The man is a monster. Surely, he won't be allowed to come back to the island."

"He won't," O'Reilly said. "Mr Hughes is going to be on license for the rest of his life. He'll be confined to the UK, and he will never be allowed to travel abroad. He'll be added to the sex offenders register and he will be closely monitored. Basically, he'll be a free man, but his freedom will be extremely limited."

"How exactly did you come by this information, Liam?" DCI Fish asked.

"An old Gardai colleague of mine," O'Reilly said. "Frank Murphy is his name, and I worked alongside him for a while back in the day. He left the guards and took a position at Belmarsh."

"That's where Len Hughes was sent," DC Stone said.

"Correct."

"What do we do with this information?" DCI Fish said.

"We look more closely at the details surrounding the investigation in 2003," O'Reilly said. "Something feels terribly wrong about it. And then I suggest we ask ourselves if the impending release of Len Hughes is connected to the recent events on the island. I can't be the only one who thinks that something stinks about the timing."

"What are you implying, Liam?" DCI Fish said.

"It's some coincidence, don't you think?" O'Reilly said. "Everything that's happened this week has its roots in what Len Hughes did over a decade and a half ago, and now the monster just happens to be eligible for parole."

"What about the two women in custody?" DC Stone said.

"Firstly, Andy," O'Reilly said. "They're not in custody. Neither of them was arrested and secondly, I suggest we let them get on their way. Belinda North and Janet North are not involved in this."

"We can't discount the fact that everyone who died bought products from their places of work," DS Skinner said.

"We can, and we will. I could be wrong, but I believe that those women were mere pawns in an elaborate chess game."

"Who are the players in this game of chess?" DCI Fish said.

"We are, Tom," O'Reilly said. "And at the other end of the board is a monster called Len Hughes. I think he's been planning this for a very long time."

"There are some major flaws in that theory, sir," DS Skinner said.

"I appreciate that, but we still need to consider it. Len Hughes gets banged up sixteen years ago. He's well aware of the terms of his incarceration and he knows if he's to stand any chance of an early release he needs to keep out of trouble. So, he does precisely that. He bides his time inside, waiting for the fateful day when he's eligible for a parole hearing. His conduct inside all but guarantees his release."

"Surely the crime he was convicted of should have put paid to an early release," DC Stone put forward.

"Twenty years ago, that probably would have applied, Andy," O'Reilly said. "But times have changed, and the justice system has changed with it. Back then it was all about punishment but now the penal system is more focused on rehabilitation. The politicians who call the shots do not want a scumbag locked up forever. They've basically created a revolving door system – the bastards commit their crime, they do their time and if they smile and wave for long enough while they're at it, they're deemed to be rehabilitated and fit to rejoin society. When they get out, they commit crime again and so the cycle begins once more."

"That's a rather cynical attitude, Liam," DCI Fish said.

"And it's one that's not going to change," O'Reilly said. "Men like Len Hughes will never change. They're predators through and through, and no amount of so-called rehabilitation will fix them."

"We cannot re-open the case against Len Hughes," DCI Fish pointed out. "He was tried and convicted in accordance with the guidelines set out in law. As far as the judicial system is concerned, what's done is done and it cannot be undone."

"I'm not suggesting we undo anything, Tom," O'Reilly said. "But there were flaws in the way his crimes were investigated and there's something they overlooked."

"And you plan to find out what was missed after all this time?"

"Not me, Tom," O'Reilly said. "Katie and I are going to be otherwise engaged for a while. I expect you to have found something by the time we get back."

"Have I missed something?" DCI Fish said.

"No," O'Reilly said. "I haven't told you this yet. Katie and I are taking a trip over the Channel."

"We are?" DC Owen said.

"You're going to love Frank Murphy, Katie," O'Reilly said. "He hates criminals, and he hates the English even more. Lord knows why he took a job at a prison in London."

CHAPTER FIFTY ONE

"How did you manage to get a visit with Len Hughes arranged so quickly, sir?" DC Owen asked O'Reilly the following morning.
They were about to check in for their 08:30 flight from Guernsey to London Gatwick. DCI Fish had been reluctant to authorise it, but O'Reilly hadn't taken no for an answer. He knew there was a connection between the recent sickness and death on the island and the upcoming parole of Len Hughes. And when O'Reilly had explained that Hughes was more than happy to speak to them, DCI Fish agreed that it could be a productive use of Island Police resources.

"It wasn't difficult, Katie," O'Reilly said. "Contrary to popular belief a police officer doesn't actually need a visitation order to be able to speak to an inmate. It helped that I have an old friend who happens to be a supervising officer at Belmarsh. It's one rank down from custodial manager and Frank has a lot of sway there."
"Doesn't the inmate have a say in the matter?"
"A convict is under no obligation to say anything during the interview," O'Reilly said. "But they can't refuse a visit."
"And Len Hughes doesn't seem to have a problem with it," DC Owen said.
"That makes me wonder what he's planning. Because the bastard is planning something – you mark my words."

The conversation was cut short by an angry voice behind them.
"Would you mind moving along a bit?"
O'Reilly turned around to face the elderly man in the queue.
"The desk is free," he said. "You're holding up the line."
"You're going to make us miss the flight," the woman accompanying the man said.

"My sincere apologies," O'Reilly said. "Are you flying over for anything special?"

"That's none of your business, mister," the old man said.

"Quite right," O'Reilly agreed. "This is the flight to Belfast, isn't it?"

"London," the man corrected. "Can't you read?"

O'Reilly nodded. "That'll do. I have unfinished business in London."

He said this in his most menacing Northern Irish accent. He gave the man his finest lunatic smile and shuffled towards the check-in desk. The elderly couple stayed well back.

"You're terrible, sir," DC Owen said as they made their way up the stairs onto the plane. "You scared the life out of that elderly couple."

"I did no such thing," O'Reilly said. "And that bloke was downright rude. When was the last time you were in England?"

"Not since I was a kid. My mum's brother lives in Southampton, and we sometimes used to spend a few weeks there in the summer holidays."

"The flight to Gatwick is just over an hour, and I must admit I have no idea how we're going to get to Belmarsh after that."

"I did some research," DC Owen said. "There's a train that goes all the way to London Bridge. From there it's another two trains to the prison. It takes just over an hour. What time are they expecting us?"

"11.30," O'Reilly said. "Loads of time. The return flight is not until six this evening."

"I hope we come away with some answers."

"I've got a feeling that we will."

As a rule, O'Reilly had never had a problem with air travel. Flying wasn't particularly unpleasant – what he hated was the rigmarole that went with it. He remembered a time when getting on an aeroplane was all part of the fun of a holiday, but those days were long gone. Now, it seemed that the companies that operated the airlines wanted nothing more than to jam the paying customers onto their aircraft and spit them out at the other end as quickly as possible, throwing in a hefty dose of rules and regulations for good measure along the way.

They were in the air, travelling west fifteen minutes later. The seatbelt signs stayed on, and O'Reilly wondered why this was. Perhaps it was to prevent passengers with weak bladders from using the toilet during the hour-long flight. It made sense – there would be less work to do after the plane landed.

"I don't suppose they're going to give us a meal," he said.

DC Owen laughed. "By the time we reach cruising altitude we'll be ready to begin the descent into London."

"I forgot to eat breakfast this morning."

"I'm sure we'll be able to find somewhere to get something to eat when we land."

"I hope so. My stomach is already growling at me."

"What's the plan when we're face to face with Len Hughes?" DC Owen said.

"I want to know what he's up to," O'Reilly said. "His reaction to the visit was a curious one. According to Frank Murphy it was as if he was expecting it, and that makes me suspicious."

"Do you really think he was involved in the recent poisonings on the island?"

"I've asked Frank to compile a list of everyone who's been to visit him in the past few years, and we'll also be allowed to see his correspondence history. Inmates are not allowed unsupervised Internet access. Mobile phones are prohibited, but we can't discount him having one. Security in somewhere like Belmarsh is strict, but it's not unheard of for someone to smuggle in a phone for an inmate."

A woman's voice announced that they were beginning their descent into London Gatwick and O'Reilly's hope of being offered something to fill the gap in his belly vanished in an instant. He would buy something at the airport. He rubbed his eyes and when he opened them, he sensed that he was being observed. He looked around and realised that two pairs of eyes were pointing in his direction. The elderly couple from the queue at Guernsey airport were taking a keen interest in him. O'Reilly grinned and waved. It seemed to have the desired effect. The man and woman looked away.

"Do you think the team have unearthed anything from the case files from 2003?" DC Owen said.

"I do," O'Reilly said. "I have every confidence in them. There will be something in those files that will help us to crack this one."

CHAPTER FIFTY TWO

"There's nothing here."

DC Stone was craving a cigarette. In his effort to try to quit, he'd neglected to smoke one when he got up that morning and he was regretting it. He was feeling irritated, and he couldn't concentrate on the pages and pages of information they were sifting through. He explained his predicament to DS Skinner, and he was informed he had ten minutes. He didn't have to be told twice – ten minutes would be long enough to smoke two cigarettes in quick succession in the car park.

"According to the witness statement," DCI Fish said. "Kelly Vole was standing by the school gates when she saw a man matching Len Hughes' description get out of his vehicle and drag Vicky Ingram inside. Classes had ended an hour earlier, but Kelly and Vicky stayed behind to participate in sports. Kelly was in the netball team and Vicky was a keen cross-country runner. The girls had planned on walking home together."

"I wonder if Len Hughes was aware of Vicky's extra-curricular activities," DS Skinner said.

"I believe he was. Kelly tried to help. She ran over to the car, but it pulled away before she got there. She managed to get the registration number, and she raced to the office to raise the alarm."

"She sounds like a smart girl," DS Skinner said.

"The admin staff were still on duty," DCI Fish said. "And the police were called."

"It was another hour before the police arrived at Len Hughes' address," DS Skinner said. "And this is where the events are a bit hazy. And when I see who the first responders were, I can understand it. PC Jack Powers was a bit of a maverick. He had the potential to have grown into a good officer, but he could be impulsive. According to PC Powers the vehicle was parked in the driveway but the gate in front of the property was closed. Instead of calling it in and waiting for further instructions PC Powers took it upon himself to climb over the gate and enter the house without back-up. He found Len Hughes in one of the bedrooms upstairs. Vicky Ingram was on the bed and after checking for signs of life and finding none, PC Powers restrained Len Hughes and only then did he call it in."

"The more I read of the initial first responder incident report," DCI Fish said. "The more I see that protocol was disregarded in so many ways. PC Powers not only entered the property without back-up in place, he forgot everything he'd ever learned about preserving a crime scene. Instead of waiting for instructions he went in like a bull in a China shop."

"He transferred to London soon afterwards," DS Skinner remembered.

"Poor London. There really isn't much here to help us. Len Hughes was arrested, and Vicky Ingram's body was removed from the property six hours later. Forensics found no indication that a struggle took place, and it was concluded that Vicky was strangled where she was found, and she didn't put up much of a fight while she was being murdered."

DC Stone came back in.

"Katie and the DI have landed in London. Katie just messaged me. They're due to speak to Len Hughes at half-eleven."

"I don't know what we're supposed to find in these reports," DS Skinner said. "The initial call-out was a bit of a botch-up but I can't see how PC Power's actions were in any way detrimental to the investigation as a whole. It appears to me that it was a cut and dry case. Hughes was seen abducting his victim and she was found dead at his house soon afterwards."

"He denied playing any part in her murder," DC Stone said.

"And this was supported by the evidence," DS Skinner said. "The postmortem determined cause of death to be asphyxiation. Vicky was strangled but there was nothing to suggest that Len Hughes was the person who strangled her."

"Do we know if the investigative team considered the theory that there was another person there that day?" DCI Fish said. "An unknown?"

"That's the part that's bothering me, sir," DS Skinner said. "All the evidence pointed in that direction, but nothing was ever followed up. As far as everyone was concerned, they had the guilty party and even though Hughes vehemently denied killing the girl, it never went any further."

"It was a case of: Hughes raped her," DCI Fish said. "He was found next to her dead body, ergo he must have killed her."

"Case closed," DS Skinner said.

"Hughes is tried, convicted and shipped off to England," DC Stone said. "He's no longer Guernsey's problem."

"Why is O'Reilly so convinced that what happened that day is connected to the recent murders on the island?" DCI Fish said. "The investigation was carried out in a rather slapdash manner, but there's nothing in the case files that can be linked to the poisonings."

"The DI is adamant that there is, sir," DC Stone said. "But nothing has caught my attention yet."

"The case went to trial just three weeks after Mr Hughes was arrested," DCI Fish said. "Which in itself is unusual."

"It normally takes months," DS Skinner said. "If not years for a murder investigation to reach that stage. Somebody wanted this to go away, didn't they? They wanted this to disappear very quickly."

"I'm still not buying it," DS Stone said. "It's all very well suggesting that some kind of cover-up occurred, but in the end, Len Hughes was sent down for a very long time. And even when he does get his parole, he's never really going to be free. He'll be monitored for the rest of his life. His freedom disappeared forever the day he was found next to the dead body of the girl he raped."

"Something is terribly wrong about the way the investigation was conducted," DCI Fish said. "But I fail to see how it has any bearing on the recent events on the island."

"Do we keep on looking through the files?" DC Stone said.

"We do," DS Skinner said. "If O'Reilly thinks there's something there, I do too. We just haven't found it yet."

CHAPTER FIFTY THREE

HM Prison Belmarsh wasn't quite what O'Reilly had anticipated. He'd heard about the prison – its reputation was unparallelled, but when the taxi dropped them off outside, the overall experience was somewhat anticlimactic. It didn't help that it was a glorious day. There wasn't a cloud in the sky and the sun beating down on the yellow brick of the prison that had housed some of the country's most notorious criminals, lent it a rather innocuous look. O'Reilly thought he could be in the car park of a shopping mall. Only the high barbed wire fence reaching out over the top of the building gave any hint of the kind of monsters that were confined within.

"Have you been here before?" DC Owen said.
"I've had no reason to, Katie," O'Reilly said. "It's not what I was expecting at all."
"Me neither. I imagined armed guards on observation posts. I thought there would at least be the sounds of gunshots and screams in the air. This could be any old warehouse. I'm disappointed."
"Don't let the exterior fool you," O'Reilly said. "There are some nasty bastards in there."
"Ronnie Biggs was imprisoned here," DC Owen said. "As was Charles Bronson. And not to mention Jeffrey Archer."
"He's got to be the worst of the lot," O'Reilly said. "Pompous upper-class twit. He should have been banged up for longer. I forget why he was even imprisoned. Probably for being a shite writer."
DC Owen laughed. "He was jailed for perjury, sir. I don't think there are any laws against being a bad author."
"There damn well should be. My Mary used to read the aristocratic tosspot's drivel, and I couldn't for the life of me understand why."

The procedure for getting inside Belmarsh was a lengthy one. After showing their IDs to a guard by the first security point and explaining the nature of their visit, they were given visitor badges and directed to the next security checkpoint. Here, they were relieved of their mobile phones and searched for anything not allowed inside. O'Reilly thought this was rather unnecessary when they were made to run the gauntlet of a further two security checks, one of which consisted of a scanner not unlike the ones found in airports.

"I fail to see how anyone can smuggle a mobile phone in here," DC Owen said. "We didn't have to go through such rigorous checks at the airport."
"There are plenty of ways to skin a cat, Katie," O'Reilly said. "A place like this has hundreds of people in its employ. You've got cleaners and kitchen staff, not to mention the guards and any one of them could get friendly with an inmate and break the rules for them. We're early. Time to introduce you to Frank Murphy. You'll have to excuse his gruff exterior – he doesn't like people very much."
"He sounds like someone I know."

One of the prison officers escorted them to the office that Frank Murphy shared with the custodial manager. They were informed that the custodial manager was in a meeting, but Frank was expecting them. O'Reilly knocked on the door, and they went into the office.

Frank Murphy hadn't changed much since O'Reilly last saw him. He was a tall, skinny man with thinning hair. His eyes were steel grey, and O'Reilly had forgotten how unnerving his stare was. He closed the door, and Frank told him and DC Owen to take a seat.
"No hug?" O'Reilly said.
"It's good to see you again, Liam," Frank said.
"Likewise. This is my colleague, Katie Owen."
"English?"

"Guernsey," DC Owen said.

Frank nodded.

"What can you tell us about Hughes?" O'Reilly said.

"The officers like him," Frank said. "Despite what he's in for. Sixteen years and he hasn't stepped out of line once. He does his work, eats his food and stays away from trouble. He's what the board would call a model prisoner."

"But you don't share that opinion?" DC Owen said.

"You're astute."

"She's the finest asset the Island Police has at its disposal," O'Reilly said.

"You don't like Len Hughes, do you?"

"No," Frank said. "I don't like him, and I don't trust him. I may not be in the ranks of the Gardai anymore, but I still have the nose of a guard. Hughes has a hidden agenda. He's not what he appears to be."

"He was sent here before you arrived, wasn't he?" O'Reilly said.

"He'd already served half his time by the time I transferred here," Frank said.

"Can I ask why you did that? I thought you hated the English."

"My daughter married one of the bastards. That's how I ended up here. Janice left me shortly after Valerie moved here with her bastard Englishman and I thought the change would do me good."

"I'm sorry about your marriage," O'Reilly said.

"I'm not. Now, what else do you need to know?"

"Does Hughes have many visitors?" DC Owen asked.

"Not really. I made that list you asked for."

He reached across the desk and retrieved a file. He handed it to O'Reilly.

"What about phone calls?" O'Reilly said.

"The list of approved contacts is on there too." Frank tapped the file.

"Are the calls monitored?" DC Owen said.

Frank nodded. "All of them with the exception of the calls to his lawyer. We're not allowed to listen in on them."

"Grand," O'Reilly said. "Is there anything else you think we should know before we speak to the man?"

"Don't fall for his charm," Frank said.

"I'm sure that won't be a problem."

"You don't know the bastard. He'll draw you in and nine out of ten people will fall for it. He'll only tell you things he thinks you want to hear, and he is a master manipulator. I'm no shrink, but I reckon if we were to get him evaluated, he'd be diagnosed as some kind of psychopath. He's definitely a sociopath with plenty of narcissistic tendencies."

"And you claim not to be a shrink?" O'Reilly said. "Thanks for the head's-up."

Frank stood up and extended his hand. "It's good to see you again, Liam."

O'Reilly shook the hand. "You too, Frank."

"And it's nice to meet you, Katie Owen," Frank added.

He didn't offer his hand.

"Likewise," DC Owen said.

"I've arranged for you to be alone in the visiting room with Hughes," Frank said. "I thought that would suit you better. There'll be an officer outside the door, but you'll have Hughes to yourself for an hour."

O'Reilly understood what he meant by this immediately.

"Thanks, Frank, I appreciate it."

CHAPTER FIFTY FOUR

O'Reilly had seen photographs of Len Hughes but the man waiting for them in the visiting room looked like none of them. The successful businessman was dressed in a white T-shirt and a pair of blue jeans. His once thick head of black hair was receding and grey at the temples. His face looked gaunt and pale. He looked like he hadn't seen the sun for a very long time. His brown eyes were so dark they were almost black and O'Reilly thought he looked every inch the monster he was.

"I trust you had a good trip," Len said. "I'm not allowed any contact, so you'll have to forgive me if I don't stand up and shake hands."
O'Reilly sat down on one of the chairs that had been provided. DC Owen sat next to him.
"O'Reilly?" Len said. "Irish?"
"Do you know why we're here?" O'Reilly said.
"I don't. But I imagine you're going to tell me."
"What can you tell us about the sixteenth of March 2003?" O'Reilly said.
"Nothing you don't already know, I imagine."
"I'll be the judge of that. You abducted Vicky Ingram from outside her school, and you took her home and raped and murdered her."
Len fixed his eyes on O'Reilly's and shook his head slowly. "Hold on there. I'll put my hands up to the rape. I did that, yes but murder? I didn't kill that girl."
"So you kept saying all those years ago. But you also didn't explain how a teenage girl ended up dead in your bedroom."
"I didn't want to talk about it."
"You're going to have to do better than that," DC Owen said.
Len grinned at her. "It speaks. You have the most unusual eyes, my dear. Has anyone ever told you that?"

"Talk us through what happened that day," O'Reilly said.

"I'd been watching her for a while," Len said. "Vicky, I mean. They say you covet what you see every day, don't they? She used to walk past my house twice a day. She shouldn't have done that. In that short skirt of hers. Some might say she got exactly what she deserved. What do you have to say about that?"

"Go on," O'Reilly said.

"I watched and waited, and I took the opportunity that arose. She was exquisite."

"You threw her into the back of your car, and you took her home and violated her," O'Reilly said. "It wasn't the first time you'd committed rape, was it?"

"You've spoken to Amy."

"She's an incredible woman. What you did to her didn't break her. She rose above it and she's living a good life despite you."

"I did not rape her," Len said. "Your legal system proved that."

"We all know what happened, Mr Hughes."

"What is it you want?" Len said. "You're asking questions you already know the answers to. Why are you really here?"

"You were a successful businessman before you got caught with a dead girl in your bedroom."

"True," Len said.

"What is it you did for a living?" DC Owen said.

"I was a broker. Finance."

"And you did alright out of it?" O'Reilly said.

Len laughed and O'Reilly wasn't expecting it.

"Is something amusing you, Mr Hughes?"

Len rubbed his fingers over an imaginary beard on his chin.

"Did I do alright? Let me see – before I was sent to this hell hole, I was making around six and a half bar a year, on average."

"Six and a half million?" DC Owen said.

"That's usually what a *bar* represents, darling."

"I'm not your darling."

Len held his hands up in apology. "Take it easy."

"What happened to your assets when you were incarcerated?" O'Reilly said.

"Is this another question where you already know the answer?"

"No, it's not. According to the terms of your incarceration you'll be eligible for parole in a few months. You'll be prohibited from setting foot on Guernsey ever again, and you'll be confined to the borders of the UK. I presume your assets will be there waiting for you."

"You presume wrong, Inspector."

"Detective Inspector," O'Reilly corrected. "There's a big difference. Well?"

"Contrary to what you think," Len said. "This story does not have a happy ending for Len Hughes. Upon my inevitable release, I'll have to start over again. None of my previous investors will touch me with a bargepole, and I'll have to consider alternative employment."

"What happened to your money?" DC Owen said.

"Ask my ex-wife."

"You're divorced?" O'Reilly said.

"I'd been in here for less than a week when her lawyer delivered the papers. So much for until death do us part."

"You can't really blame her, can you?" O'Reilly said. "I imagine when she discovered she was married to a sexual predator – a perverted monster, it came as a bit of a shock. Did she take you to the cleaners in the divorce?"

"More or less."

"That's the best news I've heard since I set foot in here. There is a bit of justice after all."

"What is it you want from me, O'Reilly?" Len said. "I've served my time – I've taken my punishment, and I'm ready to make a fresh start. You're never going to find out what really happened that day. You know that don't you?"

"I have a bad habit of getting to the truth eventually," O'Reilly said.

"I did not kill Vicky Ingram," Len said. "And you're never going to find out who did."

"But you are admitting there was someone else there that day?" DC Owen said.

Len's smile was reptilian, and the curl of his lips made DC Owen look away. "I do believe we're finished here."

"Callum sends his regards, by the way," O'Reilly said.

The change in Len Hughes' face was subtle, but O'Reilly noticed it.

"He's a good man," O'Reilly added. "I have a lot of respect for him."

"Good for you," Len said.

"Oh, I almost forgot. Callum is no longer a police officer."

"I'm sorry to hear that."

"A number of secrets that were supposed to have been kept buried have risen to the surface. It's not going to end well for DCO Dove."

"Why are you telling me this?"

"I'm just making conversation," O'Reilly said. "I think we're done talking."

He stood up and Len Hughes did the same.

"You have no idea what I've gone through in here," Len said.

"I can imagine it can't have been easy," O'Reilly said.

"This conversation isn't being recorded, is it?"

"We're not allowed. It's not a formal interview."

"If I tell you something, it won't go any further, will it?"

"Unfortunately, not," O'Reilly said.

Len leaned closer and O'Reilly wondered if he was going to whisper in his ear.

He didn't.

"You didn't hear this from me," Len said.

"Go on," O'Reilly said.

"Your top lip is bleeding," Len said.

This time his laughter was loud and somewhat exaggerated. He grinned at O'Reilly and doffed an imaginary cap.

"I got you there, didn't I?"

"Katie," O'Reilly said to DC Owen. "Could you ask the officer outside if there's any tea on the go? I could really do with a cup."

"Will do, sir," DC Owen said.

She got up and left the room. She closed the door behind her and O'Reilly could hear muffled voices in the corridor.

"The conversation isn't being recorded," O'Reilly said. "And that's for my benefit as well as yours. This is for Amy Winter."

He couldn't use his gammy leg but the aim with his left leg surprised him. He hit Len Hughes dead centre between the legs, and the effect was instant. Len doubled up and put his hands on the sensitive parts between his legs. He looked up at O'Reilly. His eyes were watering, but the defiant grin was still on his face.

He straightened up and removed his hands from his privates.

"I raped Vicky Ingram twice."

The O'Reilly manoeuvre was repeated but this time there was much more force in it. Len Hughes gasped, and O'Reilly was worried he was going to pass out.

"I would have gone for a hat trick if I wasn't interrupted," he managed.

O'Reilly was tempted to give him a third kick, but he decided he'd pushed his luck too far already.

"I'll see myself out," he said. "I'd get those looked at if I were you."

"You're going to read about me," Len said.

His dead eyes were wide, and his breathing was rapid.

"The Len Hughes story is far from over."

"You can say that again," O'Reilly said. "I would really recommend getting some medical attention for those shrivelled up balls of yours. You can consider yourself lucky I wasn't able to use my other leg."

CHAPTER FIFTY FIVE

O'Reilly was finishing off his third sandwich in a café around the corner from the prison when his phone started to ring. The screen told him it was DS Skinner.
"Will, how are things going?"
"Where are you, sir?" DS Skinner said.
"Some greasy spoon near Belmarsh," O'Reilly said. "We're flying back in a few hours."
"You need to talk to a PC Jack Powers. He was the first on the scene at the Vicky Ingram murder."
"Why couldn't you have told me this when we got back to the island?"
"Because Jack isn't on the island anymore, sir," DS Skinner said. "He transferred to London not long after Vicky's murder. He's working for the Met now out in Dagenham."
"Where the devil is Dagenham?" O'Reilly said.
"Less than five miles from where you are now. I'll forward his details."
"What has this PC Powers got to do with the investigation?"
"I've not long got off the phone with him," DS Skinner said. "He knows something about what happened that day – something that was never brought up during the course of the investigation, and he's willing to talk about it now."

After a brief phone call to PC Powers O'Reilly realised that they had a problem. PC Powers couldn't get away until half-four. That meant they would miss the return flight to Guernsey, and a subsequent phone call resulted in a further problem. There were no more flights to the island tonight and they would have to return in the morning. O'Reilly decided that it couldn't be helped. He would book a couple of rooms in a hotel, and they would spend the night in London.

They had a couple of hours to kill before the appointment with PC Powers, so O'Reilly ordered another sandwich and a pot of tea.

"I really don't know where you put it, sir," DC Owen said.

"I need to make up for what I failed to eat earlier, Katie."

"What did you make of Len Hughes?"

"Before or after I used the O'Reilly manoeuvre on him?"

"You didn't?" DC Owen said.

"I certainly did," O'Reilly said. "Twice, and I hit two bullseyes. He got under my skin in that visiting room."

"He knows exactly who else was there that day, doesn't he?"

"He does," O'Reilly said. "And he's got something up his sleeve."

"Do you still think he was involved in the poisonings?"

"I'm certain of it, but I don't know what form that involvement takes. There is no possible way for him to orchestrate something like that from Belmarsh. A quick look at his visits over the years didn't sound any warning bells and his list of approved contacts is equally silent. His phone calls are monitored, so he wouldn't be able to give out instructions that way. He's involved but I'm finding it hard to see how he did it."

The sandwich and tea arrived, and O'Reilly tucked in.

"Do you want some?" he asked DC Owen.

"I'm full," she said. "What about his lawyer?"

"Whose lawyer?"

"Len Hughes can't make unmonitored phone calls," DC Owen said. "Apart from the ones to his lawyer. Communication between a lawyer and a client is bound by lawyer-client privilege and prisons are not allowed access to it."

"You can't think his lawyer is involved in this?"

"It's worth considering. Do we know how often he spoke to his legal representative?"

"It'll be easy enough to find out," O'Reilly said. "And if there was any communication between them in the weeks before the poisoning started, we'll have something to look into."

He took a sip of tea and picked up his phone. He dialled the number and Frank Murphy answered straight away.

"Sorry to bother you again," O'Reilly said. "But can you find out when Len Hughes and his lawyer spoke to each other recently – specifically in the past few weeks or so?"

"Hold on."

The line remained silent for quite some time.

"Are you still there?" Frank said eventually.

"Still here," O'Reilly said.

"According to the records, Len Hughes spoke to his lawyer nine times in the last month."

"What about before then?" O'Reilly said.

"The communication wasn't as frequent, but that's not particularly unusual. With his parole hearing coming up it's understandable that he'd be in contact with his lawyer more often."

"Do you have the name of the lawyer?"

"Downing," Frank said. "Peter Downing. Works for a firm called DDR Legal Services."

"Can you send me the call log?"

"Not without a warrant, Liam," Frank said. "You know that."

"Come on, Frank," O'Reilly said. "For old times' sake."

Frank sighed. "OK, but I'm not doing it officially. I'll take a photo and forward it to you. But this never happened, understood?"

"It never happened. Thank you."

He ended the call and shortly afterwards his phone beeped. He tapped the screen and handed the phone to DC Owen.

"Could you send this to Will for me?"

"Of course."

She composed a short message and forwarded the photo of the call log to DS Skinner. She handed the phone back.

"I added a bit of context. It shouldn't be difficult to track down this Peter Downing."

O'Reilly had just paid the bill when his phone started to ring again.

"That was quick," he said to DS Skinner.

"We've got a problem, sir."

"When don't we have problems. Go on."

"DDR Legal Services don't exist."

"Are you sure?"

"Positive, sir," DS Skinner said. "I couldn't find any legal firm called DDR, and I also couldn't track down any lawyers called Peter Downing."

"Have you tried phoning the number?" O'Reilly said.

"Not yet."

"Don't worry about it," O'Reilly said. "I'll give it a ring."

It was a mobile number, and it looked like a Guernsey one.

"How do I make it so they don't know who's calling?" O'Reilly asked DC Owen.

She took the phone, changed the settings and handed it back.

"It's ringing," O'Reilly said.

The ringing stopped and then there was silence. O'Reilly waited. After a few seconds he heard what sounded like someone clearing their throat. It was a familiar sound. O'Reilly could feel his stomach heating up and his right fist had clenched without him realising it. He waited a moment before he spoke.

"Good afternoon, sir."

The persistent drone told him the person on the other end of the line had hung up.

CHAPTER FIFTY SIX

PC Powers had arranged to meet them at another greasy spoon in the centre of Dagenham. For once, O'Reilly had no inclination to order any food. He settled on a cup of tea and thanked PC Powers for agreeing to talk to them. Jack Powers was a stocky man with eyes that were too close together. O'Reilly wondered if this was why he was unable to maintain eye contact for more than a couple of seconds. His pale blue eyes darted back and forth permanently.

O'Reilly was still finding it difficult to comprehend how a legal firm that didn't exist could manage to fool an establishment like Belmarsh prison. He assumed they would have measures in place to prevent that from happening. He made a mental note to bring it up with Frank Murphy when he had a chance. This should never have been allowed to happen. More concerning was the man who'd answered the phone earlier. O'Reilly didn't know the exact significance of it yet, but he had a good idea, and it made him sick to the stomach. He would deal with that later too.

"You were in the Island Police in 2003," O'Reilly got straight down to business.

"I joined up right after university," Jack said. "It was all I ever wanted to do."

"Tell us about the day of the sixteenth of March."

"We got the call about half-four in the afternoon," Jack said. "I was in the patrol car with PC Ben Grange, and we were only half a mile away from Len Hughes' house."

"What was the nature of the call-out?" DC Owen said.

"We were informed that a girl had been abducted from outside her school. A witness got the registration number, and the car was registered to Hughes."

"Were you the only ones who were sent out?" O'Reilly said.

"We were the closest," Jack said. "We were told to stand by and wait for reinforcements."

"But you didn't do that, did you?" O'Reilly said.

"I made a mistake," Jack said. "But I would do it again in a heartbeat if I was faced with something similar. Ben advised against it, but I couldn't stand by when a young girl's life was in danger."

"It was a difficult call to make," DC Owen said.

"The car was in the driveway," Jack carried on. "But the gates were locked. I climbed over and went inside the house. I found Vicky in one of the bedrooms upstairs. I checked for a pulse, but she was already dead."

"Where was Len Hughes?" O'Reilly said.

"Standing there like nothing had happened," Jack said. "I had to use every ounce of self-restraint to keep myself from killing the bastard right there and then. I couldn't look at the smug grin on his face – it would have sent me over the edge. I told him to get on the floor, I cuffed him and called it in. I sometimes wonder if maybe I'd acted a bit quicker, Vicky would still be alive."

"It wasn't your fault," DC Owen said.

"Backup arrived and I was practically dragged out of the house. I lost it a bit, and I couldn't bring myself to leave her there."

"My DS told me you had something to tell us about that day," O'Reilly said. "Something that wasn't brought up during the course of the investigation."

Jack nodded. "I only thought about it afterwards, when Hughes insisted that he didn't kill Vicky. At first, we all thought he was lying – he was trying to get a reduced sentence, but I soon realised that he could have been telling the truth."

"Why is that?"

"Because I did see someone else there that day," Jack said.

"You saw someone inside the house?" DC Owen said.

Jack shook his head. "Outside, driving away from the property. It was just as we arrived, and I didn't give it much thought at the time. I was more concerned about getting to Vicky, but afterwards I wondered if it was important."

"Did you get the registration number of this vehicle?" DC Owen said.

"No, but I recognised it. It wasn't a car you'd easily forget."

"Who was driving, Jack?" O'Reilly said. "This is incredibly important."

"It was the car belonging to a senior officer in the Island Police."

A waiter approached the table and asked them if they wanted anything else. O'Reilly replied in the negative.

"What did you do with this information?" he asked Jack.

"I didn't know what to do with it. I wondered if I was mistaken. Everything happened so fast, and I knew that I couldn't go around making accusations without being absolutely certain."

"What did you do?"

"I approached the officer in private," Jack said. "I explained to him what I thought I'd seen, and I was told to forget about it."

"You were ordered to disregard what you'd seen?" DC Owen said.

"I didn't have much choice. And I wasn't a hundred percent certain it was actually his car."

"What happened after that?" O'Reilly said.

"I was given a bollocking for my conduct that day, and I took it on the chin. I acted impulsively and I was out of order. I should have waited for further instructions, but I couldn't."

"Is that the reason why you transferred to the Met?" DC Owen said.

"One of them," Jack said. "I was skating on thin ice as it was, and it became unpleasant just going to work. A position in the Met came up and I applied. I've always liked London, and I've been here ever since."

"You were never promoted?" O'Reilly said.

"I'm not interested in rising through the ranks," Jack said. "I like being a PC and I'll be a PC the day I retire."

"You're not telling us everything," O'Reilly said. "You didn't just up and leave the island because you'd always been a fan of London. What is it you've left out?"

Jack didn't answer straight away. He ran a finger over the rim of his teacup and nodded.

"I was threatened. It was a veiled threat, but I knew what was being implied."

"I think I can guess the rest," O'Reilly said. "The senior officer you saw driving away from the scene of a murder made you an offer you couldn't refuse."

"Something like that," Jack said. "My time in the Island Police would have been very short-lived if I'd stuck around. I took the job in London, and I've never been back to the island since."

CHAPTER FIFTY SEVEN

O'Reilly was not a happy Irishman. After a lengthy discussion with the officious man at the booking desk at Gatwick airport he admitted defeat and resigned himself to the brutal reality that meant the old saying *the customer is always right* no longer applied. He'd explained his predicament with the return flight and was told in no uncertain terms that a refund would not be forthcoming. The flight had already left, and the seats that he and DC Owen were supposed to be sitting in had been sold to someone else. He would have to book a flight for tomorrow morning, and he would have to pay the full price for it.

"That man back there is what's known as a prize dickhead, Katie," he said.

"That's how it is these days," she said.

"It's not like they're out of pocket. They sold our fekkin seats to someone else."

"Where are we going to stay tonight?" DC Owen changed the subject.

"PC Powers advised me to check into a hotel close to the airport," O'Reilly said. "The flight leaves at eight, and he warned me about the morning traffic in London. There's a Premier Inn within walking distance from here. I'll book us a couple of rooms there. I hope they've got a good restaurant."

The Premier Inn was definitely not within walking distance, as the advert promised, but there was a transfer bus from the airport that ran every thirty minutes. O'Reilly and DC Owen got off outside the hotel and went inside. O'Reilly managed to get them adjoining rooms and after getting the electronic keys from reception they got in the elevator and O'Reilly pressed the button for the fifth floor. He needed a shower to wash off the London grime. He arranged with DC Owen to meet downstairs in the restaurant at seven.

After gaining access to his room on the third attempt O'Reilly cursed modern technology.

"What is wrong with a normal damn key?" he asked nobody in particular. He took in the room. It was nothing special, but it would do. The large windows offered a view of the airport a couple of miles away. Planes were taking off and landing and O'Reilly watched them for a while. He'd always been fascinated by aeroplanes. He still couldn't comprehend how something so huge was able to stay up in the air for so long.

He took a long shower and put on some clean clothes. He glanced at the contents of the mini bar but resisted the urge to crack open one of the miniature bottles of whiskey. He knew how much hotels usually charged for the drinks in the room, and he didn't think the Island Police budget would stretch to it. He'd already abused it by missing the original flight. He picked up the key card and went downstairs to meet DC Owen in the restaurant.

She was already seated when he went in. Her hair was still wet from her shower, and she looked a lot more refreshed than O'Reilly felt.

"I think I might have found something, sir," she said.

"Can I at least sit down first?" O'Reilly said. "And perhaps order something to drink."

"Sorry. This place is quite nice."

"Airport hotels are all the same. The waitress is coming over."

There wasn't much on offer as far as beer was concerned unless you were partial to lager. O'Reilly wasn't, so he ordered an IPA beer for himself and DC Owen. It took less than a minute for the drinks to arrive at the table.

O'Reilly took a sip and smiled. It was good beer.

"Right," he said. "What's on your mind, Katie?"

"It came to me in the shower," she said. "I like to test my brain while I'm showering, and I often do maths problems and word games in my head. It helps me to unwind."

"You're a peculiar young woman, Katie Owen. I like to sing songs from the old country, but whatever floats your boat I suppose."

"I got to thinking about the odd amount the poisoners are demanding," DC Owen said. "And I think I've figured out where the amount comes from."

"It is a strange sum to ask for," O'Reilly said. "Why not just ask for a hundred million?"

"After a bit of mental arithmetic, it came to me. Sixteen times six and a half million is a hundred and four million."

"Am I being a bit thick?" O'Reilly wondered. "Or is that supposed to mean something to me?"

"It was the conversation with Len Hughes that made me think of it. When Hughes gets his early release, he'll have served sixteen years. And he told us that his average earnings were six and a half million before he was imprisoned."

O'Reilly thought about this for a minute. He took a long drink of beer and a smile formed on his face.

"I do believe you're right, Katie. When Hughes gets out, he'll be broke. His ex-wife made sure of that. He wants what he was denied while he was inside, doesn't he? Six and a half million for every year he was banged up."

"A hundred and four million," DC Owen said. "On the dot. He's definitely involved in the poisoning."

"And you don't need to be a genius to figure out who he had working for him on the outside. Peter Downing of DDR Legal services who just happens to be a high-ranking officer in the Island Police."

"And if we follow the logic behind this," DC Owen said. "We can safely assume that the person helping Len Hughes out is the same person who was at his house on the day of Vicky Ingram's murder."

"We're close to cracking this one," O'Reilly said. "I just need to figure out a way to get the bastard who killed Vicky Ingram exactly where I want him."

The waitress returned and asked if they were going to have something to eat. O'Reilly replied by asking her if it was a rhetorical question.
"Sir?"
"Never mind," O'Reilly said. "Could you bring us a couple of menus please. And two more of those exceptional beers."
She nodded and walked away with a bewildered expression on her face.
"It makes you wonder what they teach them in schools these days," O'Reilly said. "For this to work, we need to work smart. And I think I may have a plan."
"Why don't I like the sound of this?" DC Owen said.
"It's only slightly illegal, Katie," O'Reilly said. "And the lawbreaking isn't going to be done by me."
"What did you have in mind?"
O'Reilly told her. He decided to interpret her silence when he'd finished as a positive sign. He also made up his mind to put the investigation out of his head for the evening. Tomorrow was another day.

CHAPTER FIFTY EIGHT

The flight from London was delayed, and it was almost eleven when O'Reilly and DC Owen got to the station the next morning. After a quick cup of tea in his office he headed for the briefing room to bring the rest of the team up to date with the new developments. The trip over the Channel had been a productive one, and O'Reilly was confident that the investigation would be concluded very soon. But he still needed to put his plan into action, and he knew he couldn't afford to make a mistake.

"Len Hughes is definitely involved in the recent poisonings," he said to start off the briefing.

"Can we prove it?" DCI Fish said.

"Unfortunately, not. It was Katie who figured it out in the shower. Would you care to explain, Katie?"

"My brain works a bit differently to most people's," DC Owen said. "And I got to thinking about the odd amount the poisoners were demanding. One hundred and four million. I figured that there had to be a reason for it, and I came up with a theory. Len Hughes told us he used to make six and a half million a year on average."

"I'm in the wrong job," DC Stone chipped in.

"You're in the only job that'll tolerate you, Andy," O'Reilly said. "Let Katie finish."

"Hughes will have been locked up for sixteen years when he's allowed out," DC Owen said. "It's simple maths."

"Sixteen times six and a half million is a hundred and four million," DS Skinner calculated.

"Precisely, Sarge."

"But," O'Reilly said. "As I mentioned earlier, it doesn't prove anything. It's circumstantial at best and we're going to need a lot more to implicate Len Hughes."

"What did you have in mind?" DCI Fish said.

"We also discovered that the security measures Belmarsh has in place are somewhat flawed. All of Hughes' phone calls are monitored with the exception of the ones to his lawyer."

"It's standard practice," DCI Fish said. "Lawyer-client privilege applies. How is the system flawed?"

"The person listed as Hughes' legal representative is no more a lawyer than you or me, Tom. And the legal firm he's supposed to represent doesn't exist. Hughes figured out a way to orchestrate the terrorist attack on the island while he was banged up in Belmarsh."

"Who is the phony lawyer?" DC Stone said.

"I'm coming to that, Andy. I phoned the number listed, and I got a nasty surprise. It's someone we all know well, and we also suspect it's the same person who was present that day when Vicky Ingram was murdered."

"We spoke to the officer who was first on the scene," DC Owen said. "PC Jack Powers. He transferred to the Met soon afterwards and he didn't do it willingly. He was forced out because of what he thought he'd seen that day."

"A car driving away from Len Hughes' property," O'Reilly said. "A very familiar car. PC Powers brought it up with the senior officer in question and he was told to forget he'd ever seen it or face the consequences. The threat was implied, but there was little doubt what would happen if PC Powers disregarded it. Once again, there is very little evidence value in this and that's why we need to change our tactics and play a bit dirty."

"We'll do this in accordance with the law or not at all, Liam," DCI Fish said.

"I appreciate your concerns, Tom," O'Reilly said. "But we need to take the gloves off for this one. We have no concrete proof that the main players did anything illegal and the way I see it – there's only one move left to make."

"Len Hughes lied about his lawyer," DC Stone said. "We can have him for that."

"I don't want him for a petty fib about one of his contacts, Andy. I want him for nine murders, and I'm going to make damn sure he spends the rest of his life in Belmarsh because of it."

He spent the next thirty minutes explaining what he had in mind. When he was finished, he prepared himself for a barrage of objections, but none came. Even DCI Fish appeared to be considering his idea.

"Are you absolutely certain you can arrange this, Liam?" he said.

"Positive, Tom," O'Reilly said. "You leave the nitty gritty up to me. Like I said to Katie, it's not strictly legal but it won't be the Island Police who will be partaking in the lawbreaking."

"It's risky," DS Skinner said. "But I'm with you all the way."

"Me too," DC Stone seconded. "I think this will work."

"I'll get the ball rolling then," O'Reilly said.

He got up and left the briefing room.

The first phone call was to Frank Murphy. The prison officer answered after a few seconds.

"Frank," O'Reilly said. "Have you got a minute?"

"You're like the rain over Dublin Bay, Liam," Frank said. "Just when you think it's drifted off, it comes back even harder. What is it now?"

"I want you to make sure that Len Hughes isn't allowed to make any phone calls – not even to his lawyer."

"You know I can't do that. If an inmate wants to speak to his lawyer, we can't stop him."

"Let me put it another way," O'Reilly said. "Very soon, a shitstorm is heading your way. The person listed as Len Hughes' legal representative is really a high-ranking officer in the Island Police. The firm he's supposed to work for doesn't exist. I'm telling you this out of professional courtesy so you're prepared for the backlash your prison can expect when the truth comes out. Hughes has been masterminding a plot to extort millions out of the people of this island from the comfort of Belmarsh. He's responsible for the deaths of nine islanders, and he orchestrated the whole thing from your prison."

Frank didn't say anything for a while.

O'Reilly spoke first. "This isn't going to go away."

"Jesus," Frank said. "Are you sure about this?"

"Positive. I'm working on a plan but it's imperative that Hughes has no contact with anyone. I don't know if anyone else inside Belmarsh is involved, but we have to work on the assumption that it's possible."

"I'll arrange for him to be kept in isolation. I'll think of something. This is bad, Liam."

"You can say that again," O'Reilly said.

They said their goodbyes and O'Reilly dialled another number. This conversation was going to be a lot harder, but he couldn't think of another way to proceed. If the plan was going to work, he needed to sell his soul to the proverbial devil.

CHAPTER FIFTY NINE

The Boathouse was quiet and O'Reilly was glad. The weather gods also seemed to be playing along, and it was still warm without a puff of breeze in the air. That would work in his favour. He'd called ahead and reserved the outside seating area. There was no chance of them being overheard there, and that was essential if his plan was going to work.

O'Reilly got a *Scapegoat* from the bar and took it outside. He'd asked one of the waiters to bring out a couple of menus even though he suspected he wouldn't be eating anything. He sat down with his back to the restaurant. The boats in the marina below were still and the rigging was silent. Vessels were returning to the harbour after a day out at sea. O'Reilly had never been keen on boats before, but he could see the attraction, especially on a day like today.

He checked the time on his phone and saw that he'd received a message from his daughter. Assumpta was wishing him luck. O'Reilly smiled. He would need all the luck an Irishman has if this was going to work. He replied to the message with a thumbs up. The sliding door opened behind him, and it made him jump. It was the waiter. He placed the menus on the table and asked if O'Reilly wanted another drink.

"I'll have the same again, thanks," he said.

When he'd asked the soon to be ex-police officer to meet him at The Boathouse, he hadn't expected him to agree to it so quickly. He'd lied and told him he had some information that he would prefer to discuss in private. The officer in question had fallen for it hook, line, and sinker.

The waiter reappeared with his beer and O'Reilly's heartbeat quickened when he saw the man making his way to the doors that led outside.

Chief Officer Robert Johnson sat down opposite O'Reilly without greeting him. There were no handshakes and no pleasantries.

"What is it you've got for me, Liam?"

"Relax, Robert," O'Reilly said. "You don't mind me calling you Robert, do you? Now you're no longer a police officer, I mean."

The waiter came outside again. CO Johnson told him they were not to be disturbed. He didn't ask for anything to drink.

"Spit it out," he said.

"I spoke to Len Hughes yesterday," O'Reilly said.

"And?"

"He's under the impression that he'll be released soon."

"I was under that impression too."

"He told us something very interesting," O'Reilly said. "Without even realising it. We also had the pleasure of meeting a police officer by the name of Jack Powers. Remember him?"

"What is this, Liam?" CO Johnson said.

"Why didn't you mention your relationship with Len Hughes?" O'Reilly said. "Not once did you admit that you knew the man. I'm talking about before you even met your future wife."

"We were barely acquainted. He was my broker, nothing more."

"Is that why you were at his house that day?" O'Reilly said. "The day that Vicky Ingram was killed."

"I have no idea what you're talking about."

"PC Powers told us what he saw," O'Reilly said. "He wasn't a hundred percent certain it was your car, but your reaction afterwards when he brought it up with you all but confirmed it."

"Why are you so obsessed with a sixteen-year-old case? It happened, Len Hughes was convicted, and he served his time. End of story."

"But it's not the end of the story, is it? This story still has plenty of pages left. You made a mistake answering the phone yesterday. I must admit, I didn't expect you to. I withheld my number, but it could have been anyone calling you."

"You're talking in riddles, Liam."

"The Irish do that a lot. Peter Downing. Does that name ring any bells?"

"You tell me."

"What about DDR Legal Services?" O'Reilly said. "Let me tell you what's going to happen now. Your association with Len Hughes is going to come out, as is the fact that you were at the house when Vicky Ingram was murdered. Then we're going to prove how you and Len Hughes hatched a plan to poison random islanders in order to blackmail the island."

"Are you drunk?"

"I've never been more sober in my life," O'Reilly said.

He looked out onto the boats again. He wasn't going to say anything else for a while. He hoped that CO Johnson would make the next move.

"You can't prove anything," he said. "You know that don't you?"

"I do. But I'm hoping you're going to do the right thing. I had you down as a man of integrity. What happened that day, Robert?"

"You've got nothing to link me to the murder of Vicky Ingram."

"She was fourteen years old," O'Reilly said. "She had her whole life ahead of her and you and Len Hughes put an end to that for the sake of a few minutes of twisted pleasure."

CO Johnson shot up in his chair. "I am not a rapist."

"Sit down, Robert."

CO Johnson obliged. "I am not a rapist."

"No," O'Reilly said. "You're a murderer. What happened? What were you even doing there?"

"You do realise that nothing I tell you will be admissible as evidence."

"I'm aware of that," O'Reilly said. "Even if I were secretly recording this, it would be thrown out quicker than you can say *Vicky Ingram*."

CO Johnson looked like he'd been physically slapped.

"Why?" O'Reilly said. "Nine people are dead. Len Hughes is a monster. He was a monster back then and he will never change. But you – what happened to you, sir?"

CO Johnson rubbed his eyes.

"I owe him, Liam. Len Hughes raped that girl, but he didn't kill her."

"No," O'Reilly said. "You did. And you feel a twisted kind of obligation, don't you? Hughes wanted what was denied to him for sixteen years. Six and a half million for every year he was inside. Does one hundred and four million Euros ring any bells?"

CO Johnson nodded.

"You're going to tell me everything, Robert. And you're not going leave anything out."

CO Johnson nodded his head again. Then everything came flooding out. O'Reilly sensed that he'd been waiting to tell this story for a very long time.

CHAPTER SIXTY

"I hadn't been on the island long."

O'Reilly decided to let him talk. It was clear that he needed to offload, and he would let him do just that.

"I'd known Len for a while before I came here. He was recommended to me by a colleague in Edinburgh. I'd recently come into some money – an inheritance and I'd heard about the favourable tax laws for investments in Guernsey. We had a few business meetings, and I suppose you could say we became friends."

He stopped there and O'Reilly didn't push him to continue.

"That day was the worst day of my life," CO Johnson carried on. "I never could have imagined how it would turn out. I needed to discuss a few things pertaining to my investment portfolio and I couldn't get hold of Len. He wasn't answering his phone, so I decided to pop round to see if he was at home. His car was parked in the driveway but the gate at the front was closed. I was ready to drive away when it slid open."

"You're referring to the gate?" O'Reilly said.

CO Johnson nodded. "Not a day goes by that I don't wish it had remained closed. I would have driven away, and I wouldn't have suffered from recurring nightmares for sixteen years. It was an automated gate, and I assumed that Len had seen me and opened it for me. I drove in and got out of the car."

O'Reilly took a sip of his beer and waited for CO Johnson to tell him more.

"I went inside the house, but Len wasn't there. I called his name, and he told me he was upstairs. Never in a million years did I expect to find what I found when I went into that bedroom."

O'Reilly could imagine. "Vicky Ingram?"

"I asked Len what was going on, and he asked me if I fancied a bit of pleasure before we got down to business. I was sickened. The girl was on the bed with her underwear stuffed inside her mouth. Her hands were bound behind her back. My first reaction was to reach for my phone. It was clear that a horrible crime had been committed, and I had to call it in."

"But you didn't, did you?"

"I'd left my phone in the car."

"And you didn't think to go back outside to retrieve it?" O'Reilly said.

"I didn't know what to think. I must have panicked. None of it seemed real. I need a drink."

"I'll go," O'Reilly said. "What will it be?"

"Something strong. Brandy. A big one."

O'Reilly was glad to be away from Chief Officer Johnson for a while. He'd hoped for a full confession, but when it came, he wasn't prepared for it. He got a triple brandy from the bar and took it outside.

CO Johnson drained half the glass in one go. "She wasn't as sweet and innocent as you think."

"She was fourteen," O'Reilly pointed out.

"Fourteen going on forty. I told Len that I couldn't ignore what he'd done, and he didn't seem particularly perturbed. He told me to calm down. He said he would fix it – he would make it go away."

"And you agreed to that?" O'Reilly said.

"Of course not. I was ready to leave. I was prepared to do everything I could to do the right thing but then things took a turn for the worse. The girl managed to get free. She yanked her knickers from her mouth, and she spat at me. She asked me if I wanted a go. I was horrified. Then she started to laugh. She was mocking me – telling me that I probably couldn't get it up anyway. It was unbelievable. Len had raped her – he'd violated her, and she was acting as though it was something she did every day."

"What happened next?" O'Reilly said.

CO Johnson finished his brandy.

"I turned to leave. I had to get out of there. The abuse followed me out of the room. The girl was taunting me. Calling me things you would never expect to hear from a fourteen-year-old's mouth. Then I made the worst mistake of my life. I went back inside the bedroom, and I told her to shut up. She didn't, so I grabbed her by the throat. She mocked me with her eyes while I throttled the life out her."

He took a drink from his glass even though it was empty.

O'Reilly saw that he had tears in his eyes.

"I'm sorry," CO Johnson said. "It wasn't supposed to happen."

O'Reilly felt ill. This was a man he'd trusted. He respected him and he never would have imagined him to be a cold-blooded killer. There were still a lot of questions that needed to be answered though.

"What happened after you killed her?"

"Len said he would fix it. He told me to leave and said he could make it go away. Nobody knew where the girl was, and he would sort everything out. I didn't know then that someone had phoned the police. I got out just in time. I saw the patrol car in my rearview mirror when I drove away from the house."

"Then what?" O'Reilly said. "Len Hughes was arrested, but he denied murdering Vicky. And he was telling the truth, wasn't he?"

"It was the most stressful time of my life."

"Poor you." O'Reilly couldn't help himself.

"I spoke to Len only once after that before he was shipped off to Belmarsh," CO Johnson said. "But once was enough. He told me he would take the fall for what I'd done but it was far from over. I would owe him and that debt would need to be repaid when the time came."

"How did the idea of holding the island to ransom come about?" O'Reilly said.

"As the years went by, I thought less and less about what happened that day, but then I was stopped in the street one day by a complete stranger and told that Len Hughes was expecting a visit from me."

"When was this?"

"About two months ago," CO Johnson said.

"And did you go to see him in Belmarsh?"

"I didn't have much choice. The man who passed on the message was an ex-con. Len knew he would be released soon, and he asked him to have a word with me. I visited Len once a week for six weeks. He reminded me of my debt, but he said there was a way to make good on it. That's when he came up with the idea of the random poisoning and the ransom demands."

"You're married to his sister," O'Reilly said. "How did you explain the visits to her?"

"I made up something about meetings in London. I hated myself for lying to her."

"I imagine you did," O'Reilly said. "She wanted nothing to do with him, and she had good reason. Tell me about the poisoning and the ransom demands."

"It was all Len's idea. He said it was an easy way to get the money."

"A hundred and four million," O'Reilly said. "You didn't do this alone. Who contaminated the products?"

"I can't tell you. In fact, that's all I'm going to tell you. Are you happy now?"

O'Reilly wasn't. In fact, he'd never felt so sick in his life.

"You played a part in the murders of nine people. You killed a fourteen-year-old girl. You're the chief of the Island Police. This is going to destroy the reputation of the Island Police when it sees the light of day. You're sick. The recent sickness on the island pales into comparison compared to the sickness inside you."

CO Johnson's facial expression changed in an instant. The penitent man was gone and replaced with a defiant one.

"It's not going to see the light of day, Liam. Everything I've just told you is worthless from an evidence perspective."

"You're right," O'Reilly said. "But I'm not really concerned about that."

He took out his phone.

"You recorded our conversation?" CO Johnson said.

"I already told you I didn't," O'Reilly said.

He dialled a number and put it on speakerphone. The call was answered immediately.

"Fred," O'Reilly said. "Did you get all that?"

"Pure gold," the editor of the Island Herald said.

"Don't forget what we discussed."

"I'm a man of my word," Fred said. "The video footage will be forwarded straight to your lovely daughter at the Gazette."

O'Reilly looked CO Johnson in the eye. "Is there anything you'd care to add for the record?"

"You can't use this, Viking. Filming a police officer without prior permission happens to be against the law."

"I was under the impression that you were no longer a police officer," Fred said.

"Filming a citizen in a public place with the purpose of broadcasting it is also illegal. You will pay for this."

"I looked it up," O'Reilly said. "You'll probably get a fine of a few hundred quid. Can you live with that, Fred?"

"Best few hundred I've ever spent. I'll get this off to Assumpta asap."

O'Reilly stood up and walked up to the sliding doors. He removed the tiny camera and placed it on the table.

"Perhaps you want to keep that, sir," he said to CO Johnson. "A little memento of your final moments as a free man."

CO Johnson looked at the innocent looking camera.

"That footage cannot be used as evidence, Liam. And you know it."

"I'm not overly concerned – I already told you that. Once that footage is out there for the whole island to see, it's game over for you anyway. You don't mind picking up the tab, do you – I seem to have left my wallet at home."

CHAPTER SIXTY ONE

O'Reilly parked his car outside number 17 Harrow Road in Delancey Park and got out. It was late afternoon and there wasn't a puff of breeze in the air. He walked towards the house and stopped. The gargoyle was looking right at him and O'Reilly thought it looked different. It didn't seem so sinister today. He leaned over and rubbed its head without knowing why.

It had been a demanding couple of weeks since the video of CO Johnson's confession was aired for everyone on the island to see. The chief of the island police was arrested shortly afterwards and after a lengthy series of interviews, he'd eventually cracked. Everything was made clear in one six-hour interview. Robert Johnson had told O'Reilly everything. Afterwards, the Irish detective had gone home and stood in the shower for almost an hour.

Len Hughes had mentioned the idea for the poisoning during CO Johnson's first visit to Belmarsh and he'd also reminded the chief officer of the deal they'd made. Hughes wanted his money, and CO Johnson was going to get it for him.

There were two more players in the sick game – a brother and a sister. John and Maggie Green were more than willing to play when they learned of the money involved. Len Hughes had met John in Belmarsh. He was released shortly before the sickness on the island started after serving six years for GBH. John was an IT expert, and his sister was a biology student who also happened to have a dubious moral compass. It was the siblings who'd played the role of the poisoners. John and Maggie had contaminated the food and drink in Fresh Life Supermarket, and they were also responsible for the lethal ginger in *Nature's Gifts*.

The choice of shops was Len Hughes' brainwave. He knew that the Island Police would look closely at Belinda North and Janet Ingram, and it would be a wild goose chase that would cost them a lot of time and resources.

John and Maggie Green had no intention of releasing ricin onto the island. O'Reilly's suspicions had been correct. The threat of such a horrendous attack was enough though, and the Island Police were on the verge of giving in to the demands of the poisoners. Len Hughes and CO Johnson very nearly got away with it.

Len Hughes wasn't going to get his parole or his money. In fact, Belmarsh was going to be his home until he took his final breath. In a bizarre twist of fate, CO Johnson would soon be joining him. He too was never going to see the outside of a prison cell.

O'Reilly was never going to forget what had happened on the island in the past few weeks and it was going to take a long time to even begin to comprehend the sickness that he'd witnessed. It was difficult to rationalise the actions of two human beings, one of whom he'd always held in such high regard. It was going to leave a bitter taste in his mouth, and he hoped he would be able to move past it in time.

Callum Dove had resigned, and O'Reilly suspected that it was a case of jumping before he was pushed. The punch he'd thrown hadn't been reported and O'Reilly didn't think it was necessary to make it official. The ex DCO was not out of the woods yet. There was the matter of his involvement in the travesty of justice that was the Amy Winter rape case. And that's why O'Reilly was in Delancey Park right now. He cast a final glance at the gargoyle and walked down the path to the front door.

Amy Winter opened the door and invited O'Reilly inside. Someone was singing somewhere close by and O'Reilly assumed it was Amy's daughter, Millie.

"She has a beautiful voice," he said.

"I think so," Amy said. "Can I offer you something to drink?"

"I've not long had a cup of tea."

"There's a fresh batch of biscuits in the kitchen," Amy said. "Chocolate."

"Now you're talking," O'Reilly said.

"Let's sit in there then."

O'Reilly sat down at the table. Amy sat opposite him.

"I felt that I needed to come and see you," he said.

He helped himself to a biscuit and took a big bite.

"Delicious. You have a say in what happens next."

"I've thought long and hard about it," Amy said. "And nothing will change what happened that night."

"I'm so sorry for what you had to endure," O'Reilly said. "You were let down by the people who were supposed to protect you."

"What's done is done. Len Hughes isn't going to get out of prison, is he?"

"He'll die in Belmarsh," O'Reilly said. "But you can still get the justice that you were denied. The man who helped Len Hughes get away with what he did to you may not get the punishment he deserves. He's resigned, but the Island Police won't want to make a big fuss out of it. He'll probably still get a full pension. We can insist that the original case is reopened if that's what you want."

Amy shook her head. "No. I'm doing just fine. It won't do anyone any good bringing it all up again. The officer you're referring to may have got off lightly, but he still has to sleep at night. He has to live with what he did. Your daughter called me earlier."

"I gave her your number," O'Reilly said. "I hope you don't mind. The Herald has put out nothing but dirt and scandal, and I know Assumpta and the Gazette will tell a different story – something to uplift the people of the island. God knows, they need it right now, and your story is exactly what they need to hear. Assumpta will do you justice."

"I get that feeling too. She sounds lovely."

O'Reilly stood up. "I'll leave you in peace."

"You can stay as long as you like," Amy said. "There are still plenty of biscuits."

"Maybe just one more. You've been a shining light through all of this – you really are an incredible woman."

"And you're an incredible man. Will you be OK?"

"Me?" O'Reilly said. "This isn't about me."

Amy stood up too. "Can I give you a hug?"

O'Reilly wasn't expecting this.

"You don't want to do that."

Amy took a step closer. "You look like you need one."

She wrapped her arms around him and squeezed him tight.

"What are you doing?" It was Millie.

O'Reilly hadn't heard her come in.

"Detective Inspector O'Reilly is sad," Amy said. "He needed a hug."

O'Reilly felt tiny arms around his waist. Millie had joined in too. He could feel tears building and he had to use every ounce of self-control to keep them at bay.

Amy and Millie broke the embrace at the same time.

"Feel better?" Amy asked.

O'Reilly managed a smile. "I do. Thank you – I feel a whole lot better."

THE END

Printed in Dunstable, United Kingdom